BACK AGAIN

BACK AGAIN

A NOVEL

JAMIE STOUDT

Beaver's Pond
PRESS

Book design and typesetting by Mayfly Design
Cover image by Mandy Guth Photography
Edited by Kari Cornell
Managing Editor: Laurie Buss Herrmann

ISBN 13: 978-1-64343-834-4
Library of Congress Catalog Number: 2020919437
Printed in the United States of America
First Printing: 2020
25 24 23 22 21   5 4 3 2 1

Beaver's Pond Press
939 Seventh Street West
Saint Paul, MN 55102
(952) 829-8818
www.BeaversPondPress.com

To order this book, visit jamiestoudtbooks.com. Reseller discounts available.

To Irene Sanchez, who cheered me on from the first word through the last edit. Thank you.

PROLOGUE

Wendy Halstad was in church, up front, all alone in a jar. She was dead, ashes to ashes and all that. Massive heart attack, fifty years old, no warning, no symptoms, no time to say goodbye. Just *kerplop*, and that was that.

She had been an ardent churchgoer, everybody's friend, and the most capable, cordial, and thick-skinned employee of the Stillwater, Minnesota, DMV Regional Office. Thick-skinned, as in she could take more crap than a honey wagon and still remain capable and cordial. And that was good, because every third person coming into the DMV was pissed off. Well, 33.78 percent, actually. They keep very close track. The theory was that internalizing all that crap was probably what killed her. The coroner checks for cause of death—in this case, a massive heart attack—and not the cause of the cause of death.

Regardless, here they all were, three hundred strong, in a church, saying goodbye too late to a friend in a jar on an altar. Those three hundred would go home, changed and humbled and nervous. Wendy was a saint, one of the good ones, and yet there she was, up front, room temperature. The change in the attendees would last a day, maybe even two, because this was Wendy. They'd be nice to their spouses, appreciate the April warmth, and let their kids stay out till nine, the thought being, If Wendy got pulled out of the race this early, then I'm toast, buttered, sliced, crusts removed. Waiting to be chewed, swallowed, and pooped back out. Or even a worse analogy—or maybe not.

Wendy had had a good husband, Michael. Michael was often between jobs, and thus available to friends, neighbors, stray dogs, and Jehovah's Witnesses. If you needed a ride, or an ear, or the wax ring on a toilet replaced, you called Michael. The DMV paid Wendy pretty well, what with all the crap and such, and she and Michael were in need of nothing. So being a "good guy" came naturally to a good guy with lots of spare time.

But Michael, in the front row, staring at the jar, was a mess. He and Wendy had always been a pair. People seldom mentioned one name without the other. Like Heckle and Jeckle. Amos and Andy. Captain and Tennille. They were of the same mind, the same life view, the same bank account—and they were not meant to be separated, one in the first row, the other the center of attention up front. His thoughts were of nothing, quite literally, as if his mind had been wiped clean. No thoughts of his future. A past that went *boom*, gone, much like four coronary arteries inexplicably blowing out at the same time. He had been thrust into *The Twilight Zone* by Rod Serling himself. And those three hundred nice folks behind him, they expected something. Tears? A grimace? A nod of acknowledgment? Whatever. There was nothing there to give.

Wendy and Michael's kids, Andrea and Andrew—Andie and Andy—were there too. Their names were Wendy's idea. Her all-time favorite name for a child was Andy, and she didn't have a second all-time favorite name for a second child. Naming the second one Burt or Winslow or Garth would have been giving him less than an all-time favorite name, and that wasn't something that Wendy would ever do.

The kids were a little more cognitive than Michael at the moment. Grown up, out of college, pursuing careers and calendar entries, with kids of their own. Reality would not allow them to zombie out like their dad. They loved Wendy with all their Andie/Andy hearts, but their kids were here, staring at the jar, and at Michael, and at the guy up front in the toga robe trying to explain why God had killed Grammy Wen.

CHAPTER ONE

Three Years Later

Michael pulled the Blue Bird into the Stillwater School District bus barn at 4:03 p.m. Except for snow days, Michael made the barn at 4:03 p.m. every school day, give or take three minutes. On snow days, there was no schedule, and weekends, summer, and teachers' convention days, there was no school at all. He was still trim, with sandy hair that got a bit lighter each year, some crow's feet evidence of smiling eyes, and a nose that pointed a bit west of true north.

Michael had been driving school bus for two years. His kids talked him into it. Not physically demanding, what with the power steering and Allison automatics. Not too time-consuming, with only two several-hour shifts per school day. It paid better than Walmart, and he liked the noise that happy schoolkids made. He had a civil engineering degree from Minnesota State, Mankato, but had not worked as an engineer for ten years now. He was never one to chase a dollar or grovel for a promotion.

His personality was, obviously, pretty laid back. He didn't worry about things he couldn't control, like death or weather or a neighbor's dog pooping on his lawn. Now, if a neighbor did that himself, Michael would attempt to exert some control. He sometimes pondered whether driving a bus was his calling, but always came to the same conclusion—there was no such thing as a calling.

The bus barn was behind the Orchard Mall, where he spent a lot of time. After each morning's bus run, he'd head to the mall

3

and settle into his favorite chair at Barnes & Noble, grab that day's *Star Tribune*, and read every word. For lunch, the mall offered two dozen restaurant choices, his favorite being Salad Days. Then back to Barnes & Noble to read a hundred pages of his current novel of choice before the quick hike back to the barn for the afternoon middle school deliveries.

Today, as he left the barn after depositing his bus for the night, he noticed a woman leaning against his car. He absently thought, "A beautiful day, giggling kids, a good lunch, a good read, and a woman leaning against my car—I might have to invest two bucks in a Powerball on my way home." As he approached the car, though, his composure got a little hinky, and his mind started playing those old tricks again. He had "seen" Wendy several times since she died—a hairdo that looked similar but belonged to someone else, or a voice that sounded uncannily the same but belonged to an eighth-grade boy on the bus—but this time, each step closer confirmed the thought rather than exposed the nonsense of it.

"Hey, sailor, can a girl get a ride without getting molested?" Michael stopped ten feet away, his mind racing, his composure more hinky. This *was* Wendy. She had used that line on him a hundred times. The face was *not* someone else's, and the voice did *not* belong to a middle schooler. She was still five foot two, still trim, and still wore her blonde hair in a page-boy cut. And she wore a summer pants suit that Andie had removed from their closet within weeks of the funeral. Wendy Halstad was leaning on his car.

He didn't speak and stood statue-still. She said, "I was doing a little shopping and was hoping I didn't have to walk home. I'm happy I caught you!"

"Wendy?" Michael said, his voice weak.

She giggled. "Duh, but you can call me Lucille if that trips your trigger."

He stammered, "Wha . . . how . . . you're . . . oh my god. What . . .

what's going on?" And he started to cry. Wendy walked to him and took his hand, and immediately he suffered a dizzying adrenaline rush. "You're . . . real. You're here. Wh . . . where did you come from?"

"I told you, bozo, I was at the mall, and I respectfully request a ride home. You're acting like I just got off a ship from Denver!"

"Uh, yeah, well, uh, you can't actually get on or off a ship from Denver . . ."

"That's what I'm saying, dummy. What's up with you?"

She was still holding his hand, and it was tingling like it had fallen asleep. The sensation went up his arm, engulfing him. An adrenaline rush. A runner's high. A nicotine buzz while smoking *and* wearing a patch. A patch on each arm. And then everything just seemed to work itself out. Like searching your mind for your third-grade teacher's first name, and then it hits you—Mildred! Or like when you buy a Powerball ticket and the numbers match. He grabbed her, hugging her tight, and confirmed that yes, she was real, and he was still crying, and it was okay.

Wendy chattered all the way home. She'd bought some sensible shoes, and angel-hair pasta for dinner, and an Annie's pretzel, which she teased she might be persuaded to share. Michael drove and smiled and breathed deeply and drank in the chatter. The earth had just cracked open, but he was fine with it. The world—everything—had just turned upside down, and that was okay. His life just completely changed all over again, and he was fine with it.

Still, he knew he was in for . . . something. Maybe she was here to take him with her? Into the urn? Nah, he didn't believe that stuff, but whatever, he was fine with it. An old Bill Withers lyric bounced around in his head: "Well you can just keep on using me . . . until you use me up." And if that's what it was, Michael was fine with it.

When he was seven or eight, he'd had a tough year. Measles for ten boring days, then he broke an arm falling off a roof he was climbing on because it was there, and his grandpa died, and even his dog ran away. Or so his mom said. He'd always thought that she'd told him kind of strangely, like she had information she wasn't sharing. But he was seven, and back then seven-year-olds were not allowed to interrogate their mothers. As difficult as it was, that year prodded him to accept life as it came, and be cool with it.

He wondered for a moment if the urn would still be on the mantel when he got home.

CHAPTER TWO

Wendy started making dinner when they got home—"they" sounded strange. Michael hadn't thought of himself in the plural since . . . that day. But he didn't ask any more questions. He just figured things were okay. The completely nonsensical made sense. Why would he waste a moment's energy questioning the best thing that had ever happened to him? Marrying Wendy had previously been the best thing. But this, this was a whole 'nother level. World-class baklava. Angel-hair carbonara. "Hmm," he said. "Must be hungry."

He thought of a story he'd read years before about Bob Kerrey, then the governor of Nebraska and a presidential contender. Debra Winger was supposedly living with him in the governor's mansion, and a reporter asked him, "Governor, you were once thought to be dead on a hill in Vietnam with your leg shot off. Now you're a governor, living with Debra Winger, and being pushed to run for president. What are your thoughts on your future?" Kerrey looked to the side for a moment, then looked back at the reporter and replied, "I have no idea. I'm just enthralled watching my life unfold."

After the pasta and the pretzel and an intense viewing of the evening news, Wendy suggested they have Andie and Andy over for dinner the following day. Michael pondered that. Like winning the Powerball, he felt the kids might need to be eased into this situation more carefully than just "dinner tomorrow." They were going to freak. Yeah, pretty much everybody was going to freak.

Andie was a private practice attorney, handling a little bit of everything, except divorce. She wasn't a "sock it to 'em" kind of gal. Andy was an investment counselor for a small firm, licensed to sell securities. His success was based less on knowing the stock market (he said privately that anyone who *did* claim to know the stock market was a liar) than on learning the names of his clients' children. They had turned out pretty damn well, Michael knew. The two were both smarter than he was, as Andie and Andy would often agree, usually followed by a "duh."

In spite of the curious calm he felt, Michael was intrigued that Wendy didn't act as if she'd ever been gone, or like she really was— whatever. Should he give refunds to the people who'd bought flowers for the funeral? Should they send out apologies? Should they act like, "What you talkin' 'bout, Willis?" when people asked, "What's up?" Well, Wendy didn't seem too distressed about it. She looked like she did three years ago—a lovely fifty, five-foot-two, packed tight, with a mischievous twinkle in her green eyes.

So he said, "How 'bout we play that dinner thing by ear and come up with something fun to do tomorrow?"

Wendy said, "You read my mind!" Which prompted Michael to think, "My dear, there is zero chance in hell that I just read your mind." Wendy continued, "I'd like to visit Pastor Conlin at the church for a bit tomorrow morning. Can you drive me?"

Again, Michael pondered. Visiting Pastor Conlin was way down on his list of fun things to do the next day. But he said, "Sure! That'll be a hoot! At least to watch." And he decided, if you're out of the jar, visiting your pastor would logically be your first stop. Logically, right. He'd pinched himself so many times in the last several hours, he had a welt on his arm.

Wendy looked at him curiously, but continued, "I'd like to talk to him about some ideas I have on making better use of the church facilities. You know, there are three services on Sunday, and the Wednesday evening stuff, but that amazing campus is basically unused for most of the week."

Michael responded, "Is he expecting you, or aware of what you're up to?" He stopped himself from asking, "Does he know that you exist—again?"

Wendy giggled. "Michael, I'm not *up* to anything! I just have some ideas, and I'm comfortable that Pastor Conlin will be receptive. Just common-sense stuff like repurposing the Great Hall, and opening up the gym to the neighborhood, and some minor architectural modifications."

Common-sense changes like architectural modifications, Michael thought. Sure. He closed his laptop. "I just sent a note to Student Services that I'm taking a week of personal time, so I'm at your service. And I'm already smiling at the pastor's response." Faking a yawn, he said, "So, I'm kinda tired. I think I'm going up to bed."

Wendy didn't look up, just said, "I'm going to hang out down here and read. I picked up a couple amazing books at the mall, and I can't wait to dig in."

Michael went up the steps, curiously relieved. After three years of recovery, celibacy, anger, grief, frustration, adjusting, and Zoloft for breakfast, he had no clue how he was going to handle that whole horizontal-in-the-dark thing.

CHAPTER THREE

As they pulled up to the church Monday morning, Michael turned to Wendy and asked, "Have you thought of how you're going to, ah, handle Pastor Conlin? I mean, he's going to be . . . surprised." Or just drop dead from the shock, he thought.

"Not really," she replied. "He's always been good at handling stuff on the fly. I'll just see how it goes. Maybe I won't bring up the architectural suggestions if he's not fully receptive."

"Mmm," Michael said, thinking, "Holy shitstorm, Batman, this is going to be mind-bending."

The church was monstrous. It had a five-acre campus, including the Great Hall; a smaller four-hundred-seat chapel; a separate gymnasium / recreation center; and four wings off the Great Hall that housed the church business offices, the outreach and fundraising programs, the music rehearsal and recording studio, and the facilities maintenance staff and equipment. The grounds were manicured. There was a gazebo and a fountain and even a small fleet of shuttle buses.

They walked hand in hand from the parking lot to a side door of the office wing. Holding Wendy's hand, after so long, was like being in high school again. Michael thought how lucky he was and hoped she'd never let go.

There was no one at reception or in the hallway, but it was nine on a Monday morning, and churches weren't known for Monday morning hubbub. He hadn't been here in three years. His religious beliefs had taken a turn south at the same moment as Wendy's untimely exit.

Michael knocked lightly on Pastor Conlin's open door. The pastor was sitting at his desk in a golfing polo (Michael thought, What the heck, I guess ministers can't really golf on Sunday, can they?) and reading glasses, a pen in one hand. He looked up, recognized Michael, and immediately stood, a smile on his face and a hand out as he walked around the desk.

"Michael Halstad! It's good to see you again. You're looking healthy and bright-eyed . . ." and then Wendy stepped up beside Michael and said, "Hello, Pastor Conlin. May we come in?"

Conlin froze, like a freeze-frame in a stuck projector, dropped the pen and all pretense of cordiality, and stared at Wendy for two, three, maybe four seconds. In that time, his smile faded, his outstretched hand dropped, and his eyes widened more and more as each second passed. And then his face turned red, and he barked, almost growled, "What is the meaning of this? Who are you, and what are you trying to do?"

Wendy reached out and took his limp hand. "Pastor Conlin— Daniel—I'm Wendy, Michael's wife, and I was hoping we could talk for a few minutes."

She held his hand firmly, and after an initial arm spasm, and a gasp, he didn't pull away. The blood vessels in his neck slimmed back down, the red faded from his face, and his eyes mellowed from rage to curiosity, and then to intrigue.

"Please, sit down, and, we . . . well, what would you like to talk about?" The intrigue was still on his face, and as he stepped back to his chair, he took off his glasses. His hands were shaking slightly. Michael thought that the whole encounter had gone rather well, considering. The pastor had shown a hint of dropping dead from shock, but he recovered nicely, which meant Michael wouldn't have to explain the situation to a police investigator.

"Daniel, I've been doing some reading, and some pondering, and I wanted to get your take on what's going through my head. I've always known that you're a ponderer, that you sometimes reach outside the box for answers."

Conlin nodded, encouraging her.

"Well, one of my dilemmas is that we know the earth is billions of years old, right?"

"Agreed," Pastor Conlin responded immediately.

"And the Bible says earth is five thousand five hundred years old."

"Yes," he laughed. "I've counseled many a parishioner on that little discrepancy. And I believe, and preach, that the Bible is not only the most important document ever written, but it's also a guide for morality, and order, and the rule of law, and personal fulfillment . . ."

"But?" Wendy prompted.

"Well, I differ from many in the clergy in that my emphasis is on *guide*, and not cast-in-stone absolutes."

"But weren't the Ten Commandments literally cast in stone?" Wendy asked, seeming to coach as much as inquire.

"Exactly!" he said, sitting up a little straighter in his chair. "The Ten Commandments were contemporaneous, by all accounts put to stone tablets as they were divined—pardon the pun—by Moses. But the Bible is not accurately represented as a historical document. Remember, it was written in hundreds of sections, often hundreds and in some cases thousands of years after the events occurred. There was no education system at the time. No science. No understanding of physics, or geology, or genetic adaptation, or, or . . ."

"You've scratched the itch I've not been able to reach, Daniel! If we take the Bible literally—"

He finished her thought: "—then we have to discount most scientific discoveries, yes, and landing on the moon and Mars, and petrified dinosaurs, and even oil—a process of biological decay that takes millions of years—yes! The Bible provided focus, and a consistent theology, if you will. It was—is—a collection of facts and stories and narratives that occurred over many, many years, not a document written in one sitting by the original players."

"And the strict adherence . . .?"

"Pushed by goodness and best intent, but also by zealots and manipulators to establish and exercise control and power. But keep in mind, the writers of the Bible only knew what they knew at that point in time. No advances in the human existence are factored into any part of the original document. To take it literally is to ignore its intent, and to ignore the need for humanity to grow and improve, and search, and discover. What I preach is that the Bible, and in fact God itself, is too complex for us mere humans to—to grasp the depth and unfathomable intricacies of our world, and, even more challenging, the universe."

Wendy sat back, staring intently into Daniel's eyes. It was clear she had started at the right church, with the right man. Daniel was—confident?—that people could only pretend to understand God, let alone interpret intent. She believed him to be an extremely intelligent, thoughtful, practical, and charismatic champion for positive change.

Michael, on the other hand, was more confused than when he walked in, but he accepted his new role (confusion), and he figured he was dealing with it pretty damn well, considering.

Wendy suggested that Michael investigate the rehearsal hall and recording studio while she and Pastor Conlin walked the campus, excitedly talking, gesturing, laughing, and pausing to think. Her hand was occasionally on his shoulder, encouraging and prodding.

When he and Wendy returned to the church office, Daniel said, "I'm thinking of calling a meeting of the church directors for Wednesday evening, to go over our ideas. I'd appreciate it if you'd join us."

"Sure!" she said. "But, for some obvious reasons, and some less than obvious, my hope is to be . . . *peripheral* to your decision-making. The focus should not be on me."

She looked firmly into his eyes for a moment, and he said, "I understand."

■ ■ ■

On the short drive home, Michael asked, as casually as possible, "So, what's the plan?"

Wendy laughed and said, "Oh, you know me, Michael. I'm no good at plans. I'm just working on a . . . concept. I'll leave the plans to Daniel Conlin. By the way, he's calling a vestry meeting of the church deacons for Wednesday evening, and would like us to join them."

"Well, I remain captivated. What have you *conceptualized* for tomorrow?"

"I'm thinking of going over to the synagogue. I don't know Rabbi Berg as well as Pastor Conlin, but I've met him, and I think I'd enjoy chatting with him. Drive me?"

■ ■ ■

That evening after supper, Michael was exhausted—too much brain work—and Wendy was energized, as she had been every moment since she appeared by Michael's car. He again said he was going up to bed, and she again said she had some fascinating reading to do. As he walked past the back of the couch on his way to the stairs, he looked down at Wendy's "fascinating" reading collection: *Introduction to Plasma Physics and Controlled Fusion* by Francis Chen. *Peace Dividend Economics* by Ron Volker. *Fast Track Research Initiative (FTRI)* by Dr. APJ Abdul Kalam.

"Fascinating," he mumbled. "Makes perfect sense. Not."

CHAPTER FOUR

There was no synagogue in Stillwater, so Tuesday morning they drove to the Temple Shalom in St. Paul. Rush hour was behind them, and traffic was light.

The building was large and ornate and unique to the area, and Michael thought it looked like a mausoleum. He figured he would keep that image to himself, though. Through the front door, they followed a beautiful Persian carpet runner—Michael raised his eyebrow at the irony of this carpet from Persia, now Iran, carpeting the hallway of a Jewish synagogue. The carpet led down a hall, past several offices, to a reading room, where they found Rabbi Berg, reading.

Michael did his modest knocking thing (I'm an asset in so many ways, he thought), and the rabbi looked up—though he definitely did *not* look like a rabbi, to Michael's sensibilities, anyway. He was maybe forty, with a full head of closely cropped dark hair, and broad shoulders. He was buff and square jawed with intense eyes. He looked like a Navy SEAL wearing a yarmulke. "Maybe he stole the rug," Michael thought irreverently. And he glanced to see if he could make out what Berg had been reading. Dead Sea Scrolls? *Golan Heights Tribune*? No, he could just make out the author—Baldacci. "I think I like this guy," Michael chuckled to himself.

Berg, wearing faded jeans and a black Def Leppard T-shirt, tight in the pecs, stood. Michael said, "Rabbi? I'm Michael Halstad, and this is my . . . wife, Wendy. She's wondering if you might have a few minutes to . . . conceptualize with her."

The rabbi looked at him quizzically, and Wendy looked at him with mock indignity and a twinkle in her eye. She quickly interjected, "Rabbi, please forgive Michael. I've always been attracted to dorks, and he's, like, a professional. I was hoping I could pick your brain a bit and learn more about your faith and your synagogue." She shook his hand, slowly and firmly, and his eyes blinked, like he and Wendy had just exchanged a carpet shock.

"Absolutely," he said, beaming. "But there is one condition I must insist on."

Wendy's twinkle faded. "What's that?"

He looked at her grimly and said, "You need to call me Jake." He smiled and waved a hand toward an overstuffed leather couch. "Have a seat and start picking."

They sat, and he looked at her expectantly. Wendy paused a moment to conjure up the right words. "What's your view of this whole 'Son of God' thing?"

Berg stared, blinked again, and bellowed out a heartfelt belly laugh that filled the room. He struggled to compose himself, while Michael rolled his eyes and mumbled, "Oh Lordy. No reason to wade in if you'd rather cliff dive."

Berg said to Wendy, "As you know, the Jewish faith does not assume that Jesus was the son of God, which is an interesting study in 'different paths taken.'"

Wendy raised an eyebrow to encourage an expansion of the statement.

"Christians and Jews agree with the Old Testament word for word, in theory, but when the Jewish faith marched straight ahead, the Christian faith took a left, you might say, around two thousand years ago. I've always been fascinated with the result, or the subsequent interactions of the two religions . . . believing extremely different historical interpretations as 'fact,' yet still, and always, getting along."

"While other religions . . ." Wendy prodded again.

"Exactly. Rejected each other's beliefs, and waged wars to prove who was right. You think 'Jews and Muslims,' right? But more curious antagonists are the Protestants and Catholics. From a thousand feet above, they believe exactly the same things. But as you bring the view down to street level, you see the devil is in the details."

Wendy laughed out loud. "Ending that thought with that phrase promotes you to 'philosopher' category."

The few minutes of mind picking lasted three and a half hours. Early in that marathon, Michael asked Jake if there might be a music rehearsal room he could peruse. Jake shook his head but said there was a Jewish deli next door (location, location, location) that served world-class matzo ball soup, and Michael left them to their pickin' and grinnin'.

■　■　■

On the drive home, Michael said, "Say, why don't I order up a pizza for tonight, and we can have Andie and Andy over for dinner?"

"Great idea!" she said. "I've been so busy the last few days, it seems like ages since I've seen them."

"Uh, yeah, I bet it does. You have a topping preference?" he asked.

"Same as always. Old habits die hard, you know?"

Michael coughed. In fact, he seemed to be coughing more and more. For a moment, he thought about pulling over to the curb and having "the talk." But then he figured the shit would hit the fan at dinner—why fill up the car with it, too?

"Your talk with Jake seemed to go well," Michael said.

"Yeah, he's a great guy. Really smart with a surprising background. Can you believe? He was Special Forces! Served in Iraq, and 'two quiet trips across the border into Iran,' as he called it."

"Whoa! That blows me away," Michael lied, recalling the pecs like a gladiator's, hair tight to the sides, stolen Persian rugs. "So, I'm guessing tomorrow morning is the Al Hakeem Mosque?"

"Ha, ha," she laughed. "You've always been able to read my mind. And I bet it's pretty light reading."

Yeah right, he thought. Plasma physics and the female psyche—all combined into one light read.

CHAPTER FIVE

At Michael's suggestion, Andie and Andy left all their kids with Andy's wife. Andie's husband was in the National Guard, currently deployed in Kuwait. They rode together, and Michael met them at the car as they pulled into the driveway, climbing into the back seat before they even got unstrapped.

"Hi guys!" he said. "And have I got a surprise for you!"

"Ooh! Meat lover's stuffed crust?" Andie licked her lips. "That was always Mom's favorite."

"Yep. That's the pizza, but it's not the surprise." Both of them raised their eyebrows in the front seat, inquiry written on their beautiful faces. "Your mom is here."

"Yeah, she's been on your mantel for three years, Dad," Andie said. Her smirk settled to a neutral look.

"There's no way for me to explain, but I didn't want you to be completely blindsided. Wendy is here—in the kitchen, not on the mantel. I . . . I just need you both to keep your shit together. Let's go in."

They both stared at him, not understanding, both thinking the same thing—that Michael was into the sauce. He climbed out, then they did, and they fell in beside him on either side, walking to the front door. Michael leaned over to Andy and whispered, "Catch your sister."

Through the door, across the living room, and into the kitchen. Wendy was sitting, facing the backyard, doodling on a notepad. She stood, turned to them, and exclaimed, "Well there you are! It seems like forever since I've seen you!"

Andie froze, stared hard, analyzing Wendy's nose and lips and hair and skin pores and the little mole on her right cheek. Then she collapsed. Andy, always good at taking direction, caught her before she hit the floor. He handled the shock much better, like, well, like he had an assignment. Saving his sister from linoleum burns and chair-leg trauma.

Wendy didn't miss a beat, saying, "Andie, you're pregnant! How wonderful! When is it due? Tell me! Tell me!"

Andie was still being propped up by Andy. Her legs were gone. Alpha Centauri–gone. And she was crying like a baby. Like Wendy's baby. Wiping her eyes, wiping her nose, snot and salt water falling to the floor. Her lips moved but made no sound, other than the sobbing, of course. She stopped for just a moment, wiped her eyes again, took full measure of Wendy's essence, and went back to sobbing. Her legs were trying to find footing, but between her lack of muscle control and the fluids on the floor, she was helpless.

Andy choked out a "Mom!?" but that was it. He had to concentrate on saving Andie from the floor, and the chair.

Michael finally got it together and said, "Let's all sit down, right here around the table." He pulled out a chair for Andie, and Wendy settled back down into hers. As he and Andy sat, Michael said, "Ah, when I came out of work on Friday, there was a familiar figure leaning against my car. Wendy, your mom, well . . . she asked me for a ride home."

Wendy held out her hands, one to each of her babies, and took an Andie and an Andy hand in hers. They both grabbed tight, to prove to themselves she was there, and they felt the energy, the pain-numbing, fear-soothing transfer of essence, and the four of them sat for several minutes, soaking in the reality of what could not be real.

Andie spoke first. "I'm not pregnant, Mo . . . mom. I just di . . . I didn't expect to see you again. Ever."

"I know." Wendy said. Finally, Michael thought, Wendy gave some acknowledgment of her . . . status.

"At your . . . well . . . your funeral, I came to grips. Right there. I came to grips." Andie was coming around, somehow accepting whatever this was.

Wendy gave a small laugh. "You know, I really don't have any memories of that day."

Michael coughed and went to the sink for some water.

Andy asked, "Sooo . . . what are you . . . *doing*?"

She glanced at Michael, then dove right in. "Well, I'm conceptualizing. I've got some ideas, some thoughts, about making some changes, some improvements." She glanced at Michael again.

He jumped in, like Rowan to Wendy's Martin. "You know, changes at our church, for instance. Repurposing the Great Hall, architectural modifications"—he coughed again—"and, you know, discussions with Rabbi Berg."

The doorbell rang, and Michael jumped up, glad to be saved by the bell. A young man clad in a Paul's Pizza jacket chirped, "Hi! Paul sent me!" That was their delivery catch line: "Hi! Paul sent me!" It was on bus stop benches and in the flyers for the local high school teams. It was even in church bulletins. Michael wasn't sure how appropriate that was (Paul sent me?), but it hit a captive audience.

Chirpy said, "Twenty-two dollars, and the sauce is on me!" Another slogan, required at every delivery.

Michael vowed that this would be the last time for Paul's. "I'm switching to Frank's," Michael thought. He gave Chirpy thirty dollars and said, "Keep the change—*and* the pizza. We all just figured out that we're really not hungry." He looked across the living room into the kitchen, and Wendy, Andie, and Andy all nodded agreement and gave Michael the slash-across-the-neck sign, which he chose to believe was "Right. No pizza."

Chirpy shrugged his shoulders and was on his phone before

he'd fully turned around. Michael heard him say, "Hey, Gordo. You want a meat lover's stuffed crust for ten bucks?" And then, "No joke, dude. Be at your curb in eight minutes." And he was gone.

They talked late into the evening, Andie and Andy quickly learning that Wendy's answers to all questions about her "excellent health" would be deflected. But no matter. They sat back and smiled and laughed and reveled in the sound of her voice. By ten o'clock, Andy was getting concerned that his wife would be starting to worry. They pushed their chairs back and called it a night.

Michael walked them out to the car, and his two kids just stared at him, waiting for answers. He stared back with a bit of a smirk, being the old hand at dealing with the new Wendy. "I got nothing," he said. "She reads all night, and we're on a mission all day. All I can say to you is 'Take it as it comes.' Every minute with Wendy back again is a minute to treasure. Are your lives not fuller now than they were yesterday?"

"'Fuller,'" Andie said with a scoff, "like the parting of the Red Sea was 'cool.' How are we supposed to deal with this?"

"You came to grips with it after she was gone. This is a whole lot better, isn't it? Focus on 'fuller' and 'better,' and let's appreciate the ride. Okay?"

Andy said "Okay, Pop. Fuller and better. We'll focus. Fuller and better." He seemed unconvinced but agreeable. They climbed into the car, backed down the drive, and headed home.

Michael walked back to the house, talking to himself. "Fuller and better. Fuller and better . . ."

CHAPTER SIX

On Wednesday morning, Wendy asked Michael to drive her to the Al Hakeem Mosque in Minneapolis. From a worldview perspective, the mosque was . . . interesting. It was a strip mall. It wasn't *in* a strip mall. It was the whole mall, maybe a block long, single story, and fifty feet deep. A two-story entry had been added to the center, along with a modest pond or fountain in front.

The lobby was not opulent, but it was comfortable: several long couches, two table-and-chair groupings, and a blond maple reception desk. Standing at the desk, working at a power-raised desktop, was a tall thin man wearing a traditional throbe, a long floor-length cotton robe, in white. He was not wearing a ghutra and agal, the common Muslim male headgear of a rectangular scarf secured by a ropelike tie. He had a black beard and mustache cropped close.

"*Ahlan wa sahlan,*" he said. "Welcome to the Al Hakeem Mosque. How may I help you?"

Wendy responded, "*Assalamu alaikum,*" which drew a sharp and immediately regretted head turn from Michael. "My name is Wendy Halstad, and this is my husband, Michael. I was hoping to chat with your imam, about your services and teachings and such."

"To what end?" he asked cordially. The gatekeeper.

"I'm a student of theology, interested in learning about all faiths—your successes and challenges, and integration with the 'modern' world." She nodded at the man's high-tech desk and computer gear.

"I understand. Let me confer with Imam Kourash to see if he's available. Please have a seat." He gestured toward the nearest couch, then went back to his desk, picked up a black hijab scarf, and handed it to Wendy, smiling but not speaking. He turned right, down a short hallway, and into the first office (or boutique, back in the day).

In less than a minute, the man returned with the imam in tow—no question who he was. The imam was a short, round fiftysomething with a full gray and bushy beard, the robe, the hat, and the rope. The encyclopedia definition of an imam. "*Ahlan wa sahlan*," he said. "I am Imam Kourash."

"*Assalamu alaikum*, Imam," Wendy said, still adjusting the hijab over her blonde hair. "I'm Wendy Halstad, and this is my husband, Michael. I'm hoping I might sit with you for a bit, and learn about your mosque."

"Certainly," Kourash said. "Come with me, please. Abid, bring us three teas, if you will," he said, raising an eyebrow at Michael.

"None for me, thank you," Michael said, and, pointing to his feet, he added, "I'm taking my dogs for a walk."

Imam Kourash chuckled and led Wendy into his office. He held out his arm to shake hands, and as they shook, he stopped abruptly and looked intently into her eyes. "I believe we are going to have a very interesting chat." Only after several more moments did he release her hand.

As they sat, facing each other in overstuffed lounges separated by a small table, Wendy started in without preamble. "Why do you believe Christians and Muslims have been killing each other for two thousand years, Imam?"

He gave a single laugh, a gleam in his eyes. "Interesting, indeed!" he said. "And you're in luck. I have some very strong, personal opinions on that issue." He looked at her with a question, and she responded with a "go ahead" nod.

"This may surprise you, coming from a Muslim cleric, but my belief is that Allah—God, to you—invested all of us with the ability to think for ourselves. That is, frankly, heretical to many of my more zealous brothers." He paused to choose his words. "I believe in Allah and the Quran, and the Prophet Muhammad, of course. Yet combined with that strong faith is a personal belief that all that is Allah is beyond the understanding, the comprehension, of we mortals.

"There is often no acknowledgment that *faith* and *fact* are two different words, with very different meanings. Fact is akin to a stone. It is there, it is heavy, it has color and texture, and it contains a combination of elements to give it presence. Faith, while very real, has no presence, no calculable weight, no color or texture or minerals. Faith is in our minds—and yes, in our hearts, but the contents of our hearts, other than tissue and blood and possibly some cholesterol, are a creation of our minds . . . Are we still tracking together?"

Wendy nodded. "Yes, we are, Imam. Please go on."

"Because faith—firm faith, of heart, soul, and mind—cannot be touched or held in one's hand, it is held even more firmly, strongly, within one's being. Christian or Muslim, if you believe to your core that your faith is real and correct, then you must also believe that the others with a differing faith *must* be wrong.

"There are 1.8 billion Muslims in the world—and I hope I've not left any out!" he said, winking at Wendy. "And there are 2.4 billion Christians in the world. By definition, each of those believers must know, as strongly as their own religious beliefs, that those other billions of people follow a false god.

"One can't have it both ways: 'I am firmly correct in my beliefs, but those who follow a different faith may be correct.' It is as firm as the laws of physics. There cannot be two 'correct' realities."

Wendy was glad that Michael was not present to disagree.

"And hence comes the rub. A nonbeliever in one's religion becomes, to the believer, an infidel, a godless savage, a pagan, or a devil worshipper. They become disposable, subhuman, a threat. Whatever the description, the justification, they become easier to kill. Ironically, neither Muslim nor Jew accepts that Jesus was the son of God. Yet many Christians loathe Muslims and adore Jews. And Muslims and Jews seem to be enemies of the ages. Beneath all the hatred and nonacceptance, the three religions are remarkably similar. In fact, they have near incestuous beginnings."

"I understand," Wendy mused. "But I'm surprised to get that philosophy from a Muslim cleric. You obviously don't speak for, or in concert with, all 1.8 billion Muslims."

"Correct, young lady, and that brings us back to where we started. I believe, unlike many, that we are imbued with the ability—actually, the expectation—to think for ourselves. Common sense is often very radical."

"So," Wendy said, thinking hard, "you earlier referenced Allah and 'my' God as one and the same. *That* is radical as well!"

Imam Kourash took that lead-in. "Not really, if one can accept the concept—what I believe is the reality—that Allah or God is too complex to quantify, to identify in human terms, to refer to as 'He.' We humans have decided to make God easy for *us* to understand. We give 'Him' human characteristics, mannerisms, looks, and even voice. How ridiculous!

"I teach a . . . less traditional Muslim doctrine. That of living by the guidance of the Quran, but with the belief—not shared by all, mind you—that God doesn't write. Not with chisel, pencil, or crayon. God's word is written by humans who have interpreted the true Word of God at a time when there was hardly any written word, no liberal education, no understanding of science, or the universe, or the elements that make up a stone.

"I teach a doctrine of love, and acceptance, and adherence to the Quran, without imbuing it with the fanciful 'Word of God.' It is the 'Word of God' as interpreted by mere mortal men."

"Wow!" Wendy blurted out.

"Yes, 'wow' is an appropriate summary. And praise Allah," he said as he winked at Wendy, "that I am leading a mosque in Minnesota. In much of the Middle East, I would not *be*. I'd be a head over here, and a body over there . . ."

"I think, Imam Kourash," Wendy drawled, "that you and I have some conceptualizing to do!"

He gave a quizzical smile. "Will that include explaining how you fit into all of this?"

"More likely, it will explain why I do not . . . cannot fit in . . . to any of it."

"I believe we will require more tea," he said, and he called to Abid.

■　■　■

Wendy found Michael resting his "dogs" out front. As they headed to the car, Wendy bubbled, "Remember what we've got scheduled for this evening?"

"Dinner?" Michael said hopefully.

"No, dummy. Pastor Conlin invited us to meet with him and the church directors at seven o'clock."

"Oh yeah. Then dinner?"

Wendy was lost in thought. "Hmm? Sure."

He took another prying shot over the bow. "You sure don't eat much. What's up with that?"

"Well, it's like data entry in a computer—garbage in, garbage out."

Michael coughed. "That's a terrible analogy! And gross! And . . . not an answer."

She jabbed her elbow into his side. "I'm guessing they'll feed us at the vestry meeting."

■　■　■

Wendy and Michael entered the church conference room exactly at seven, and the chatter from the group already there subsided. Pastor

Conlin said, "Everybody, this is Michael and Wendy. Wendy and I have been mulling over some suggestions for our Path Forward initiative, and I wanted to present them to all of you for consideration."

He touched her elbow and guided her from person to person. "Wendy, this is Silvia, our director of operations, kind of like our general manager."

Wendy shook Silvia's hand and looked directly into her eyes. She smiled at Silvia's rapid blinking, and then Silvia said, "Well hello, dear! Good to see you again!"

Daniel nudged her elbow to the left. "And this is Morty, our director of giving and finance."

Wendy said, "Hi, Morty. Say, can I borrow twenty bucks?"

Morty's jaw dropped, Daniel's eyes rolled, and Michael could be heard coughing somewhere behind them. "Just kidding. It's nice to meet you!" she said, and she shook his hand. He closed his mouth and smiled, and his eyes went from "Custer just hit by an arrow" to warm and knowing.

"No problem. I get that all the time," he lied.

Another elbow nudge. "Kathryn, our music director."

"Hi, Kathryn! Do you believe in rock and roll, and can music save your mortal soul?"

Everyone stared. Michael held his breath.

Kathryn responded like a champ. "You know, we never, ever sing the blues. We only sing of happy news." Then she just smiled and turned away.

The room erupted in laughter and applause, and Wendy said, "Kathy, I never knew I had a sister!"

Kathryn took on a face of Nurse Ratched and said gruffly, "My name is *not* Kathy." The room went quiet again, and then she said, "But you can call me Kate." She patted Wendy on the back and then held her hand in place for an extra moment. "Maybe sisters by different parents," she said with a smile.

Next was Nate, the director of recreation and youth services. He looked very much like Jesus, except for the red sneakers and the braid in his beard. He gave Wendy a fist bump.

"And finally, Pastor Allen. He heads our outreach ministry." Allen was maybe twenty-five and looked, dressed, and acted like the secretary-treasurer for the Stillwater Young Republicans Club. He took her hand in both of his and said oh so seriously, "May God be with you, and may his spirit shine upon you." Six sets of eyes rolled, including Michael's. Neither Wendy's nor Pastor Allen's eyes rolled. Hers stared intently into his while she held his hand. He tried a soft backpedal, but his hand was still stuck. He glanced down, then quickly said, "Ah, excuse me. I seem to have a bladder issue," pulled away, and headed out of the conference room.

Everyone took a breath, and Daniel said, "Let's all sit down, shall we? The kitchen brought up some sandwiches and sodas." Michael made a quick dive toward the table and then went into casual slo-mo as he pulled out a chair for Wendy, then one for himself.

The discussion was lively and positive, with each challenge followed by a solution. Everyone was in agreement, in part because young Pastor Allen did not reappear. And frankly, in this new concept, outreach ministry was no longer a viable department.

CHAPTER SEVEN

They got home around ten o'clock. Wendy took her reading position on the couch, and Michael headed up to bed. This was only the fifth full day of Wendy's homecoming, but it seemed to Michael that they had lived a lifetime in those five days. Five days that could never be but were. Wendy's presence was so much more powerful than Michael ever thought possible, and their connection this time around was complete and, unbelievably, natural. He felt he was in the middle of the *Wizard of Oz* tornado, and he was very comfortable, thank you.

Sometime around midnight, Wendy tapped lightly on Michael's—their—bedroom door. He stirred, and she whispered, "Hey, sailor, is there room in your bunk for two?" He hesitated for around a nanosecond, then held up the blanket to make room.

Right before dawn, Michael sensed that Wendy was awake. Still awake. He propped himself up on one arm and looked at her for several minutes. He said, "Wen, are you going away again?"

She gave it a moment, then said, "We all die, Michael. Forrest Gump's mama told us that."

"Not an answer," he said softly.

"I have loved you every minute of my life, Michael."

"And I you," he said.

"I want your best, your fondest, your most profound memory of me to be of tonight. No one has ever shared what you and I shared tonight. I am a part of your soul that can never be removed. I can't tell you what tomorrow brings, or the day after. But you know that this is not possible. It's real, right now, right here. But it's not possible. Revel in the gift, and not what it costs."

■   ■   ■

Thursday morning arrived with a cloudless, bright blue sky, and a death threat. Of sorts. A dead, bloody animal lay in the yard next to a sign stapled to a garden stake. Michael and Wendy saw it at the same time and hit the yard at a run. Upon closer inspection, the mess was less of a Mayan sacrifice than a fourth-grade science project.

The animal was a well-worn stuffed teddy bear/cow/goat/koala. It was hard to tell. The blood was the Heinz variety. One ninety-nine for fourteen ounces. The sign, however, was a bit more chilling. Black Sharpie on white paper attached to a wooden lath stake stuck in the grass, it read: "Home of the Devil." Next line: "God will strike you down." And the last line: "If God asks me, I will obey."

Forensically challenged as he was, Michael pondered the sign. Guy speaks directly to God. Could be a girl, but girls generally only killed their abusive boyfriends / significant others. This guy was waiting for a sign from God, or so said the sign in the yard. Which was obviously directed at Wendy's ecumenical efforts to unite the tribes.

Wendy said nothing and walked back into the house. Michael cleaned up the mess, pondering for just a moment nuking a hot dog so as not to waste all that catsup, but his inner adult rejected the thought.

Back inside, he found Wendy tucked into her reading chair, legs underneath her and a mischievous look in her eyes. In his worst Ricky Ricardo accent, he said, "Lucy, if we call the police, you'll have some 'splainin' to do."

She said, "No police are necessary. You can't strike down what has already been struck."

"Mama Gump?"

"No, just Wendy Halstad waxing poetic," she said. "I'm intrigued that it happened so quickly, though."

Michael looked at her. "You expected threats? Seriously?"

She nodded. "It's going to hit the fan now. The word is obviously out. Pastor Conlin, Rabbi Berg, and Imam Kourash were all about implementing our conceptualizing as quickly as possible. 'No time like the present,' they all said. And implementation will involve a lot of people."

Michael chuckled. "My grandma gave me a watch for my sixth birthday. When I opened it, she clucked 'No present like the time!' I wanted a bike."

Wendy rolled her eyes. "Back to this morning's excitement. Imam Kourash was the most concerned. Even in Minneapolis, some of his mosque members are more traditional than experimental. He asked if I would be available if he needed some help 'splainin.'"

■　■　■

Wendy spent the rest of the day at the library, buried in the three Rs—reading, researching, and reflecting. Her "concept assistance" was rolling along fine, but there was so much more to learn: Blueprints of CVN 78 (USS *Gerald R. Ford*). Latest advances in neuro-restoration. Rosetta Stone crib notes for Chinese, Russian, Pashti, Tagalog, Arabic, Canadian . . .

CHAPTER EIGHT

Friday morning, it hit the fan. Front page, below the fold, in the *Star Tribune*: "Stunning Changes at Area Houses of Worship." The byline was Micha McGuire, the *Strib*'s Religion and Faith editor. He was, in fact, the entire Religion and Faith department.

Friday, April 5   Morning Edition
By Micha McGuire

Early this week, this reporter heard a whisper of some interesting meetings at a Stillwater congregation, the St. Adolphus Free Church. Word was the church is considering truly transformational changes in its structure, focus, ministry, and even facilities usage.

I talked to 17 parishioners of St. Adolphus and got 17 similar interpretations. Pastor Daniel Conlin had met with an unnamed "concept guru" (their term), which led to a Wednesday-evening vestry meeting, which resulted in, almost immediately, adoption of these radical changes. An interesting occurrence in an otherwise slow week for church news.

But the story became larger almost by the hour. One party said they believed the concept guru was also heading off to meet with clergy at the Temple Shalom in St. Paul, and my visit there hinted that this unknown person was also meeting with Imam Kourash at the Al Hakeem Mosque in Minneapolis.

I have since spoken with a total of 39 members of the three houses of worship, and all of them convey the same story—that their church hierarchy and congregations have separately, and apparently with no coordination between them, implemented seismic and immediate changes in their missions.

Some of the changes, applied across all three faiths and facilities, include:

- Elimination of the word "worship" in their teachings and writings. The explanations, also nearly identical, were that the word and process of worship was a human construct and incorrect interpretation of the "Word of God" by well-meaning religious scholars well before the spread of the written word, formal education, scientific discovery, astronomy, or geology.

- Elimination of all depictions of God in human terms. This includes all references to God's gender, age, beard color, voice tenor, thought process, and commands. The explanations were that these groups have come to believe that the entity, the concept, and the essence of God is beyond human capacity to describe, or even to grasp.

- Elimination of outreach ministries among each of these several religions, apparently, again, with no coordination between them. This was explained by noting that all six billion people on earth have been taught or solicited to one religion or another, and outreach programs were succeeding only to "convert" prospects from one to the other. With the new "understandings" that these three groups have developed, the teachings of each religion are so similar as to preclude the need for competition.

- The acceptance of *all* religions as believing in one God, which none of these groups can now define in human terms.
- The repurposing of the three sect campuses, while retaining their communities, congregational services, and teachings. They each aspire to become centers for events, recreation, teaching, counseling, music, and public service. It is anticipated that some of the properties will be downsized by strategic selling or donation of land and buildings.

That, my friends, is mind-numbingly dramatic, but less so than what I learned as this edition of the *Star Tribune* was going to print. Since I first started researching and interviewing for this story, 13 additional religious centers in the Twin Cities have bought into the principles above!

I am continuing to investigate the identity of the mysterious "concept guru," and I will have more on this growing story in the Saturday edition.

CHAPTER NINE

On Saturday morning, Wendy and Michael drove over to the Al Hakeem Mosque. TV news reports showed a growing group of protestors, and Wendy thought that if there was trouble, it would probably be there.

Michael asked what her intentions were. "Just to calm people down," she said. "As the Soviet Union was dissolving in 1989, a Russian general was quoted as saying, 'We are going to play the dirtiest trick on the United States. We're going to deny you an enemy.' That's what I intend to do. Go one-on-one, hug, and explain."

Michael glanced sideways at her. "And you think that will save the day? They looked pretty agitated on TV."

"Sure. I just have to play rock-paper-scissors—convince them that common sense beats zealotry every time."

"Just don't get hit in the head with the rock."

■ ■ ■

As they arrived at the mosque, there were several hundred people gathered in the parking lot out front. They carried signs stating, "Death to Infidels," "The Great Satan wishes you were dead," and "Allah sent me to kill you."

Imam Kourash was walking among the protestors, unafraid, trying to engage with them. Wendy approached him, nodded, and turned to the nearest angry person. He was not carrying a sign, but had both hands raised in the air and was yelling. Wendy said, "Hi!" The paper approach, Michael thought. A unique first parry.

The protester was a young man, maybe thirty, Middle Eastern, and well dressed. He towered over Wendy, but he lowered his arms and stopped yelling. The "Hi" approach apparently caught him off guard.

"I'm Wendy," she said. "Looks like the mosque changes have you pretty pissed off."

"The changes are blasphemous," he said. "They destroy our faith, dishonor the Qur'an, and must be met with force!"

Wendy reached out and shook his hand. "What's your name?"

His face contorted into fear, like he'd just been nailed with a poison dart.

He drew his hand away, inspected it, and found no blood, so he said, "My name is Abdul. It means 'servant of God.' Why are you here?"

"I was hoping to introduce you to Imam Kourash. Do you know him?" she asked.

He hesitated. "I do not attend this mosque. But why would I want to meet an infidel who calls himself an imam?"

She led him over to Kourash, a few feet away. "Imam Kourash, Abdul has some questions for you. Do you have a moment?"

"Surely!" He looked at Abdul and smiled. "I'm betting you're concerned about these 'radical' changes, no? Let's walk away from the mayhem and talk."

Wendy's gaze followed them. One-on-one. Two hundred ninety-nine to go, she thought.

As she turned, she came face-to-face with a Saturday night special. A chrome, short-barreled, five-shot revolver, not very effective at over ten feet or so. But they were eight feet apart.

"Are you the devil who is trying to destroy our faith? Why should I not kill you at this moment, and win the praise of Allah?"

"Um . . . it might hurt?" Her face was calm, her nerves settled. She was not afraid.

Michael yelled from twenty yards away. "Wendy! Wendy! Watch out!"

The man fired three quick shots into Wendy's torso, dropped the gun, and turned to run. But he stopped, looking over his shoulder at Wendy still standing there. "Let's find a park bench and talk," she said. She lightly took him by the elbow and walked toward the front of the mosque.

In those several seconds, the atmosphere in the parking lot changed from mayhem to more frantic mayhem. People were running in every direction away from the epicenter, where the .38 Special lay on the ground. Michael had frozen in place, afraid and shocked. He watched Wendy and the shooter slowly walk away. He felt paralyzed and helpless.

Wendy and the man who shot the gun sat alone on a bench. "Why did you shoot?" she asked.

"You . . . you are the devil. You are trying to destroy my faith. And now . . ."

"What is your name?"

"Nawar. It means—"

"'Victorious,' I know. But Nawar, we've never met. You don't know me. You've never heard me speak, or read anything I've written, correct? You don't even know my name."

Nawar stumbled. "No, I—you are correct. But you *are* a messenger from Satan, am I right?"

"Nawar, you just fired three bullets into my body, yet you don't even know who I am."

"I did, and how . . . how did you . . ."

Wendy gently cut him off. "We'll get to that later. But your religion, your faith, the Qur'an, they don't advise you to kill people you do not know."

"No. But I must protect the name of Allah."

"From what, exactly? From a fifty-year-old lady who you do not know? I have studied your religion. I have read the Quran, several times. Nowhere are you directed to do what you just did."

"I heard God speaking to me. He told me what to do."

"Nawar, God did not speak to you."

"How do you—"

She took his hand. "Nawar. God did not speak to you. God does not speak to people in the middle of a protest and tell them to shoot a person they do not know. Frankly, Nawar, God does not speak to people. God is too complex to engage in word games. Do you understand?"

"I . . . I think I do. But respect for Allah is all I know! What am I to do? I will surely be put into prison—for shooting—which I deserve."

"Listen to me, Nawar. Here's what you say to the police"—she glanced to her left—"who are about thirty seconds away. You did not intend to hurt anyone, do you understand? You did not intend to kill anyone. The first three bullets in your gun were blanks, correct?"

"No, they were all—"

"Nawar," Wendy said firmly. "The first three rounds in your gun were blanks. Shells with powder, but no projectile. You wanted to scare, not kill. You may be sentenced to clean up this parking lot, but you will not go to prison. Do you understand?"

"Yes," he choked. "I am . . . sorry."

"Be a vessel for human advancement, Nawar. Embrace goodness, not thousand-year-old words that, frankly, you misinterpret. Retain your faith, but be guided by your heart."

Wendy stood and started walking toward Michael. She turned and said, "Win people over, Nawar. One by one."

She walked up to Michael, who was still frozen in the same spot, watching, and realizing. "Holy Smokes, Batman!" he said.

CHAPTER TEN

With the police noisily approaching from several directions, Wendy and Michael ambled to their car and calmly drove past the incoming brigade of vehicles.

Michael raised an eyebrow and glanced at Wendy.

"Take me home, sailor," she said.

It was about two in the afternoon when there was a knock on their front door. Wendy was upstairs reading, and Michael answered the door. Behind it was a large man holding a badge. You don't get to be a detective in any police department without eating your share of donuts as a patrol officer. This guy had a buzz cut, stood maybe six-foot-two, with focused eyes and a wrinkled sport coat.

"Michael Halstad?" he asked.

"That's me. How can I help you?"

"I'm Detective Arnold with the Minneapolis Police Department. Are you familiar with the shooting this morning at the Al Hakeem Mosque?"

"Yes, sir, I was there, but standing quite a ways back from the gunfire."

"Mind if I ask why you were there?"

Michael responded truthfully. "Well, I read the front-page story in the *Star Tribune* yesterday, and then saw a news report this morning about protests at the mosque, and I figured, Not a bad way to spend a Saturday morning."

"Yeah, so, we've gone through the available surveillance tapes that show the area, and your involvement raised a couple eyebrows in our media room."

"Well," Michael said, "I wouldn't call being there 'involved,' but it did make for an interesting morning. What raised your eyebrows?" As an afterthought, he added, "Please, come in."

Michael guided the detective into the kitchen, and they sat at the table. Arnold stared at him, appraising his demeanor, then he started his explanation. "Two seconds before the shooting, you appeared to be looking directly at the shooter. You seemed to be yelling—no audio on CCTV, of course—and you burst into a run. At the moment of the shots, you stopped and stood dead still for the next three minutes and twelve seconds. Every other person in the parking lot headed for cover, and you stood dead still. Can you explain that?"

"I guess I was just in shock. The guy with the gun wasn't looking my way, and I didn't feel that I was in danger, so I just watched. You say I stood there for three minutes?"

"And twelve seconds," Detective Arnold clarified. "Was your wife there?"

Michael looked surprised, and then took on a look of sadness. "No, sir. She's been right here for three years." He gestured to the urn on the mantel.

The detective rose, walked toward the urn, and read the inscription. He turned and said humbly, "Mr. Halstad, I'm so sorry for your loss. We've had several references to someone named Wendy as somehow involved in the changes happening at these churches. Identifying you on the video, we assumed—incorrectly, it seems—that we might have a lead. This kind of thing happens a lot in the early parts of an investigation. Two parties at the scene said they thought the shooter was talking with a woman directly before he fired, but there is no evidence of that on the tapes. People say a lot of things in stressful situations."

"Was anyone hurt?" Michael asked.

"Apparently not," Arnold replied. "No injuries identified on the tape, no emergency room gunshot victims. But the strangest thing is, we could calculate the trajectory of the shots pretty exactly, yet we found no bullets. We've had ten uniforms scouring the impact area in grids and have found no bullets, no evidence of impacts, no telltale ricochet markings. Not even stray shell casings. The gun was a revolver, but we found no ejected shells. Nothing."

"Hmm," Michael said. "Apparently the guy was a zealot, but not a killer?"

"Maybe," Arnold responded. "Hey, I'm sorry to have bothered you, and again, my condolences for your loss. Just a strange coincidence, I guess." He paused to ponder for a moment, then said, "You have a good day, okay?"

■ ■ ■

Once the unmarked car had left the driveway, Wendy came downstairs, went up to Michael, and took his hands in hers.

"Wen?" Michael said. "Are you aware that you don't show up on film? What the fuck is up with that?" He was agitated, not at Wendy, but at his total—or near total—lack of understanding of what he was dealing with.

"I wasn't, but that sure makes things easier, doesn't it?"

"Um, yeah. But what about the bullets? No bullets?" he countered.

"Oh, the bullets were real. I told Nawar to claim they were blanks, that he wasn't intending to hurt anyone."

Michael was exasperated, grasping to understand. "The bullets were real, but they can't be found. What kind of voodoo does that?"

"Michael, I didn't come into this experience with an instruction manual. I have a sense of what to do, but no plan or outline. I'm learning right along with you. And it's all very interesting!"

"So, let's go over what we know." He sat on the couch, and she followed. "You are back for a visit." He shook his head while Wendy nodded. "You have an amazing rapport with people one-on-one. You are real to the touch, but don't show up on video."

"Isn't that cool?" she gushed.

"Uh, yeah. Cool. And bullets, real bullets, don't harm you, and don't come out the other side."

"Don't forget the best part," she said, winking coyly as she snuggled up to him.

"Wednesday night, upstairs, lights off. No, Wen, I won't forget that."

■　■　■

The next morning's *Star Tribune* had more details. Michael read it like he was an insider, like he knew more than he should.

The gun was a .38 Special, five rounds, three fired, two unfired. The two unfired rounds had projectile heads. The three fired rounds gave no clue if they had originally contained projectiles or not. No evidence of stray bullets or fragments. No injuries.

The alleged gunman surrendered to police without incident, and his first words were, "I'm so sorry to have caused any fear." The MPD said the man, identified as Nawar Manook, claimed that he had used blanks. However, when asked what a blank was, he had no response. He claimed he didn't want to hurt anyone but could not explain why the last two cartridges in his weapon were live rounds and not blanks.

Asked if he held fundamentalist Muslim beliefs, he said, "I did, but no longer." When asked if he wanted an attorney, he said, "I do not need an attorney to tell you that I did not shoot anyone, that I did not intend to hurt anyone, and that I did not use real bullets."

The article ended by noting that while the police continued to investigate, they had little to charge the gunman with. Firing a non-lethal cartridge in public or inciting a riot were possible charges, but there were no victims, and there was no riot.

CHAPTER ELEVEN

Andie and Andy came over for dinner again that evening. Rather than try to explain what couldn't be explained, they again left their kids with Andy's wife. No Paul's Pizza tonight. Wendy was cooking.

After the hugs, and then more hugs, Andie slid in a question. "So, how was your day today?"

Michael responded first. "Well, pretty interesting, actually. We saw on TV that there were protests at the Al Hakeem Mosque this morning, so because your mom was, like, the catalyst and all, she decided to go over and mediate."

They all looked at Wendy, and she gave a shrug and a tight-lipped smile.

Michael continued, "It was all very exciting. Lots of yelling, signs threatening Armageddon, Wendy hugging people, a guy shooting her, people running, sirens . . ."

"Wait, wait, wait," Andie cut in. "You glossed over the part where a guy *shot my mom*. Why is that?" She was stunned, again, and wasn't getting used to it. All eyes turned back to Wendy.

"It was just a misunderstanding," Wendy started, continuing to stir a pot of macaroni.

"Three shots at her chest," Michael added helpfully, as his kids turned back to him.

"But he missed, really!" Wendy said.

"Point-blank," Michael continued.

Andy shouted, "For the love of baklava, stop!" All eyes turned to him. He was holding his arms out, palms down and flat in the "safe at first" sign. Michael and Wendy stopped their witty repartee.

"Did a guy shoot you?" Andy asked Wendy.

"Well, yes and no," Wendy said, just as Michael said "Yes."

"In the chest?" Andy demanded.

"Well, not really," Wendy responded as Michael said, "Three times."

"And you're standing here cooking pasta?" Andy demanded again.

"Yes, yes I am." Wendy said proudly.

"I agree with that part," Michael added.

Andy sat down heavily in a kitchen chair. He sighed deeply and held out his hands as if to signal safe at first again, but with palms up, demanding more information. His sister was already sitting, holding her head, elbows on the table. Several minutes passed and no one spoke. Just the puttering of pasta preparation.

Finally, Michael gave it a shot. "Look, guys. There are no answers. Wendy died three years ago. We all cried our eyes out at the morgue. She had an autopsy. She was cremated. We had a funeral."

"For the record, I don't remember any of that," Wendy inserted, almost defensively.

Michael choked, then continued. "But she's here now. And she was shot three times this morning at close range, felt no effects from the bullets, pulled the shooter aside, and actually set him up with an alibi . . ."

Andie raised her eyes to Michael's in a question.

"Blanks," Michael responded. "The police were here this afternoon and bought it."

Andie lowered her eyes again, head still propped in her hands and now moving left and right, back and forth. Finally, she raised her head, looked at her father, then her mother, and said, "I hope we have ice cream. I'm going to need ice cream." Wendy was humming over the stove. Michael stood and went to the fridge.

CHAPTER TWELVE

Michael and Wendy hit the early Sunday service at Saint Adolphus, and even at 8:50 a.m., the place was rocking. There were hundreds of people walking into the Great Hall, mingling in the lobby, or scurrying here and there doing last-moment preparations. Pastor Conlin spotted them and rushed over.

"Wendy! Michael! I'm so happy you could make it!"

"Morning, Daniel!" they both said in unison. Wendy continued, "You've got your hands full. How'd you weather the week? No gunshots, or angry protests, I hope?"

The pastor laughed. "No, no organized protests, but I've discussed the new reality with truly hundreds of people, and a handshake was the most physical we got. Hopefully you two weren't anywhere near the shots yesterday . . ."

Michael took a half step forward and said, "We weren't close enough to get shot, anyway." Then he pivoted the focus back on Saint Adolphus. "I read about your changes in the paper."

"You just got the frosting from the paper. We're in the midst of transforming our classroom wing into a homeless shelter and have brought in a team of addiction counselors from Hazelden who'll office here full time. We already have protocols in place with county services and the sheriff's office for a low-key and caring intake process, and we've staffed up the kitchen for daily operation. And if I don't stop yapping, I'll be late for church!" Conlin dashed away but stopped abruptly about ten feet away, turned, and said, "Oh, and Wendy, that musician you contacted—Zimmerman?"

He winked at her, which Michael caught but didn't follow. "He's here with a five-piece band!"

They followed Daniel into the service but stayed back behind the last row. Pastor Conlin stood at the lectern up front, only several feet from where Wendy had been so carefully placed three years ago. He scanned the congregation as they settled in with a sparkle in his eyes that said something was up. He leaned into the microphone, the band quietly plugging in behind him. In a booming voice, he introduced the day.

"'Come gather 'round people,' is the start of a prophetic anthem from the sixties. You all know it and can probably recite several verses. It embraces a romantic ideal of people learning and growing and opening their eyes and minds to change." He looked back at the band as the musicians continued to fiddle with their set-up.

"The song invites writers, and politicians, and families like us to open up our minds and our hearts . . ."

The band started softly, as background. Brushes on the snare, a soft base note, a single chord, then another . . .

Conlin continued his oration, just a bit louder. "Because to improve ourselves, to become more than we are, to embrace growth as people, as a society, and as members of our human race, we need to accept . . . embrace . . . and yes, grab on, for the times they are a-changin'."

The band ramped it up and took over. An older man at the group's only microphone looked up and ran his eyes across the congregation as gasps of recognition and yelps of excitement followed his gaze. Robert Zimmerman, or rather, Minnesota's own Bob Dylan, took up the lyrics.

Like everyone else, Michael was amazed. He was overwhelmed with emotion over the perfection of the lyrics in this moment. He looked over in awe and admiration at Wendy, and he hoped, really, really hoped, that the next song was not "Lay, Lady, Lay."

CHAPTER THIRTEEN

After he finished reading the paper, Michael looked at Wendy. She glanced up, said, "We might have a visitor or two today, Michael."

"Of course," he replied a bit sarcastically. "More police?"

"No, a little higher up."

At that moment, there was a firm *whop-whop-whop* on the front door. This time Wendy went to answer. As she opened it, a tall, gray-haired African American man in an impeccable dark blue suit held out his hand. "Wendy? My office said you'd left a message, and as I was in the Twin Cities, I decided to just stop over and see if I could catch you. My name is Admiral Hiram Brown."

As he said this, a blue late-model Toyota Corolla left the curb and drove away. "Uber," he explained with a smile. "I ditched my driver at the downtown Hilton. He's probably got my staff at DEF-CON 4 by now."

"Come in, Admiral! I'm so happy you could find the time."

Michael was looking on, listening, and absorbing. He said, "Sir, I'm Michael Halstad, and you're the secretary of the Navy!"

"Yes, sir, I am, though I prefer to go by Hiram. As you may know, I'm originally from Edina, and I was fortunate enough to get a layover to attend my church this morning. I must say, I was startled at hearing the changes, but Pastor Jenks caught up with me as I entered the lobby and gave me a big hug. 'Hiram,' he said, 'you're going to love what we've done with the place.' And I did. After the service, I had no hesitation as to where I would go next."

"Ad—Hiram, please sit down," Wendy said as she guided him by the elbow to the couch. "Can I get you some coffee?" Wendy was taking it all in stride. Michael was blown away for the . . . twelfth time? He was losing track.

"Sure, that would be grand."

The coffee came out in seconds, almost as if Wendy had been expecting to serve a visitor coffee on Sunday morning. "I've got a concept that I'd like to pass by you. You've heard of the changes—like at your church—taking place in churches across the country, correct?"

"Yes. It's astounding. And the speed of it all!" he said.

"So, as a preamble to my suggestion, are you aware that there are thirty-seven million churches worldwide?"

"I am now, and I'm surprised at the number."

Wendy continued, "Since the first three houses of worship changed their mission last Wednesday, forty-three thousand churches have adopted those core tenets worldwide. From all religions, all faiths, and most areas around the globe. And reading stock market trends—"

"She does a lot of reading," Michael said to the admiral.

Wendy went on as if Michael hadn't spoken. "I learned this morning one tiny bit of news: in the past four days, Kalashnikov rifle orders have dropped to zero for the first time in the company's history. The reason I follow the Kalashnikov is that it has only one function—killing people."

"Intriguing, but . . ."

"Hold on there, Hiram! I'm still in preamble," Wendy laughed, and the secretary of the Navy returned a chuckle. "I like the quote from Dan Brown, in one of his books. 'The path of every religious zealot is littered with dead bodies.' And that quote sort of brings the issue into focus. Churches don't start wars, and religions don't. Religious wars are started by people who misinterpret the words of their religion. But one source of ongoing warfare, that of religious intolerance, is being met head-on with the changes you saw in your church this morning. With the spread of this long-overdue change in beliefs, religious warfare is being wiped off the table. Zealots who convinced their followers that they spoke the Word of God are being shut down, replaced by a new and more sensible understanding that the entire concept and essence of 'God' is too complex to be interpreted by fringe radicals.

"There are other warfare catalysts that will soon be extinct, very quickly. There is, at this moment, a peace dividend ballooning at such a rapid pace, it will, literally, change the world."

"I'm coming around," Hiram said. "I have an idea of where you're going, and I'll tell you a fact that I've learned in my forty-one years in the Navy. No warrior, anywhere, is in favor of war. Peace is always the goal. We simply serve a need, and we would *all* love to see that need go away."

Wendy took her cue. "Okay, so now we're up to present day. A carrier strike group includes a carrier, two cruisers, two destroyers, at least one submarine—which the Navy has never actually confirmed—and a host of tenders and supply ships, correct?"

The secretary smiled. "If I confirm the submarine, I'm giving away classified information, so let's say I agree with the rest of your list—even though I confess some surprise at your abrupt segue to carrier task forces."

"Fair enough, Hiram. You have 20 carrier strike groups, which together comprise around 200 of the Navy's 335 active commissions, plus"—she winked at him—"a secret submarine here or there. A strike group has approximately 10,000 sailors manning the ships, the largest contingent being around 4,000 on the CVNs, down from 5,000 on previous carriers due to advancing robotics and electronics."

"You've done your homework, Wendy. I'm not convinced my chief of staff could cite those stats without CliffsNotes."

She glanced at Michael. "I do a lot of reading." Then she turned back to the admiral. "So let's say you took one carrier strike group and modified its mission to, say, disaster relief. Maybe keep the destroyers and the sub—sorry—in the group, to staunch some of your nervousness, and reassign the other boats."

"Wendy." He shook his head while keeping his eyes fixed on hers. "The makeup and mission of our carrier task forces are based on years of research, millions of computer runs, opinions of some of the best military minds on the planet, and, frankly, threat. Every what-if has been factored in. As much as I truly appreciate your energy, I'm afraid your proposal is too . . . idealistic."

Wendy didn't break her gaze. "Hiram, the one what-if that has never been factored in is no war. No threat. No need for hugely expensive, amazingly destructive armadas. Look, you've got twenty carrier strike forces. My proposal is to re-mission one of them. Only one, to prove the concept, and convince the skeptics. Six hulls out of three hundred thirty-five. And there's a hidden win for the Navy."

Hiram raised an eyebrow. "I'm a sucker for wins."

"If you put in place a system of repurposing your attack vessels in advance of the cataclysmic collapse of worldwide hostilities, you keep your navy relevant. One carrier can show the way."

The admiral chuckled again. "Well, you nailed me with my own worldview, there. Your phrase, 'the cataclysmic collapse of worldwide hostilities,' is our goal. But the devil is in the details."

"Correct. So, let's look at a few of those. Every business in the United States is hiring. Every single one. Should the Pentagon not need its current 2.1 million soldiers, sailors, and support staff, there has never been a better time in the history of our country to fill those civilian jobs with highly trained and potentially available former military personnel.

"Next, the cost of your most recent carrier, the *John F. Kennedy*, was 11.4 billion dollars. There are three more in production as we speak, all of which will cost more. Allowing for that cataclysmic collapse in hostilities, which is also rapidly developing as we speak, you would be the first Navy secretary in history to go to Congress and say, 'You know, we don't need that much money this year.'

"And next, the curious math of the 'peace through strength' doctrine—which I acknowledge has been very successful. But if the United States downsized based on a factual drop in world hostilities, all other nations trying to maintain their percentage of par with our military would also downsize. As the threat from opposing militaries diminishes, our need for armor diminishes, which reduces the threat even further. The human brain is a flawed and sometimes prehistoric organ that still uses the logic, with a pinch of chew between cheek and gum, 'Well, if ah got that dang sixteen-inch shooter, ah maze well use it.' By reducing our threat to others, the threat to us is also reduced.

"Hiram, now is the time. One carrier strike force out of twenty will prove the concept."

Michael was sitting across the room, his jaw nearly at his chest. She had always been confident, but Wendy was now unflappably sitting here suggesting military strategy to the secretary of the Navy.

Admiral Brown was staring at her, his chin resting on his fingertips, contemplating. "I follow the concept, and it is within my prerogative to repurpose any single ship, but the logistics are staggering. We'd need to redesign the—"

Wendy continued for him. "The entire ship, basically, yes. But I've given it a lot of thought, using the blueprints of the *Gerald R. Ford*."

Brown looked up quickly. "Those blueprints are proprietary and top secret. How on earth would you find a set?"

"Admiral, you can find everything except the Kentucky Fried Chicken recipe on the internet. You know that!" She laughed.

"Yes, I guess I do," he said, a bit frustrated.

"So let's say we were to transform CVN 78 into the world's

largest and fastest disaster relief vessel. We'll look at speed first. As a nuclear engineer, you know that the largest hindrance to higher speeds on water is hull resistance, and that increased power is not linear to increased speed. Pound for pound, to get CVN 78 to move at twice the speed of its current maximum thirty-three knots would require an eightfold increase in power. Which is achievable, but unrealistic in an existing hull."

Brown was smiling broadly, and Michael stared at Wendy, shaking his head slowly back and forth.

Wendy continued as if she were teaching a penmanship class. "However, the opportunity is to reduce resistance by reducing displacement. CVN 78 displaces 103,000 tons. But if you reduce the displacement to 72,000 tons, your top speed will increase 30 percent, to 43 knots, with no required boost in power. And that reduction in displacement is achievable strictly by removing armaments and armament systems—65 F-35 or comparable airframes, missiles, machine gun rounds, AAA, racks, aviation fuel, spare parts, catapults, and on and on."

Brown looked alarmed. "What an incredible waste! It would break my heart to disembowel this magnificent ship!"

"Magnificent *warship*," she interjected. "I'm telling you, Hiram, that ship may be obsolete in weeks. Your options will be to repurpose it or scrap it. And in fact, the 'incredible waste' is the point! CVN 78 cost 12.8 billion dollars to build, and we're not going to need it!"

"I'm following you. I'm just not liking the process," he said. "I would not be able to watch the 'repurposing' in progress. It would bring me to tears, and photographers follow me everywhere." He glanced out the window. "Except here, thank goodness." He sighed. "Go on."

"Okay. Because the ship won't be a warship, you can reduce personnel from the current four thousand to around twelve hundred fifty. A whole host of positions just won't be needed—pilots, flight deck fire crews, munitions crews, weapons and airframe maintenance crews, launch and intake crews, fueling crews, target identification teams, and several other categories.

"And next is a gift from God, if you will." Wendy smiled, and the admiral looked at her quizzically. "Because the various religious organizations will not be spending huge amounts trying to 'win' souls from other religions, they have agreed to fund a variety of public works efforts, including the International Committee of the Red Cross. As a fast-attack, disaster relief floating city, the humanitarian and medical staffs will be provided at no cost to the Navy or the US Treasury. While on board, they would report to the ship's captain, just like any other sailor."

"My god, woman!" Brown exclaimed. "How have you put all this into a realistic proposal? This is years' worth of planning!" He smiled again and said, with light sarcasm, "I assume you planned the ship's lunch menus?"

Wendy laughed. "No, I'll leave that to the cooks. However, you bring up one of the unique opportunities to repurpose this ship. It has an existing state-of-the-art food service group and infrastructure, experienced in feeding four thousand–plus sailors twenty-four seven. It's a perfect setup for feeding the crew, humanitarian staff, medical staff, and disaster relief victims. And you've got a world-class ship's hospital, existing berth for thousands—oh, and here's another one!" Wendy was smoking with excitement. "The draft of the *Gerald R. Ford* is thirty-nine feet, but not after you've off-loaded thirty thousand tons of weight. The new draft will be twenty-eight feet, and you'll be able to navigate into several hundred ports that today can't handle a supercarrier."

They discussed the pros and cons back and forth for another hour. Admiral Brown finally stood and smoothed the crease in his trousers. "Wendy, I've gotta tell you, I feel like I've just been sold a new car."

Wendy raised her eyebrows in concern.

"But the fact is, I like the car. This meeting has possibly been the singular highlight of my Navy career." He paused, then winked and said, "Well, maybe other than being sworn in as admiral. You have thoroughly convinced me, sold me, enthralled me, and energized me like no person I've ever met.

"The CVN 78 strike force is due in the Newport News shipyard in three days," he went on. "I'm going to issue a change in orders and have her berth up in the Halifax Shipyard. It's out of the way but has some of the best teams in the world to accomplish what we want to do quickly and quietly."

He fiddled with his phone, and within several minutes, another Uber driver pulled in out front. "It was a pleasure meeting you both, and I'll be sure to keep you in the loop." The admiral stooped, took Wendy's hand, and lightly kissed it. Then he turned and walked out the door.

CHAPTER FOURTEEN

Michael said, "Wen? I know where you're going with all this."

She looked him in the eye, a sideways glance, chin raised a bit. "Excellent! Because I don't. Tell me!"

"Oh, you know. On some level, you know. The insanity of war. You're clawing at it. Scratching at it. Scheming over it. Plotting. Conceptualizing. And you're making it up as you go. Right?"

She looked up at nothing on the wall. Stared at it until it went away. "I think you're right. I mean, I have no plan, other than an idea of what I want to tackle tomorrow. And that makes sense to me. However, I'm thinking that the insanity of war is just one symptom of the overriding problem—the failure of human intelligence to expand and improve itself. A cow can't improve its intelligence. A lion hunts, eats, and sleeps. But the human brain has the singular ability to improve itself."

She paused, then said, "I'm intrigued, though. It seems very strange that my thought process also makes sense to you!"

Michael nodded. "You know how you used to hate going to movies with me? Because twelve or fourteen minutes into a thriller, I'd lean over and say, 'The Russian guy drugged the cop, put the llama's body in the trunk, and will be caught by the blonde girl that swore off guns for lent'?"

She smiled. "Yeah. You always had it figured out before I'd eaten below the butter layer on the popcorn."

Michael smiled mischievously. "To that end, I've taken the liberty of inviting a guest of my own over, to maybe help put another notch in your gun belt."

Wendy said, "I think we're now even on bad analogies." At that moment, there was pronounced pounding on the front door.

Michael jumped. "Criminy," he groused. "Loud enough to raise the de—um. I'll get it."

"Hi, Michael."

"Hi, Peter. Enter!" Michael opened the door wide.

"Wendy, this is Peter Moscovi. We went to engineering school together?"

"Yes, I remember! Hi, Peter!" Wendy rose and held out her hand. His handshake was firm and confident, and the dozen or so strands of hair left on his head stood on end all of a sudden, making him look like a dying Chia Pet that just got a dose of Miracle-Gro.

Peter rolled his eyes up, as if he could study his scalp, and said, "That was weird. Uh, nice to see you again." Peter was Michael's age, but the similarities ended there. He was a head shorter and large in an interesting way. He was built like a tugboat—compact, powerful, and bull-chested with thick legs, but with the face of Dean Martin. No joke. It was a strange, disconcerting combination.

Michael invited Peter to have a chair, and they all sat around the kitchen table. "Wen, Peter has designed and built a prototype cardboard baller." Peter laid a thick manila folder on the table, as if to confirm its existence.

"Wow! I've never heard of one. Is it a game?" Wendy was not on board yet.

"Uh, good one!" Peter responded, believing she was making a joke. "I've designed—I don't like the term *invented* in this instance, because the process and mechanics are so simple—but I've designed a portable, expandable system to shred waste cardboard, compress it, and reconfigure it into eight-pound spheres the size of a pool ball."

Wendy said, "Cool. Why?"

Peter responded like she was enthralled and needed to know

more, *now*. "To replace coal mining, reduce CO_2 and mercury emissions, strengthen the power grid, and basically save the world."

She said, "Got it. Start from the beginning."

He needed no more prompting. "There are two hundred forty-one coal-fired generating plants left in the United States, right?"

Wendy's recent crash studies had not covered coal plants. "Sure."

"Well, they're being systematically phased out due to emissions issues, hydrocarbon releases, black lung poisoning, transportation concerns, and so on, but without enough viable megawatt production from other sources to offset their elimination.

"At the same time, China has stopped buying our recycled cardboard. We've gone from purchases of hundreds of millions of tons per year to basically none. And from prices around a hundred dollars per ton paid for the product, to zero. They don't need it anymore, and frankly, many shipments got there growing so aggressively, they couldn't be removed from the shipping containers."

"Growing? Seriously?"

"Correct. Put a pizza box or two in a sealed steel container of otherwise 'clean' recycled cardboard, heat it up to maybe one hundred twenty degrees, and send it off on a moisture-rich three-week journey to China, and you've got some serious pathogens to deal with."

"Yuck," Wendy said. "So?" She twirled her wrist as if to say, "Move along, little doggy."

"My process turns used cardboard, of which we're now storing hundreds of millions of tons, into eight-pound burnable coal substitutes. The raw material is nearly free, the process from cardboard to extremely compact spheres takes about two minutes, the pellets burn 26 percent hotter than coal; pound for pound, produce 30 percent more BTUs than coal; generate *no* trace mercury; burn more completely; and emit emissions that are 67 percent less toxic than coal. And the emissions can be scrubbed to 96 percent less toxic."

"Peter—I love you!" Wendy said. She glanced at Michael, then back to Peter. "As a friend. But it's love! And you too, Michael. One of the longest-running sources of conflict on earth has been resources—envy of, theft of, hoarding of, and exploitation of. Gold, diamonds, uranium, water, copper—you name it. But in the past hundred and fifty years, the most contentious culprit has been energy resources—coal, oil, and gas. And it's all so unbelievably stupid!"

"Stupid?" both men echoed in unison.

"Exactly. Stupid," Wendy said. "Unlimited energy is available for the taking—for free, in essence—but instead, men fight over it." She smiled, looked at them both, and said, "Sorry, but for the life of me, I can't think of a woman who's ever started a war."

Michael took this unintended cue to say, "Well, in Mesopotamia, there was Sheila the Bad, who—"

Wendy cut him off. "Sheila the Bad? I think she was Australian. Anyway, 'Wendy bad' for allowing you to lose your focus." She looked at him with a fake frown. "So quickly."

Michael grandly flourished one arm, extending his hand. "Proceed, my queen."

"Solar, wind, fusion, wave energy—comparatively nothing is spent researching and developing the energy sources that surround us because we're so focused on those beneath us. And, worldwide, we spend hundreds of billions a year fighting over the buried stuff while claiming there's no money to develop the other.

"When I was coaching Pastor Conlin, Rabbi Berg, and Imam Kourash over the limits of human understanding, I was barely scratching the surface. Humans would rather chase, kill, and skin a rabbit than simply eat an apple."

"And my device fits in . . ." Peter prompted.

"Michael was onto it when he invited you over, and you've already diagnosed the illness and designed the treatment, if not the cure. The insanity, for instance, of digging up, transporting, burning, and cleaning up coal when, as a temporary placeholder, a recycled waste can replace coal in an immediate phaseout while the more sustainable energy sources are harnessed and those processes refined."

"Yes! That's my goal." Peter brightened, then paused, his enthusiasm fading. "But I've had no luck convincing anyone to invest in this. I mean *anyone*. Liberals hate it, because it doesn't eliminate the power plants. Conservatives hate it because, well, they love coal—I suspect mostly because liberals hate coal. I've made no traction at all in getting this process into application."

"Your system is stuck in the middle," Michael said.

"Exactly." Peter shook his head. "No one is willing to take a really positive, interim step of eliminating the mining and burning of coal, increasing efficiency, reducing negative health effects, and slashing costs. I guess because it's not the perfect, all-encompassing fix, it's being ignored."

"You need a big hitter," Michael said. He looked up at Wendy, who was nodding.

"I've been talking with someone who could get involved in this," Wendy said, "but my concept with her was heading in a different direction. She's due here any minute."

Whop-whop-whop. Michael turned to Peter. "*That's* how you knock on a front door, not like you're trying to serve a warrant."

Peter laughed. "So sorry to have offended your refined sensibilities, Mr. Petite Knuckles."

It was Wendy's turn at the door. "Wendy?" asked the woman at the door. Wendy ushered her in, saying, "You must be Melinda. So nice to meet you! Come in! We're having a wonderful discussion, which only moments ago turned to you!"

Melinda laughed as they shook hands. "My ears were burning—huh, and they continue to burn!" she said as she caught Wendy's vibe. She was about their age, tall and trim, with eyes so intense they could slice through stone. More specifically, Melinda had a look that could cut through bullshit from a mile away.

Wendy did the introductions. "Melinda, this is my husband, Michael. And be careful, he's not stable."

Michael grimaced and rolled his eyes at Wendy, then smiled at Melinda. "Nice to meet you. It's been a busy day!"

"And this is Peter, a college friend of Michael's who seems to be a gifted inventor."

"Designer," Peter interjected. "I'm only smart enough to adapt the inventions of others."

"I'm sure," Melinda laughed. "I see MIT in your eyes and hear it in your voice."

Peter's head pulled back an inch or two in surprise. "In fact, I got my bachelor's and masters at Northwestern, but my doctorate at MIT."

Michael yelped. "Dude! Doctor Dude! I had no idea!"

Peter deadpanned, "You don't bring me flowers, you don't sing me love songs . . ."

Melinda smiled at them both. "You guys drank a lot of beer together as undergrads, right?"

"Barrels," Michael said.

"Rivers," Peter agreed.

"Melinda, have a chair." Wendy guided her to the remaining seat in the kitchen. "On the phone, we talked a bit about piggybacking on your foundation's efforts in clean water and disease prevention."

Melinda nodded.

"But we've come up with an alternative scheme that might be right up your alley."

"Tell me more," Melinda gushed. "I love schemes!"

Wendy took a deep breath. "Well, our general focus is on—how should I put it?—conflict abatement, and applying the products of those successes to enhance daily lives."

"A noble scheme!" Melinda said.

Wendy tipped her head in agreement. "To that end, Peter has developed a viable process to basically eliminate the production and burning of coal, cleanly, immediately, and economically. Peter, put it in a nutshell?"

He smiled. "Glad to. Coal mined in the United States produces 19.27 million heating BTUs per ton. I've developed a process to shred and compress waste cardboard using a misting of water and, believe it or not, cornstarch, into eight-pound burnable spheres that produce twenty-five million heating BTUs per ton and burn cleaner and more completely, with no residual toxins. The system is portable, expandable, fast, and basically trouble-free."

"Excellent!" Melinda nearly yelled. "The link between the elimination of coal and the advent of fully renewable! Why haven't I heard of this before?"

"Um . . . because I'm an itty . . . bitty . . . cog in a giant industrial conundrum?" Peter suggested.

Melinda let out a howl. "How did you get out of MIT with a sense of humor intact?"

Peter smiled modestly. "They figured they either had to graduate me or shoot me. Nobody's a very good shot up there."

They all laughed. Peter was in his element, and Melinda was on a roll. "So we just need to take your design, duplicate it—how many coal-fired power plants are left?"

"Two hundred forty-one," Peter said.

She didn't miss a beat. "Duplicate it two hundred forty-one times, expand it to scale, coordinate the supply of raw materials, and eliminate coal burning in the United States?"

"Yes, ma'am," Peter said.

"Piece of cake!" Melinda was fired up. "Money is not an issue, and I have a couple friends who can make this happen like that!" She snapped her fingers.

"Melinda, there's one more piece of this cake. If you take this on, I think you need to make a profit, then use the income to eliminate your business." Wendy was confident Melinda understood.

"Of course! And what irony. We harness the efficiency of eliminating coal to fund the research to eliminate carbon burning altogether. It's . . . genius." Melinda softened, looked to Peter. "You're okay with planned obsolescence?"

"Ha!" he chortled. "That's the whole point! Plus, I can always reduce the degree of compaction, drop the weight, paint the pellets, and reintroduce them as the first biodegradable pool balls."

The room erupted, then quickly settled into a rhythm of suggestions, discussion, modifications, and acceptance for another hour, until they'd hashed through every variable they could think of.

Wendy stole a line from *Jesus Christ Superstar*. "Then we are decided?"

Melinda responded on cue and conspiratorially: "We are decided." She stood, shook everyone's hands, and headed to the door. "I want to put this in place right now. This is game-changing. I am so happy to have met you all!"

As the door closed, Michael looked quizzically at Wendy. "Melinda . . . ?"

"Vanderbilt," Wendy replied nonchalantly. "Melinda Vanderbilt."

Michael's jaw dropped to that now comfortable place on his chest.

CHAPTER FIFTEEN

After Melinda left, Michael and Peter retired to the back porch for a late-afternoon beer and updates of their lives as bus driver and doctor of applied engineering, respectively. When Peter left, Michael plopped down on the couch next to Wendy.

"Finally!" he said. "The intensity of this day is over! Are you exhausted?"

"Not at all," she replied. "The discussion with Peter reminded me of how much I need to learn about renewable and sustainable power. I need to know kilowatt production from solar panels at various latitudes, wave energy transference, the degree that harnessing wind reduces wind speed, and the effects on the ecosystem . . ."

"More reading?" Michael asked.

She nodded. "It's like oxygen. It's what seems to rev my turbine right now."

There were three loud slaps on the front door. "Oh, for god's sake!" Michael said as he grabbed the handle and pulled the door open. "Peter, what in the hell do you . . ." but he stopped mid-tirade. It wasn't Peter, but rather two tall, fit men dressed as twins—dark suits, dark ties, shiny shoes, black belts—with matching frowns.

"Michael Halstad?" one asked. The other stared.

"Sure," he said. "Who are you? *Men in Black*? We haven't seen any otherworldly creatures in weeks."

"National Security Agency, sir," the first twin said. "May we come in?"

The other guy with no voice held up a badge.

"NSA?" Michael stammered. "I, uh, is that a smart thing, to let NSA into my home?"

"I presented it as a question out of courtesy, sir. It's not an option." Both men walked past Michael into the living room, one backing into a corner, and the other cornering Wendy. "Wendy Halstad, I assume?" the talker said.

She mimicked Michael. "Sure. What's up?" She looked up, way up, at the man's face. He was well over six feet, dark, and handsome. Wendy preferred geeks.

"Ma'am, the NSA has been monitoring your communications due to some red flags that recently crossed a threshold from innocuous to curious, and then this morning from curious to seditious. And likely criminal."

"Dang. And I was all set to curl up and read this evening." Wendy always seemed to go flippant when the shit hit the fan.

Michael came to the rescue. "Excuse me guys, but you have no right to . . ."

"Shut the fuck up and sit, or my partner will tase you to smooth out this process." This guy was one mean hombre. Michael sat and shut the fuck up.

"Ma'am, I'll put all our questions into one clear line. Who are you? Why are you impersonating a dead person? Why were you seen in consultation with an imam you've never previously met? Where did you go when shots were fired? What dealings could you possibly have with the secretary of the Navy? Or with an MIT scientist? Or, for that matter, with Melinda Vanderbilt?"

Michael, never the prudent one, responded, "Sir, you forgot Chirpy from Paul's Pizza."

The talker nodded at his quiet partner. "Tase him." And he did.

■　■　■

After several minutes, Michael groaned, sat up, and took in his surroundings. The room was the same but moving a little. The NSA team and Wendy were seated and apparently in deep discussion, Wendy saying, "So I told him, 'Nawar, you don't even know me. Why would you want to shoot me?' And I might have said, 'Plus, you're not very good at this whole terrorist thing. You're eight feet away from me, and you missed three times!' I think that's when he told me about the blanks."

Michael felt ignored. "Wendy, what the hell?"

"You're fine," she said. "It was a Taser shock. I couldn't, like, make you better. It wears off, and you're fine."

"I'm pissed," he snorted.

She smiled at him and motioned for him to sit with her. "Okay, you're fine, and pissed. Come join us. I've waived my right to an attorney, and we're having a lively discussion around the various claims they have against me."

Michael coughed. "Ah, Wendy—why would you do that?"

"It's simple, dummy," she laughed. "I've not done anything illegal, and these gentlemen are just confused by incongruous, disjointed information."

"Incongruous?" Michael had an eyebrow raised.

"Your word for the day. Come sit up here on the couch."

Michael couldn't seem to get his legs under him, but found his anger, and his smart-ass inner self, intact. "I've just been subdued by a federal agent. I'm not going to cozy up on the couch! And you two guys—wait. I know you. You're—you're Buzz," he pointed at the guy toying with his Taser. "And you're Asshole!" He pointed a jiggling finger, still attached to his tased arm, at the talker.

Asshole said, "Tase him again," and the quiet one stood.

Michael stared defiantly from his half-reclined position on the floor. "You tase me again, I'm going to shit my pants and lose bladder control. Then you'll need a hazmat team."

Wendy added helpfully, "He's right. That happens every time he's tased more than once."

Buzz looked at Asshole, and Asshole threw up his hands. "Okay, let him sit there and jiggle." He turned back to Wendy, but Michael wasn't done.

"So, you two jerks are just gonna keep doing what you do, abusing our rights, and leave me spasming on the floor?"

The talker glanced at his watch and replied without looking over, "The spasms should be about done."

"I've got a friend who's an FBI agent in Fargo. I'm—"

"No, you don't," the talker said.

"I—I don't?"

"No, you don't have a friend who's an FBI agent in Fargo. No legitimate FBI agent would admit to being stationed in Fargo. Not even to his mother. He'd admit to Denver, or Yankton, or Pocatello, but not Fargo. No way. Probably ATF."

Michael looked left and right, feeling helpless. He caught a glimpse of the agents' car in the driveway. "Wait, wait. The NSA drives a Smart car? A clown car? Are you shitting me?"

The talker looked back at Michael, an exasperated scowl on his face. "We flew in from DC—security alert and all that. The EQ 4-2 was all that Dollar had available."

"The EQ 4-2," Michael repeated. "You're a piece of work, Asshole. And your partner Buzz, the one who doesn't talk—what's up with that?" He ignored Buzz . . . continuing to stare at the talker.

"I'm senior partner, he's junior. His instructions are to keep quiet, watch, and learn."

"And tase," Michael said.

"Damn straight. 'And tase.'"

Michael was adamant. Wouldn't let it go. Tried to be insulting. "How long have you two been a pair?" he asked.

The talker answered as if talking to a second grader. "We've been *partners* for thirteen years, and he's—"

"Whaaa . . ." Michael yelled. "You've been partners for thirteen years? And he isn't allowed to speak yet? That's—that's just bogus, man!"

"I'm allowed to speak. I just don't," Buzz said. All eyes snapped his way. Then he exploded into voice. "I was told not to talk, and I don't talk. No big deal. And by the way, you got our names right. How'd you do that?"

"How'd I do what?"

"Our names. My name actually is Buzz. Well, not my given name, but my nickname, due to my expertise with, well, you know . . ." He held up the Taser. "And my partner's name is actually Asshole."

"Bullshit," the talker said.

"Okay, his name is Azolé Bertinucci. Everybody calls him Asshole. Well, behind his back. Even my wife."

Azolé looked surprised. "You've got a wife?"

"Wife and seven kids. They're one, two, three, four, five, six, and eight." Buzz was rolling.

"What happened with seven?" Azolé asked.

"Remember, we were stationed in Afghanistan seven years ago? It kind of messed up our rhythm. But they're such wonderful little humans. Three are boys, three are girls, and one is still undecided."

Michael coughed.

Buzz deadpanned, "I don't get to tell many jokes."

Bertinucci broke in. "A wife and seven kids? And your wife calls me Asshole? And you didn't even invite me to your wedding?" He sounded hurt.

"I do what I'm told, Ass . . . Azolé. I kept my mouth shut. And there are so many things I need to tell you! Remember the perp in that counterfeit passport thing? He had an accomplice, his girlfriend, a real looker. I pointed her out to you, but you didn't respond, probably thought I was just ogling, even though I don't ogle. I'm married with seven kids, for goodness' sake. And that deal in Waco? I wrote down the phone number of the witness, but you crumpled it up, thought I wanted you to order pizza. And when that guy shot Senator Holcomb, he told me about four other people he'd shot, but you—"

Azolé shouted, "Buzz! Shut up. We'll talk about all that later!"

Buzz clammed up and moved back into the corner.

Bertinucci got back to business. "Mrs. Halstad—or whoever you are—I should take you down to the federal building in St. Paul, but the EQ 4-2 doesn't have a back seat."

Michael interrupted, and said to Wendy, with no informative intent, "That's what the '2' stands for, honey: two-passenger."

Bertinucci ignored him. "So for now, I'm going to release you on your own recognizance, and I'll be back with you in a day or two. I need to talk this whole mess over with my partner."

Michael coughed. Buzz winked at him.

Wendy piped up, "Well, this really has been enjoyable."

"That wasn't the intent," Agent Bertinucci groused.

"Be that as it may, you know your way out, so I'll administer to my husband." Wendy stood, walked past the two NSA agents, and crouched down by Michael. "Would you like a pillow, dear?"

The feds walked out the door, squeezed into the clown car, and pondered whether they should write a report or just claim they'd flown to Minnesota for coffee.

CHAPTER SIXTEEN

"I've been researching," Wendy told Michael the next morning as he was searching a cupboard for coffee. Still half-asleep, he responded, "Hmm?"

"International law. It's extremely interesting," she said, scrolling through some tome or other on their computer.

"No doubt," Michael said from the kitchen. "Bilateral trade agreements, adjudicating in absentia from The Hague, maritime transportation licensing. I've been wanting to read up on all of that."

Wendy sensed some sarcasm but ignored it. "I'm specifically looking at semi-consensual expatriation. The laws are very murky."

"No shit?" He was now overtly sarcastic. "I'm getting a vibe that you have sensed the concept of an opportunity. Is it . . . dangerous?"

"Well, possibly. I called Hiram again last night. He's back home in Bethesda. He's just a wonderful, open, creative man. I wish we could have known him when I was, well, you know."

"Yeah, I know." Michael entered the living room, pulling his first taste of his Folgers dark roast. "You could have maybe helped him get his car licensed."

Wendy gave a dismissive laugh. "Now I know you're being sarcastic. No, we talked about this concept, and he gave me some insights. For instance, back in the early 1950s, the United States bought a small island in the central Pacific, to use for nuclear weapons testing."

"Similar to Bikini Atoll?"

"Exactly. But intriguing. The island was never used for bomb testing, yet it's still listed not only as property of the United States, but also as contaminated." She was reading some background as she talked. "It's two miles by two miles, has no inhabitants, is lush with vegetation, and even has a 1940s-era military landing strip, abandoned since the mid-1950s."

"Interesting. Are we moving?" Michael was engaged but had no idea what her "concept" might be.

"No, dummy. But I'm thinking about visiting. In the next day or two."

Michael put down his coffee and appraised his wife. She was focused, engaged, determined—and no question, she was going to—he looked over her shoulder at the computer—"Ekman Island." He came to full neurological attention.

"Hiram put me in touch with Richard Crowley—" Wendy began.

Michael interrupted. "Sir Richard Crowley, of Crowley Airlines, of course."

"Exacto. There's a six-hour difference between Stillwater and London, so I was able to chat with him for a couple hours this morning. He's picking me up about noon. Would you like to go with?" Wendy looked up at Michael and smiled.

There was no question. He'd go to the end of the earth with her. "Sure. So, where are we going?"

She resumed her reading. "To the end of the earth and back. A couple of times."

"Of course. I'll grab a toothbrush and some extra underwear."

■　■　■

They drove to Holman Field in St. Paul, a small commuter airport, and were just pulling up to a commercial FBO as a Crowley-tagged twin-engine jet floated in for a landing. The engines were winding down as Wendy and Michael walked through the fixed-base operator lobby and out to the tarmac.

The plane was big, about the size of a shortened 727, but sleek and looked brand new. The FBO team pushed a rolling ladder to the front cabin door, which opened inward as the ladder arrived. Crowley was the first out the door. He was only five foot eleven, but he looked taller, larger than life, with hair flying and a toothy smile from ear to ear. As he hit the asphalt, his crew of five followed him down the steps.

Wendy and Michael approached, and Crowley held out both arms and gave her a hug. While it was only for a moment, Crowley's eyes widened in surprise, catching Michael's gaze over her shoulder. Michael simply nodded, and then held out his hand.

They shook, and Crowley's first words were to Michael, more quietly than expected. "What the bloody hell was that?!"

Michael smiled. "Sir Richard, welcome to the expanding circle of amazing people captivated by Wendy Halstad."

He looked back to Wendy. "Wendy, it's a pleasure to meet you in person."

"Sir Richard," she said brightly. "Thank you for agreeing to work with us on this project. It could be world-changing and will definitely be exciting!"

"I'm an excitement junkie. I could never have said no. Let's relax in the terminal while my crew takes a break and the base operator fuels us up."

The fixed-base terminal was privately owned, luxurious, and accommodating. An attendant brought coffee, tea, and a selection of meats and cheeses. Crowley and the Halstads sat in a triangle of overstuffed leather chairs that seemed to beg for a good book and a hearth fire.

"Sir Richard, tell us about your plane!" Michael said with unreserved excitement.

"Folks, we don't need to be so formal. You may call me 'sir.'" Both Michael and Wendy froze for just a moment, and Crowley broke into a loud and mischievous laugh that they would soon learn was an integral part of his nature. "Richard is fine," he said, still chuckling. "However, I rather enjoy the Queen adhering to 'Sir Richard.'" This got the laugh again.

"The Gulfstream G700 is the first prototype of this model of luxury jets. It has a stateroom with sleeping quarters for two, and it caters adeptly to an entourage of an additional twelve, plus crew, which in this case will be four. The engines are rear-mounted Rolls-Royce power plants manufactured in Derby, England, my hometown. This model, the first G700 to complete testing and certification, is perfect for this ambitious effort, as it's hands down the fastest, most luxurious, and most bloody expensive private-use platform in the world."

Wendy broke in. "You said fast?"

Crowley took his cue. "Mach point ninety-three, or around seven hundred miles per hour, in your less-than-logical rating for speed."

Michael raised an eyebrow, and Crowley smiled. "The civilized world uses kph, not mph."

"Got it." Michael chuckled. Brits, he laughed to himself—and immediately chastised his inner sarcasm. Sir Richard Crowley wasn't merely a Brit; he was an enigma, and had earned every right to say anything he damn well pleased.

"And range?" Wendy pressed.

"Seven thousand five hundred nautical miles as configured, plus I'll have my staff in Honolulu secure an additional ten-thousand-gallon fuel tank in the baggage hold to increase our maximum to nine thousand nautical miles."

Wendy nodded. "That should be fine. Crew?"

"I've brought two flight crews, basically two pilots and two co-pilots, plus one steward in addition to you. We'll have the pilots rotate out after each exfil, so one crew will always be on ground resting while the other is on task."

Wendy nodded again, calculating distances and flight hours in her head as they talked. "Oxygen canisters?"

"Already modified and waiting to be installed at my Honolulu FBO. By using my own staff and facilities, we'll keep curious eyes at bay."

Michael was beyond confused. He'd had no clue their little vacation was a mission, and had known no other details before he'd sat down in this awesome chair. He wondered if this would all go away if he took a nap.

Wendy finished her math and visibly relaxed. "Admiral Brown speaks almost fondly of you. You two must have some history."

"Farther back than I bloody care to admit," Crowley responded. "We've done a couple projects together, one of which was very hush-hush, and my aerospace firm, Crowley Zero Gravity, is working two contracts with NASA. Hiram taught me how to land an A-6 taildragger on a carrier back when he was a mere captain. Without question the most frightening thing I've ever done. But if one doesn't challenge themselves, one ends up gumming noodles in a home."

The plane's crew ambled back into the private terminal's lobby. "We're fueled and ready to go, sir," said one of the two captains.

Crowley stood. "Marvelous. Shall we?" He motioned to Wendy and Michael. Wendy popped up, but she and Sir Richard had to each offer Michael a hand. He was buried so far back in the cushions, he was struggling to escape on his own.

"Next stop?" Michael asked. He was learning to keep his questions short and focused on the near term.

"My terminal in Honolulu, Pac-Comm Air Services. We'll refuel there, scrape off my three-day-old beautiful lettering, install the extra fuel bladders, and head back out." He looked at Wendy. "Probably a two-hour stop at Pac-Comm."

She nodded. "At that point, our timing becomes critical. Admiral Brown will be meeting with the president"—she looked at her watch—"right about now. He doesn't anticipate any delays on that end, thanks to your involvement."

Michael coughed, then stared at her. "The president. As in POTUS?"

"Yeah! Isn't that cool?" Wendy was ebullient, like a high schooler on the way to her first Sadie Hawkins dance.

Michael was not ebullient. He had this feeling, deep in his bowels, that he was about to get tased again.

■ ■ ■

Halfway to Hawaii, Sir Richard turned to Wendy again. "Tell me about the president's involvement."

Wendy looked over at him. He was seated in the most luxurious, comfortable airplane chair ever invented, with his feet up on an opposing one. Wendy had received a satellite call from Admiral Brown a few minutes ago but had asked very few questions, so there was little information to be gained from listening to her side of the call.

"Hiram was pleased with the meeting. He had met with President Gallagher, her chief of staff, and her national security advisor. Pretty tight group. He explained the concept of our trip, but also explained that the fewer details they had, the more deniability they had if things didn't go as well as expected."

Crowley raised an eyebrow, still relaxed with his feet up. "How concerned are you?"

"Somewhat," she replied, "but not overly. The danger is minimal. The potential gain is substantial, and if it doesn't work, we just fly away. You're out about a hundred grand in expenses, but you've still got your plane, and we just fly home."

He nodded. "That works for me."

"Hiram said the president's team liked the cutout—you. With

you handling the logistics, the United States is clear of any traceable involvement, and your position is mostly legal."

He raised his eyebrow again but didn't speak.

"Look, you're doing a favor to the president, and to Hiram, while fulfilling your lifelong passion of making the world a better place."

Crowley smiled at her. "I'm not arguing, Wendy, and frankly, not terribly worried, either. This could be the most fun I've had in several years. My first, and only, concern is the safety of my crew, and I think we've covered that pretty well."

"I understand," she replied. "I've got a thought or two in my half-empty head that should soften any issues that come up."

Crowley leaned back in his seat and closed his eyes. Michael continued staring at Wendy until she finally looked over at him. "What?" she asked.

He shook his head. "Nothing. All good." His head continued shaking back and forth.

■ ■ ■

Once the plane was cleared for final approach into the Daniel K. Inouye International Airport in Honolulu, Wendy tapped Michael on the shoulder, waking him from a fitful sleep. "Once we're done at Pac-Comm, we're going to drop you and Sir Richard at Ekman Island."

"I thought you said Ekman was uninhabited."

"It is, other than a squad from the Naval Mobile Construction Battalion ONE, the Seabees that Admiral Brown diverted for a few days. They're doing some reconditioning of the runway to allow several takeoffs and landings of this G700, and our thought is that you and Sir Richard would oversee that effort out of harm's way until the plane comes back tomorrow with some passengers to drop off. Then we'd pick you back up, and drop you both at Pac-Comm."

Michael perked up. "I finally get to use my engineering degree?"

Wendy shook her head. "The Seabees are just filling potholes. But you might get to drive an asphalt compactor."

Michael was less than enthused. "That's been on my bucket list," he said drily. "Any chance I can paint some crosswalk markings? That'd be a twofer."

"Sorry, babe. It's a compactor or nothing." Wendy secured her seatbelt, glanced at Michael's, and gave him "the look." He dutifully buckled his seatbelt.

■ ■ ■

The larger of the Pac-Comm hangars was buzzing with activity as the G700 taxied into it and shut down. The terminal manager, Nigel Miller, rolled the stairwell to the plane's door himself and greeted Crowley as he stepped off. "Sir Richard, great to see you again! We've got everything ready for a quick turnaround, and a lunch prepared in the conference room. If you can find your way there, I'll get my crew working on the modifications immediately." Miller turned to head off, but stopped short and turned back to Crowley. "Ah, I did take the liberty of modifying your instructions on one item, Sir Richard."

Crowley raised his head in inquiry, and his FBO manager took his cue. "In the interest of safety, we looked at the prints on the G700, and came up with a way to securely fasten the replacement oxygen canisters next to those from the factory, so as to avoid replacing the originals that continue to hold oxygen. Thus, in the case of an actual loss of cabin pressure, you'll have oxygen available, and still have your . . . 'backups.'"

"Activated by?" Crowley pressed.

"A simple toggle in the cockpit, which will activate a servo to change the draw from the original canisters to the second set. Also, because of the rear-engine design of this airframe, the fuel lines run from the wing tanks, beneath the cabin floor, and back to the engines. When we install the additional fuel bladders in the hold, we'll install a similar toggle and servo switch up front. As the wing tanks hit 'bingo'"—Miller smiled at Crowley—"or preferably a moment before, toggling the servo will switch the fuel flow from the wing tanks to those we'll install in the hold."

"Thank you, Nigel," Crowley said with a wink. "I appear more intelligent to the world, because I'm smart enough to hire good people like you." They both laughed, and Miller headed off to supervise the upgrades.

The conference room had a bay of windows that overlooked the brightly lit, cavernous hangar. Its eighty-foot door was closed. While the passengers and the crew for the first flight ate, the two second-phase pilots retired to their quarters, which Miller had set up in the rear of the private terminal. The current team watched a crew of fifteen technicians scrambling around the plane. One team had pre-positioned a motorized bucket truck and was already in the air, removing the "Crowley Airlines" decal from the left side of the craft.

While working on a roast beef on rye straight from heaven, Michael asked Crowley, "Will removing the lettering damage the paint at all?"

Crowley laughed. "As classy as those logos look, they're only adhesive-backed vinyl. They're removing them with Sharper Image hair dryers, which Nigel ordered from Amazon yesterday. Though Bezos and I are competitors in our aerospace efforts, I must credit him with building from scratch the most innovative and successful retail business in history. Yesterday, we needed half a dozen hair dryers. Today, we have them." To himself, Sir Richard murmured, "Wish I'd thought of that."

Michael continued chewing. "And they're installing a new tail number?"

"Yes," Crowley confirmed. "It will read 'DPRK 1.'"

Michael turned and looked at him quizzically.

"For Democratic People's Republic of Korea."

"That's . . ." Michael blurted.

"Correct. DPRK is North Korea."

■ ■ ■

Two hours later, Nigel Miller strode into the conference room and announced, "Lady and gentlemen, your G700 is modified, fueled, relettered, and ready to fly." He said to the captain flying the first route, "Cliff, you'll use the tail number that came with the plane for take off. For landing in Pyongyang, you'll use DPRK 1, and back to the original when you arrive back here. My understanding is that any tail-number readers in the Honolulu tower will be in the restroom when you take off and land."

"Got it. Thank you, sir," the captain responded. Cliff Mattern had been a pilot and then a pilot instructor in Britain's Royal Air Force, from which he retired after twenty years. Richard Crowley had met him previously and had convinced him to keep flying after retirement from the service, not as a Crowley Airlines pilot but as Sir Richard's own personal pilot. Mattern was tall, solid, and around forty, fitting the description for almost every retired soldier in the world. Crowley liked him because he was affable, unflappable, and a top-notch flyer.

"Well, Michael, you and I will tag along as far as Ekman Island, where we'll deplane in order to sit on our arses until my beautiful Gulfstream returns from Pyongyang." He looked sternly at Wendy, who nodded.

"Don't worry, Richard. We'll bring your plane back."

He turned back to Michael with his broad smile, "And don't you worry. I've packed an umbrella, two lawn chairs, and four pints of Guinness stout."

"And our job?" Michael asked, assuming he would *not* get to drive an asphalt compactor.

Crowley nodded. "We'll be on communications and signaling. Not much to do until the plane arrives on its return route, which will be late this evening. We'll put out some digital flares, set up a radio link with the captain, and make sure there are no Seabees or wild boars on the repaired runway when the wheels hit."

Michael turned his gaze to Wendy. She refused to meet his eyes.

■ ■ ■

The landing at Ekman was uneventful. A first pass over the field confirmed that the repairs had been made, and Captain Mattern kissed the asphalt on the second pass with an amazingly light touch.

They rolled to a stop on an apron that used to be the access lane to a Navy hangar, but the hangar was now two long rows of concrete footings about one hundred feet apart, with the center of that space filled with a tangle of galvanized sheet metal, light girders, and several mature trees. Death had not been swift or kind to this once sturdy structure.

Off to the side of the field, the ten Seabees abandoned here two days earlier were standing at parade rest. Their equipment included a propane-powered air compressor, which they had used to first blow off the runway, then clear the various potholes and surface cracks of debris. Their hot-tar wagon was also propane powered, and when heated to boiling, the pungent aroma had filtered over the entire airfield. They'd gathered gravel from around the sides of the expired hangar, mixed it with the hot tar, and filled the holes and cracks with the mixture. The final step was to drive the gas-powered packer back and forth over the repairs.

The result was not pretty but would serve as an acceptable surface for the three landings and takeoffs anticipated for this mission.

The equipment would be abandoned on the island, but this was the US Navy, and they were accustomed to abandoning equipment all over the globe. As many as twenty-five thousand Jeeps were left in the Philippines after World War II, and a good portion of the carrier planes remaining after the war were pushed over the sides of their floating airstrips into the Pacific.

The field repairs on Ekman Island involved hot, sweaty work, but the ten Seabees knew what they were doing.

Mattern kept the engines running. The plane was large enough to require a rolling ladder for egress, but there was no rolling ladder anywhere on Ekman Island. The Seabees had found an old eight-foot aluminum ladder, and as Steward Swenson opened the cabin door, the Seabees set up the ladder, which extended about a foot above the cabin floor. Mattern chuckled at the irony of using a two-dollar ladder to get out of a seventy-five-million-dollar airplane.

Michael climbed down, followed by Crowley. It wasn't lost on Crowley that one of the richest men in the world was being deposited on a deserted island, thought to be radioactive, in the middle of the Pacific.

Crowley looked up at Mattern, as serious as a man with a near-permanent smile could be. "Cliff, you're coming back for us, right? You're not using this opportunity to take over my company?"

Mattern laughed at his response. "Sir Richard, you deal with more crap in a day than I choose to encounter in a lifetime. You can keep your company, sir."

Crowley laughed and waved a goodbye. To Wendy, he simply gave a thumbs up. Michael looked up at Wendy and thought, too late, that he'd not even given her a hug goodbye. But frankly, he thought, he had not been brought into the secret "need to know" group on this adventure, which apparently included everyone but him. And in that case, he tried to convince himself that if there was no need to know, there was no need to worry about what might or might not happen. It wasn't working.

He gamely waved at Wendy, and she threw him a smile and a kiss. Turning around, Michael finally noticed the group of sweaty construction workers standing to the side, once again at parade rest.

Mattern took his seat, strapped in, and watched as Swenson pulled the ladder and secured the door. With no tower to worry about, he throttled up to maximum taxi speed, turned a 180 at the end of the runway, and gave the two Rolls-Royce engines full power. The takeoff required all 1,300 repaired feet of the runway, but they lifted off with what seemed to be little effort.

Like a servant he'd long been accustomed to having, Crowley set up the umbrella and lawn chairs himself and in a mock deferential air said to Michael, "My lord, might you be thinking hot tea or cool Guinness?"

Michael laughed and said, "I'm willing to save the tea until the beer's all gone," and he accepted an open pint from Sir Richard Crowley.

Crowley then turned to the ten Construction Battalion noncoms and said, "Sorry, blokes, but I failed to bring enough for our full contingent." He held up his beer.

A US Navy chief petty officer, nametag of Baker, responded, "Not a problem, sir. We're Navy. We never forget the beer." With that, he nodded at a seaman, nametag of Ortega, who trotted over to a very large footlocker and dragged it back to the group. He opened it and revealed that what looked like a traditional Navy gray-green footlocker was in fact an Igloo cooler, filled with what appeared to be several cases of Coors packed in ice.

Crowley laughed out loud and, half-mocking, said, "That's all?"

Very seriously, Baker said, "No, sir. We're a squad of ten, sir, working diligently for two days to ensure that your Cessna was not scratched or . . ."

"Gulfstream," Crowley corrected.

"Gulfstream, yes, sir," Baker responded. "The manual says that a hardworking squad of ten sailors of the US Navy requires hydration in the amount of . . ." He looked at his seaman, who immediately responded, "Two gallons, sir."

Baker nodded to the corporal and continued. "Two gallons *per day* of liquid, sir. The manual specifically does not dictate the type of hydration, because the manual was written by a Navy chief petty officer, sir, who, as you may be aware, runs this man's Navy. As such, and being an expert marksman and mathematician, I had logistics air-drop, along with our equipment, gear, and hot tar, thirty gallons of Coors. On ice."

Michael choked on his stout. "Thirty gallons? Did you bring any food?"

Baker looked sternly at Ortega and asked, "Corporal, did we bring any food?"

The corporal responded just as firmly. "Unknown, sir." There was a two-second pause, and then the entire group of twelve, marooned as they were, broke into laughter so fierce that two of the sailors were rolling in the grass.

■ ■ ■

During the flight from Ekman Island to Pyongyang, Wendy was able to talk at length with Steward Swenson, who was actually Thomas Swenson, forty-one years old, and late of the British SAS, one of the UK's special forces contingents. Swenson was six foot four with brown hair and piercing blue eyes and built like a brick shithouse.

Wendy said, "You don't look like a flight attendant."

Swenson tilted his head. "No?"

"No. You look like a brick shithouse. No offense intended."

"None taken, ma'am. I'm actually Sir Richard's personal assistant."

"Bodyguard," Wendy said, as a statement of fact.

Swenson smiled for the first time since they'd met. "Yes, ma'am. I've worked for Mr. Crowley for six years now. He's a good boss. It's a great job, and occasionally, it's exciting."

"Married?"

"I am, actually. I'm based in the UK, and in spite of Sir Richard's reputation, we're probably 80 percent in-country. My wife's name is Connie, and we have two girls, eight and eleven. And no, in response to your next question, I've had no occasion to fire a weapon in anger. Since my SAS time, that is."

Wendy liked him. He wasn't brash or full of himself. He was confident, polite, and soft-spoken. "Are you carrying a weapon now, Thomas?"

"Yes, ma'am. Always. Sir Richard and I believe that just an occasional glimpse of my Sig, or the bit of a bulge from my shoulder holster, may be enough to convince somebody to, well, go be mad at someone else."

"Sig?"

"SIG Sauer P320. It's a nine-millimeter semiautomatic, with a fifteen-plus-one shell capacity. It's a little heavier than some handguns, but the weight helps with aiming."

"You don't plan on using it on this trip, do you?"

"No, ma'am. Not unless you need me to. And frankly, discharging an undeclared firearm in North Korea would create a real mess."

Wendy gave a sigh of relief. "Good. The concept of this . . . exercise . . . is to stop people from killing each other. It would be a contradiction of purpose to kill people in order to make that happen."

"No argument there," Swenson replied simply.

"And as backup, defer to me." She put her hand on his forearm, and the hair on his skin raised like he was in a wind tunnel.

He took in a quick breath. "I think I've got it. You carry a little firepower of your own."

Wendy laughed lightly. "I'm pretty persuasive one-on-one."

They flew on for another half hour without talking. Eventually, and without preamble, Wendy said, "Thomas, I'm counting on you for three things. First, the good news. You won't be serving any coffee."

"I'm happier already, ma'am."

"Keep in mind, you're a full head taller than any of our guests. I suggest that you try to make yourself as invisible as possible as they board. Probably being seated will help. You only look big when seated, not like the mountain you are when standing. Nonintimidating is the goal."

He gave her a sly smile. "I'm pretty good at imitating Pee-wee Herman's voice."

Wendy laughed. "I don't think our guests would get the nuance. You can't do Dennis Rodman, can you?"

"Ma'am?"

"Scratch that one."

"Yes, ma'am."

"Anyway, several in the entourage will likely be carrying some weapons."

Swenson raised an eyebrow.

"We'll potentially have some high-ranking people touring the plane. In North Korea, no high-ranking official goes anywhere without security—I suspect because they're hated by pretty much everyone in North Korea. Should the cabin door close, which at this point is still an if, and if the captain announces a loss in cabin pressure, you'll first want to put on your steward oxygen mask. One from the galley—*not* one of the drop-down cabin masks. Clear?"

"Yes, ma'am."

"Then, as you're able, I need you to disarm those with weapons and dispose of them."

He held up a hand in a "stop" signal. "Two questions there. First, what am I disposing of?"

"Ah. Got it. My fault for not being clear. By 'dispose of them,' I mean the weapons, not our guests. And the second question?"

"Do you have a thought as to how I'll be disarming the passengers?" he asked, just a bit sarcastically.

Wendy smiled at him. "Don't worry. You'll know."

"Yes, ma'am." Swenson sounded unconvinced. "And I think you said there was one more task for me?"

"Correct. When, and if, we land back on Ekman, and if we do so with our passengers, I need you to get them off the airplane as quickly as possible."

Swenson nodded. "Down the ladder?"

"If they choose to do so, that would be great. If they hesitate, you can be as intimidating as you feel is necessary."

Swenson smiled. "I was hoping that at least part of this would be fun."

Wendy smiled again. "Should we land on Ekman with passengers, feel free to release the inner Thomas Swenson. Discretion is not required. Just don't shoot anyone."

"Yes, ma'am," he said.

■　■　■

As the plane closed in on North Korea, Wendy went to the cockpit. "Cliff, how you doing?"

"No problems at the moment. Can you go over the process one more time?"

"That's why I'm up here. Sir Richard's flight operations manager has cleared the way. You're approved for flying over North

Korean airspace, and we've been assured that there will be no issues getting to Pyongyang."

"Getting out?"

Wendy gave a bit of a grimace. "We're counting on the charm of Wendy Halstad, DMV Clerk of the Year 2007. Anyway, you'll identify us at sixty miles out, using the current tail number, and request clearance to overfly their airspace."

"Got it."

"Which they'll grant. Assuming we're not shot down . . . "

Mattern visibly dropped his shoulders and groaned.

"Assuming we're not shot down, you'll do the normal approach you'd use at any international airport. As you know, all international flights use English for tower communication, so no issue there. Uh, other than that the Pyongyang tower will be speaking the North Korean interpretation of English, not King's English, so you'll need to be on your toes."

She looked over at Eric Coventry, the copilot, and said, "Eric, you'll be a second set of ears on that North Korean English."

"Got it," Coventry said.

"Cliff, if you feel the need, you can schmaltz up your request for landing: 'Gulfstream G700 gift for the Democratic People's Republic of Korea,' yada yada."

Mattern deadpanned, "Assuming we make it to the terminal without being killed."

"We'll be approached by some North Korean dignitaries, and I presume their security—maybe ten or twelve people is what Crowley Operations was led to believe—and they'll board to inspect their 'gift.'"

Mattern then asked, "Do the dignitaries include the little guy, the one who's deathly afraid to fly?"

"He's not so little, but yes, that's the plan."

The captain prompted. "And . . .?"

Wendy smiled at him. "He's going to have a profound change of heart. And if he doesn't, we'll give him Richard's brand new seventy-five-million-dollar plane and figure out another way home."

Mattern was now concerned. "Um, this 'plan' is all based on the little guy being so excited about getting a gift—granted a very expensive gift, but a gift that he knows he'll never use—that he'll agree to all of this?"

Wendy nodded. "Correct, although Sir Richard sweetened it a bit."

The captain shook his head. "He's as good a salesman as I've ever met."

"He's got skills," Wendy agreed. "He represented that Crowley Zero Gravity would assist the DPRK in establishing a space-based missile defense system that would guarantee 100 percent interdiction of any missile fired at North Korea, in exchange for 'favors to be determined at a later date.'"

"What?" Mattern shouted. "That's against all international sanctions! Crowley would be in prison for the rest of his life!"

Wendy put her hand on his shoulder. "Cliff, Sir Richard 'represented.' He hasn't yet lifted a finger. But the North Koreans believe him. They believe all Westerners to be money-hungry, soulless mongrels, and Western billionaires to be the leaders of the mongrel pack."

The captain visibly calmed down. "Okay. I got it. Hell of a time for me to find out, though."

Wendy agreed. "As they say in the spook books, 'need to know.' If you don't know, you can honestly say 'I don't know.'"

"Unless there are bamboo shoots under my fingernails." Mattern winced.

Wendy nodded. "Yes, there is that. If you truly don't know, it takes them a lot more time and energy to determine that."

Mattern casually examined his cuticles and replied, "Yes, ma'am."

■ ■ ■

"Pyongyang Tower, this is Crowley Gulfstream Delta Papa Romeo Kilo One; we are fifteen kilometers west-southwest, requesting preauthorized permission to land on runway two-two-zero. Over."

"Crowley Gulfstream Delta Papa Romeo Kilo One, this is Pyongyang Tower. Do not land. Repeat, do not land. Circle tower at one kilometer, altitude three thousand. Acknowledge."

Off mic, Mattern hissed at Wendy, "Is this where they shoot us down?"

Wendy hesitated before responding. "Well, Cliff, I'm thinking that if they wanted to shoot us down, they would have done it over a rice paddy or somewhere remote so as not to shower itsy-bitsy metal pieces all over Pyongyang. But I'm not real up on military strategy."

Mattern groaned, "Oh my god."

"Cliff, let's ask them why."

"Oh, let's," Mattern growled, off mic and out of Wendy's earshot.

"Roger, Pyongyang Tower. Crowley Gulfstream Delta Papa Romeo Kilo One to circle at one kilometer, altitude three thousand. May I ask why? Over."

"Crowley Gulfstream, yes, you may ask why. Over"

Mattern turned to his copilot and said off mic, "Eric! Just shoot me! Please!" Coventry chuckled.

Mattern took a moment to calm down. "Ah, Pyongyang tower, why do you request Crowley Gulfstream to circle at one kilometer, altitude three thousand? Over."

"Crowley Gulfstream, we would like to visually inspect your tail number. Over."

"Roger, Pyongyang Tower. Crowley Gulfstream is circling now, at one kilometer, altitude three thousand. Over."

CHAPTER SEVENTEEN

A vehicle with roof flashers pulled in front of the Gulfstream as it taxied. Captain Mattern followed it past the main terminal about a quarter mile to an obvious military facility. Parked out front of two large hangars were two fast-attack helicopters and a military transport plane. There were also four army personnel carriers with roof-mounted cannons and four black Chinese Hongqi limousines.

The captain powered down the engines and had Swenson open the forward cabin exit door. There was a rolling ladder about fifty yards away, but it was stationary and unattended.

Four uniformed soldiers got out of the lead APC. Two appeared to be senior, in that they did not carry machine guns and wore traditional Korean officer caps. The two thugs behind them, apparently the officers' guards, had both hands on their forward-facing rifles and wore helmets and boots. All four approached the plane but did not look toward the cockpit. They walked from nose to wing and along the entire left wing, both of them dragging a hand across the leading edge. They followed the trailing edge of the beautifully swept wing all the way back to the rear fuselage, walked on toward the tail, and repeated the tour, very slowly, around the right side. They did not appear to be looking for anything specific, but it was obvious they had been instructed to circle the plane slowly, touching everything. Good dog. Sit. Good dog. Touch wing.

Back at the nose, one of the officers nodded to the lead limousine, and then to two military ground crew, who ran to the rolling ladder and pulled it toward the plane. Once the ladder was in place, the lead officer motioned to the two guards to climb the stairs and enter the plane. The officers' food tasters, it appeared.

Wendy and Thomas were sitting in the front two leather seats, Wendy on the aisle and Thomas near the wall. He was making himself as small as a six-foot-four, 250-pound man could accomplish and made no eye contact. Wendy, on the other hand, smiled and gestured to the rear, inviting the thugs to have a look.

The guards walked slowly from seat to seat, looking under and around each, into the sleeping berth, and in the rear toilets. They came back laughing and talking quietly, probably at the Western decadence of a seventy-five-million-dollar toy. The smiles were gone by the time they neared the open cabin door. One of the guards signaled to the two officers. They each pulled sidearms and slowly climbed the ladder. As they did, the other three APCs emptied, and another eighteen soldiers armed with machine guns and scowls circled the plane.

The two officers did the same tour as the guards, invited by Wendy's same smile and hand gesture. As they worked their way back toward the front, they stopped and stared at Swenson, talked softly between themselves, and then aggressively pointed their handguns at him, motioning him to stand. Which he could not do. Even in the largest Gulfstream ever built, the sidewalls were not quite five feet tall. Swenson stood, hunched over, following the contour of the cabin wall. The good news was that in that position, he did not look six foot four.

One of the officers yelled in Korean. Thomas looked at them with doe eyes and mock confusion. One officer yelled again, and motioned with his pistol for Swenson to kneel, which he did. Then he motioned for him to put his hands behind his head. Assassination position, Thomas thought to himself, except he was facing forward. Bad guys seldom had the guts to shoot a man from the front, he thought. It was almost always from behind.

Then the officer yelled again and motioned for him to turn around.

The officer ordered one of the guards to search Thomas. It dawned on him that they might have had him kneel, venturing that he was too tall for any of the soldiers present to search without a three-step stool. He smiled to himself and breathed out.

Wendy was now agitated, however. If the guard found Thomas's gun, it would not be good, and it could get bad very quickly. She was about to try to intervene when Thomas caught her eye and gave her a slight shake of his head. She leaned back into her seat.

After an aggressive and thorough search, the officer motioned for Thomas to sit back in his chair. Now it was Wendy's turn to release a deep breath.

The security team moved past them, through the galley, and toward the cramped cockpit. The lead officer slid into the space between the pilots' seats, pistol at the ready, and looked over the two aviators. Mattern, former military, saluted, and the officer saluted back. Score one for the good guys.

However, a salute could only go so far. The lead officer backed through the galley and directed one of the goons to go forward and search the two pilots, which the man did, aggressively and thoroughly.

The officer then apparently directed his second to remain on the plane and ordered the two guards off and into the circular firing squad surrounding the Gulfstream. He followed, then strutted to the lead Hongqi limousine. The front passenger window rolled down. There was a quick conversation, and then the officer moved to the rear passenger door and opened it like a valet at a crab house. Trickle-down military authority, from puffed-up lead dog to lowly doorman in twelve seconds.

A general climbed out the door and immediately started his show. He oh so slowly scanned the plane and every person, place, and item within it in a 360-degree turn. They were in the capital of North Korea, in a secured airfield, surrounded by two dozen armed soldiers, and further protected by four armored personnel carriers and two gunships. But still he did his full 360, his submarine periscope routine.

Once his pirouette was complete, the general nodded to his doorman—the lowly colonel—to proceed to the next Hongqi. He opened the rear passenger door, and out stepped a short, obese, round-faced, small-mouthed man with a ridiculous rapper's haircut—North Korea's Supreme Leader, Kim Jong-un.

After Kim stepped out of the limo, all of the other limo doors opened immediately, producing a scrum of uniformed attendants, two of them generals, and all wearing enough shiny pot metal on their chests to impress any fifth grader. They each carefully assumed their assigned positions according to rank. The three generals stood to either side of Kim, and the other eight attendants formed up loosely behind them.

Kim warily scanned the beautiful G700. He inspected the armed guard standing at the open cabin door and turned his head left and right to make sure there was an adequate number of machine guns in sight. With a nod to his generals, he proceeded to the rolling ladder. His face was grim, and his movements were tentative.

At the top of the ladder, he turned, gave his best "I'm not scared" smile and a dramatic wave to the thousands of his adoring followers who were not there but could be assumed to be directly behind the supreme leader's cameraman. With the photo taken, the smile disappeared faster than a Paris tourist's wallet, and Kim ducked his head inside the plane. Only his head, for now. Checking for snakes and demons.

Wendy, wearing a huge smile, reached for his hand with both of hers, and physically pulled him into the Gulfstream. She helped him keep his balance by giving him a hug, which brought three machine guns up to port arms and three generals reaching for their sidearms. An unforgivable breach of protocol—and by a woman, no less! She released him before she was shot, knowing that the Koreans shooting her would muddy the plan.

However, they had hugged and held hands, and Kim had his happy face on—a real one this time, a wide, lascivious-looking grin that made even the unflappable Wendy Halstad take an unintended step back. Thomas Swenson sat low in a far-side leather seat, seriously studying a G700 training manual the captain had slipped him.

Wendy gave a Vanna White wave down the aisle, and Kim worked his way aft, smiling and yabbering at his generals, apparently explaining the accoutrements of his new toy. His entourage now included his three generals, two colonels, and two machine gun–toting guards.

Wendy smiled broadly and motioned for the Koreans to try out the seats. They all looked at the supreme leader for permission. The smile had not left his face, and he grandly gestured for them to sit.

Now came the moment of truth: either Kim would say yes, or Sir Richard would be down seventy-five million.

Wendy again clasped both of her hands around Kim's and repeated the only Korean words she knew, learned from a Google search two hours earlier: "Ssi Kim? Bihaeng-gileul tasibsio seupin?" *Would you like to take your plane for a spin?*

Kim responded with the excitement of a *Price Is Right* contestant who just won a barbecue grill. "Nae bihaeng-gi?" *My plane?*

"Ye, Ssi Kim, dangsin-ui bihaeng-gi." *Yes, your plane.*

"Ye!"

His generals, who had been listening closely, became loud and animated, shaking their heads and waving their hands.

Without taking his eyes off the G700 manual's table of contents, Thomas Swenson spoke quietly but firmly. "Now would be a good time to use your curious charm on the blokes with the guns."

Wendy took the cue and put her hand on the shoulder of each member of Kim's entourage one-by-one, nodding and smiling and saying "Ye! Dangsin-ui bihaeng-gi!"

They kept their concerned looks but quieted, looking at Kim for guidance.

From a galley cabinet, Wendy pulled down a wireless microphone that Nigel Miller had installed during their stop at Pac-Comm. She handed it to Kim, pointed to the tower, and, using her practiced girlish giggle, said, "Allida." *Announce.*

Kim Jong-un was a kid in a very expensive candy store being told he could have ten of everything. With no hesitation and a bit of bravado, he clicked the mic and said, "Tab, Kim. Chwideug *nae* bihaeng-gileul tasibsio seupin!" *Tower, Kim. Taking* my *airplane for a spin.*

Wendy got right to it. "Thomas, door. Cliff, fire 'em up. Quickly! No pre-check, no tower approval. Let's boogie, and don't hit the rolling ladder!"

The engines were singing by the time the cabin door was secured. Swenson had managed to kick the ladder back a few feet, to the surprise and confusion of the troops on the ground. As the plane started to inch forward, the nearest soldier looked left and right, and then, with initiative not trained in the North Korean army, he ran to the ladder and pulled it out of the way. Swenson thought they'd probably shoot the poor sap.

Captain Mattern had his headset off. Nobody in Pyongyang to talk to at the moment. "Heading?" he called to Wendy.

"Same way we came in. Two-two-one, east-southeast. The Yellow Sea is about fifty miles. I'm betting it will take them twenty minutes before they conclude that their supreme leader is not on a 'spin.' And here's the deal, Cliff. The North Koreans fly the MiG-21 fighter. It's a little over twice as fast as we are but only has a range of one thousand miles. That means they can only fly five hundred miles over the Yellow Sea before turning back, or they'll get very wet.

"Our presumed twenty-minute head start, getting up to maximum speed, puts us about two hundred miles in front of the MiGs, but their scramble from stasis to wheels up will take them, what, eight minutes? Ten minutes?"

"Agreed."

"That puts us out another 115 miles," she said, quickly doing the math in her head, "so we'll fly for thirty minutes and be 315 miles in front, okay?"

Mattern had turned onto two-two-zero and was applying full power as he responded, "Agreed."

"So, once they're up to speed, they can cut our lead by twenty-five miles per minute. But by the time they're at speed, we're also at speed, doing eleven miles per minute. Got me?"

Mattern looked at his copilot. "Eric?"

"She's correct, Captain." Then he looked back and said, "I'm with you, Wendy."

She kept calculating. "It takes them twelve minutes to cover our 315 miles, but in those twelve minutes, we'll have covered another 132 miles, which takes them another five minutes—"

Coventry broke in. "Which puts them at bingo fuel at the point that we're visible."

Wendy nodded. "And then what do they do? If they shoot us down, they kill their supreme leader. So, they're thinking firing squad, wet landing, or turn around and call it a day. I think they turn around."

Mattern was all business. "Agreed. Better get your masks on. It's Korean bedtime in two minutes."

Wendy turned toward Thomas, put a hand on her face, and gave him a nod. He stood, more or less, and stretched, stealing a look at the pensive, heavily armed Koreans. He ambled to the galley, where he and Wendy both stood with their backs facing the main cabin, opened two upper cabinets, and pulled down their oxygen masks, out of view. They laid them on the serving counter. Swenson also retrieved his pistol from its shoulder holster in the cabinet and glanced at Wendy. She acknowledged with a nod, but then a slight headshake meaning, "don't shoot anyone."

At that moment, an earsplitting klaxon sounded in the cockpit and rang through the galley into the cabin. Above each seat, a compartment popped open and an oxygen mask dropped down, scaring the Koreans into yells and several screams.

Wendy grabbed her mask and held it up in front of the frightened Koreans. She yelled in English, "We've lost cabin pressure! Put on your masks!" while demonstrating how. She feigned abject fear, and the passengers mimicked her apparent fear for her life.

And in fact, the cabin pressure did drop to zero. Wendy's and Thomas's masks were self-contained to allow mobility. Several members of the North Korean security team refused to put on their masks—until they could draw no more air and quickly gave in. At that moment, the copilot flicked the toggle installed below the G700's flat-screen avionics array, and a servo in the hold quietly switched the flow from the oxygen canisters to the supplemental canisters containing halothane-oxygen, a basic but extremely effective medical anesthesia.

Every one of the Koreans was out in less than a minute. Wendy let the captain know, and he brought the cabin pressure back up to standard. Eric left the passenger masks toggled to keep releasing the mix, and Swenson went to work, relieving the unconscious security team members of their weapons and searching for any other lethal accessories. The easiest approach would be to simply lower the weapons into the cargo hold, but at Mattern's suggestion, the crew agreed to dump the guns in the Pacific during their lower-altitude approach to Ekman Island.

They never saw the MiGs. Two very fast chase planes showed up on radar but never got close enough for a visual.

Substantially more relaxed now that they were a thousand miles from North Korea, Captain Mattern yelled back to Wendy in the galley. "Ah, Ms. Halstad, your MiG information was extremely helpful—and very timely. Where'd you come up with all that?"

Wendy didn't look up. "I looked it up on Google, right after we were wheels up. Isn't Google just amazing?"

Mattern slowly shook his head. "Agreed."

Now it was time for her to work the phones.

CHAPTER EIGHTEEN

"Admiral? This is Wendy Halstad. I'm glad I could track you down!"

Brown chuckled. "Wendy, my dear, under the present circumstances, my staff is instructed to put your calls through immediately, whether I'm asleep, meeting with the president, or seated on the porcelain throne."

Wendy laughed right back at him. "Too much information, sir. Let's keep it to 'need to know.'" Both were laughing now. "I just wanted to let you know that phase one actually worked. We're about halfway to Ekman. Now everything depends on some pretty tight timing."

Brown cut his laugh short. "I'm with you, Wendy. We've got our ambassador in South Korea up to speed, and he's met with President Park to work out logistics. We've got the trinkets secured, and I must say, President Park is ecstatic."

"That's great, Hiram—as long as he knows to keep a lid on it until we give him a go."

Admiral Brown was nodding over the phone. "Park understands that the next twenty-four hours will define his legacy if all goes as planned. He's fully on board."

"Super. And thank you. Ah, any word on the progress of the *Ford*?"

"Yes," he replied. "She made it to Halifax, and there's a crew of fourteen hundred welders, pipe fitters, and crane operators on the project twenty-four seven. What took three years to install we'll have removed in three days. You know you've broken my heart, don't you?"

"Change, even positive change, is often a horse pill, Admiral. But when you combine the now complete collapse of nonsecular hostilities with this current project, do you have any doubts about where we're headed?"

"No, Wendy. I agree, we're on the cusp of a time that no one ever imagined. And at the speed of light. I'm . . . I'm . . ."

"You're making it happen, Hiram, that's what you are. I'll give you a call once we leave Ekman. Goodbye, sir." She broke the connection.

The next call was to Crowley. "Greetings, Richard. Are you two drunk yet? I heard some extra beer showed up."

He chortled in response. "We're competing with the US Navy for the beer, and we're losing. A bunch of good lads, though. I trust things went well in Pyongyang?"

"Extremely, Richard. Your team is world class and cool under pressure. And we didn't have to give away your baby. We were a bit nervous about the MiGs, but your bird outran them by minutes."

"MiGs?" Crowley echoed. "This connection is a mite scratchy. Did I hear you say 'MiGs'?"

Wendy pivoted. "Yes, Richard, but there are no holes in your Gulfstream. I'll fill you in later. We'll be on the ground on Ekman in less than three hours. Might you find a way to get yourselves up to the rear cabin door while Thomas boots our guests out the front? I'm thinking that the North Korean People's Liberation Army and the US Navy don't need a face-to-face."

"Good idea. I think I know a way we can all get up through that rear hatch without harassing the new inhabitants of Ekman Island."

"Please tell Michael that nobody shot me and that he may be more involved in phase two." She broke the connection.

Her final call was to Pastor Conlin in Stillwater. "Good morning, Daniel. This is Wendy Halstad, just checking in. What's shaking?"

"Wendy, I'm happy you called. I've got some interesting news, and a question as well."

"Tell me! You sound excited!"

"Energized is the better word," he replied. "So, remember the last time we spoke, there were forty-three thousand churches that had repurposed their missions?"

"Yes. Amazing."

"Amazing is a relative thing," the pastor said in joking disagreement. "It's been four days since then, and now a total of two million one hundred twenty thousand churches have picked up the banner. Two million! And interestingly, many of the new number had no direct contact with our initial flurry of congregations that embraced the changes."

"Interesting in what way?"

Pastor Conlin was truly energized. "Well, recall that the first day we met, there was a world convocation of ecumenical bishops going on at the Minneapolis Convention Center. I visited with many of them the following day, a 'laying on of hands,' if you will, and they seemed to spread the new understanding like fire in a tumbleweed patch. But this most recent expansion of . . . of agreement that God is beyond the limited capacities of humans to grasp? There seems to be minimal hand-to-hand, or one-on-one, connection to the initial group of receptive congregations."

"That *is* interesting," Wendy replied.

"What I'm hearing is that congregations around the world are approaching their pastors, priests, rabbis, and imams and demanding the refocus. Initially, the push for change was from the top down, and now it seems to be from the bottom up!"

"That's heartening, Daniel," Wendy gushed. "Millions of congregations are choosing to remove their blinders and, hopefully, expand the human intellect. I'm very pleased."

"So, that brings me to my question." Conlin backed off his energy somewhat. "I've been asked a thousand—rather, many thousands of times—what is your involvement in all this?"

"It hasn't changed, Daniel. I'm not involved. I simply asked some questions, and you, and untold numbers of others, came to an understanding, a realization, that is circling the globe. My desire, should people continue to ask you what Wendy Halstad's involvement is in all this, is that you say, 'Who?' Does that make sense to you?"

"Yes, Wendy, it does. It's contrary to what we're used to, but it does make sense."

"Now, I have a question for you. Your outreach director, Pastor Allen? I'm recalling that he never returned from the men's room the evening of our meeting with your church vestry."

"Former outreach director," Conlin said. "There was a letter of resignation under my door the next morning. It said he had decided to write a blog to establish a worldwide online outreach ministry of his own."

Wendy wasn't terribly interested. "Interesting! How's it doing?"

"Uh, yeah," Pastor Conlin said. "As of today, the blog shows total subscribers at—let me punch it up—yeah, here it is. Still stuck at three."

"Oh my! So, his mom, his dad, and . . ."

Conlin stifled a chuckle. "His sister, correct. But I do wish him the best."

"Daniel, I'm on a plane about ready to land, so I have to say goodbye," Wendy said. "I might call you again in a few days." She broke the connection.

■ ■ ■

Captain Mattern called back to the galley again as they began their final approach to Ekman Island. "Wendy, Thomas, we're down to three thousand feet. I suggest it's time to dispose of that excess hardware. I shut off the flow of the passengers' 'sleep aid' about twenty minutes ago, and I suspect we'll be dealing with some confused and angry communists very soon."

Swenson jumped up from his seat. "I'm on it, Cap." He made his way through the litter of dozing Koreans, through the luxurious private quarters, and to the rear cabin door, where he had stashed the weapons. Just like the front hatch, this one opened inward, and it made a whoosh as he broke the seal. However, at this altitude, the cabin was no longer pressurized, and the in-cabin turbulence was minimal.

He threw the pistols and machine guns out one by one, appreciating the process of disposal as much as taking the guns off his guests. He pulled the hatch closed, secured it, and made his way forward. To Wendy, he said, "I wonder how these louts will function without guns in their hands." He clicked his tongue several times.

Wendy responded, "It will be a study in humans' ability to adapt. Or failure to adapt. I'd love to be a fly on the wall . . . except there are no walls down there." The passengers were waking and looking around in confusion.

At two miles out, Mattern quickly depressed his mic button twice, and two rows of small but bright LED lights blinked on. Sir Richard had remembered to bring a mic-activated "on" switch for the solar-powered runway lights, as the plan was to use the field two more times after the current landing.

The tires chirped on the patched but adequate old runway, and the plane rapidly slowed, dropping to a steady taxi rate of about twenty miles per hour. Michael and Sir Richard were each waving flashlights, guiding the Gulfstream to its prescribed stop point. Thomas Swenson was waiting at the forward cabin door, and the moment the plane stopped, he swung the safety latch and pulled the door inward.

Dim moonlight snuck into the opening, along with the top of

the old "boarding" ladder. Looking down, all Swenson could see was two legs racing to the rear of the airplane. He kept his pistol holstered as he turned back toward his passengers, selecting the most alert of the group for "first off." He motioned to the man to come his way, but apparently, he was one of the generals and did not take direction well.

Swenson then took two quick steps forward, grabbed the general by his tunic, and lifted him out of his seat several inches into the air with one hand. The general squealed, more out of fright than anger. In mock cordiality, the steward motioned for the man to come forward, which he did. Swenson stepped aside and pointed to the ladder protruding from the open cabin door. The general vigorously shook his head, and Swenson took one aggressive step forward, bumping his chest into the general's nose.

"Out!" Thomas yelled, and he pointed at the ladder again. The man let out a squeak similar to a rusty hinge and started down. He looked up as if asking permission to take the next step, and Swenson again stepped forward and yelled, "Down!" while pointing at the ground. The general's ability to take direction was improving by the second, and he slipped from view.

Swenson pounded back into the cabin and selected the next soldier, who also refused to stand. The man received a half-power fist to his face, then found himself airborne, flying toward the galley. Thomas lifted him off the cabin floor; deposited him at the door; yelled, "Out!" and pointed to the ladder. The soldier looked over his shoulder at the flimsy ladder, turned back to the steward, and shook his head. Vehemently.

Without hesitation, Thomas gave the man a flat-footed kick in his midsection, and the soldier flew out into the night. Thomas did not watch him hit the ground, as he was already pointing at the next man to "come hither."

Things were definitely improving. The man stood without physical incentive, walked through the galley and to the ladder on his own, and climbed down. Thomas repeated the process, pleased that he'd not yet had to shoot anyone.

As the Koreans were off-loading, US Navy Chief Petter Officer Baker pulled the motorized asphalt roller up to the aft cabin door, which Wendy had opened. The roller rig sat four feet off the ground, front facing the jungle, and the driver's seat was another eighteen inches above the body. It was an easy boost from standing on the roller's seat to climbing into the G700 cabin. Each of the ten Seabees took their turn, moving forward into the private quarters but stopping before entering the forward cabin.

Michael followed the sailors aboard, and Crowley came up last. With one arm secured by Michael, Crowley used his other to shift the asphalt roller into gear. It moved slowly forward, away from the plane, as Crowley swung his legs into the cabin. Because the construction battalion squad and their beer, packs, and heavy equipment were air-dropped onto Ekman, the roller and tar cooker would remain with the island's new population.

Kim Jong-un was the last of the Koreans to leave the Gulfstream. He'd apparently never climbed down a ladder before but seemed eager to avoid the free-fall option offered by Thomas Swenson. Wendy and Thomas looked through the open door at the small group of confused and homeless North Koreans. Wendy said to Thomas, "How long do you think it will take before his underlings figure out that Kim Jong-un has no authority and no skills?"

"And a huge appetite," Thomas added, continuing to gaze upon the bedraggled group. "I say . . . sometime around breakfast." He then kicked the ladder away from the plane, scattering the entire population of Ekman Island.

As Swenson was about to secure the front door, Seaman Ortega approached him and said "Hey, boss, hold on a sec."

Swenson looked at him, shrugged, and let the seaman past

him to the open door. Ortega looked down at the group and yelled "Hey!" to get their attention. They all looked up. He pointed to the nearby jungle and yelled, "Ba-na-nas!" He nodded at Swenson, who closed and secured the door while giving him a curious look. "No reason to be impolite," Ortega said before walking back to the cabin.

Crowley secured the rear door, the asphalt roller puttered along out of sight, and the new passengers picked their seats. Wendy gave the thumbs-up to Captain Mattern, and the Gulfstream was immediately in motion.

"Hawaii, Cliff?"

Mattern give his typical stoic reply. "Agreed."

Michael pulled Wendy into a long embrace, and they dropped into adjoining seats. She said, "Tell me about the island."

He nodded. "It's small. Sir Richard and I walked across it from north to south, and then east to west yesterday. It's apparently volcanic in origin, but dormant. It rises to maybe eight hundred feet from the water, and there's a beautiful spring-fed stream that works its way down the slope. As Seaman Ortega noted, there are banana trees, but only in one area beside the cleared airstrip, so they were probably planted or brought in by the previous population. And for such a modest space, there is quite a large number of wild boar, which actually aren't so wild as they are curious."

Wendy was tight-lipped, listening and nodding. She eventually said, "I guess it's good that there's food, though every one of the men we just left there are thugs. I can't necessarily wish them well."

Michael held her hand and did not let go until they were forced to leave the plane at the Honolulu Pac-Comm terminal.

CHAPTER NINETEEN

Crowley's Pac-Comm team attacked the Gulfstream as soon as it rolled into the big hangar. As the engines wound down, rolling ladders were slid under the front and rear cabin doors, and the motorized aerial bucket lift was moving into position. Everyone deplaned: Captain Mattern and his copilot Eric Coventry, Thomas Swenson, Wendy and Michael, and the ten Seabees, who would be repatriated with their construction battalion shortly. This layover would take less than an hour.

The DPRK 1 tail number came off both sides with the help of the Sharper Image hair dryers, and vinyl RBDV 1 tail numbers, for República Bolivariana de Venezuela, were glued in their places, along with the tricolor Venezuelan flag. The wing tanks and cargo bladders were filled, the halothane-oxygen canisters were topped off, and the restroom holding tanks were relieved of their cargo. At Swenson's suggestion, Nigel Miller also loaded a sturdy collapsible ten-foot aluminum ladder into a forward galley pantry. Plus, four North Korean People's Army infantry helmets and three general's hats were removed from the forward cabin, sure to be prized souvenirs for several Pac-Comm employees. Kim had not been wearing a hat, in order to keep his high-maintenance coiffure in place. In some photos, Kim had been shown wearing a porkpie fedora, and the hat's ridiculous look and history would have required a lottery among the terminal staff.

In the Pac-Comm conference room, the off-duty phase one pilots were briefing the fresh phase two team. Swenson had managed a fair amount of sleep and would remain as the flight's armed and hard-working steward.

Crowley thanked his phase one team. "Cliff, Wendy tells me that your performance was brilliant and unflappable."

Mattern looked over at Wendy, his scowl back on his face. "She did her damnedest, sir, to prove me unworthy of that praise."

Wendy gave Mattern a smirk.

"But all said and done," Mattern continued, "Wendy Halstad is the most amazing person I've ever met. No insult meant toward you, of course, sir. But I would fly to the end of the earth for her." He coughed. "Which I just did."

"Any guidance for us, Cliff?" The new pilot asked. She seemed a tad edgy.

Mattern took a breath to speak, then paused, looked at Wendy, and finally responded. "Rocky, what I just said is all you need to know."

Crowley broke in with his big smile and overwhelming presence. "Wendy, Michael, this is Rocky Donnel, your phase two pilot. She used to be a fighter jockey, but we've knocked some sense into her, and knocked the need to fly upside down out of her, and I suspect she'll be adequate." Sir Richard winked at Donnel.

She was around thirty-five years old, five foot two, and maybe a hundred fifteen pounds dripping wet. Michael had a thought that she might need to sit on a New York City phone book to see out the cockpit window. She had short black hair, unreadable near-black eyes, and an intensity that explained how she'd excelled in such a testosterone-dominated vocation.

Wendy smiled and said, "Rocky, are you as tight-lipped as Captain Mattern?"

"Yes, ma'am," she replied, with no hint of humor or disagreement.

Crowley continued, "Michael, congratulations on your recent appointment as the new vice president of Drummond Petroleum SA."

"Yeah, about that," Michael said. He looked at Wendy. "You're okay with this? I mean, the only thing I know about oil is that if you spill it on yourself late at night, you wake up oily in the morning." Wendy smiled. None of the Brits got it.

More for the rest of the team than for Michael, she responded, "Sir Richard is persona non grata in Venezuela due to that presidential dinner he held in Colombia for Juan Guaidó. So in phase two, the Gulfstream is a gift from Drummond, which is ostensibly bidding, with gifts and bribes, to manage the Venezuelan oil production and refining businesses. The way Venezuela has remained socialist for twenty years—"

Crowley scoffed. "An insult to socialists everywhere."

Wendy rolled on. "—is oil revenue. It pays for the free health care and education, subsidized utilities, housing assistance, and even guaranteed minimum incomes."

"Sounds like utopia," Michael said.

Crowley let out a harrumph.

Wendy would not be sidetracked. "However, under Hugo Chávez, and now his handpicked successor, Nicolás Maduro, Venezuelan socialism means making the leadership fabulously wealthy and using the 'gifts to the masses'—thirty-one million of them—to keep the population at bay. In the meantime, the fraud and graft all but killed the goose. Inept management has nearly destroyed oil production and refining, and political imprisonment and thousands of 'disappearances' have created a huge humanitarian crisis—food shortages, medicine shortages, and inflation that has turned the Venezuelan bolivar into burnable heating fuel and bonfire kindling."

Crowley took up the narrative. "That creates our unique opportunity. Management of the Venezuelan oil apparatus is in flux, and I have convinced my friend, the CEO of Drummond Petroleum, to offer his company's name to repair the damage caused by Maduro and restore the country to its previous position as the largest and most vibrant economy in South America. And Maduro's appetite for bribes falls right into our wheelhouse." He smiled at Wendy. "Understanding, of course, that I really, really want my Gulfstream back."

Crowley then turned directly to Michael. "You're simply the man offering Maduro a seventy-five-million-dollar bribe to get a management contract. He knows exactly as much about oil production as you do. Your job will be to frost the cake—not discuss ingredients."

Wendy changed topic. "And our copilot?"

Crowley introduced him. "William Butters. Goes by Will or William. Never Billy."

Michael stifled a laugh. Butters stared him down until Michael quietly said, "Sorry, Will."

At that moment, Nigel strode into the conference room. "Sir Richard, ladies and gentlemen, you are locked and loaded. Have a safe and successful adventure."

Everyone stood, serious, confident, and a little nervous, except Swenson. He leaned toward Wendy, tapped his left shoulder, and said, "I'm okay to bring my friend?"

Wendy nodded. "But it stays in your holster."

"Yes, ma'am." Thomas was smiling. He liked this gig.

■　■　■

The flight was direct, Honolulu to Caracas. No need to stop at Ekman Island, as the landing strip was already prepared, the landing lights remained, and the Seabees were on to their next project. Plus, Ekman was in the wrong direction.

Wendy decided to make another call. "Melinda? This is Wendy Halstad. How are you?"

Melinda Vanderbilt responded enthusiastically. "Wendy! Nice

to hear from you! They're going at full speed at the Alan King Power Plant."

"Any problems?" Wendy asked.

"Well, the owner wasn't much interested in changing over to the new fuel, so the foundation just bought the plant."

"Yikes! You had to buy the whole power plant?"

"It was a no-brainer, actually," Vanderbilt said. "In addition to the 46 percent increase in efficiency from switching to the pellet spheres, the cost of fuel—formerly coal and now locally sourced cardboard—will be down 80 percent on day one, which was today. The price was several million over our estimated value, considering the plant is obsolete, but they weren't aware of all the efficiency increases." She stopped to laugh. "So the net is we're operating, we're green, we're immediately profitable, and we're proving the concept for the other two hundred forty plants."

Wendy asked, "Are you there at the site?"

"No, I've got a lot going on, what with the kids' band concerts, after-school sports, cooking dinner . . ."

Wendy wasn't buying it. "Melinda, your net worth is one hundred forty billion dollars."

"Yeah," she said coyly. "I hire help for some of that. Which is what I did for the Alan King Plant. Kept their management team—great group of engineers and technicians. Hired a new general manager who's responsible for not only the plant operation but also the production of the new on-site fuel manufacturing. And you and Peter were correct. The process is simple in concept, simple in application, expandable, and should be easy to replicate. And Wendy?"

"Yes?"

"We're just getting started!"

Wendy was excited. "Thank you, Melinda! Really. You're making a difference!" And she broke the connection.

■　■　■

Max Dorado, the CEO of Drummond Petroleum and its subsidiary, Drummond SA, was a hard-charging, take-no-prisoners veteran of the Texas oil business and was not lacking in confidence, intelligence, charisma, or success. He, his CFO, and two high-level Drummond project managers had put the plan together in a day while Sir Richard's team was still en route to Pyongyang. Armed with the results of phase one, the team tweaked their plan for Venezuela, and they were queued up for Crowley's call that the Gulfstream was on its way to Caracas.

"Hello, Max. Are things falling into place?"

"Hello, Sir Richard. And yes, all systems are go. You're not on the plane yourself, are you?"

"No, Max. I've learned that a long life is enhanced by staying away from people who want me dead. I'm slaving away in Honolulu."

Dorado laughed. "I trust my new vice president of South American operations is up to speed?"

"Actually, Max, he's not! We concluded that no finesse was necessary when offering a seventy-five-million-dollar bribe to a dictator. He's fluent in Spanish and can spell the words *oil* and *Drummond*, but otherwise, he's going to wing it. Pun intended."

"I trust your judgment, Richard. The overflight and landing arrangements were SOP as, unlike North Korea's airport, Maiquetía's Simón Bolívar International is a fully functioning and busy airport, right outside of Caracas. And as of this morning, your Gulfstream is registered in the name of Drummond Petroleum SA." Dorado chuckled again. "Ah, say, if Maduro doesn't like it, can I keep it?"

Crowley's response was clipped and immediate. "No."

"Roger that, Richard." He was still laughing. "Please let me know how things turn out."

"Will do, Max. And thank you." Crowley broke the connection.

■　■　■

"Maiquetía Tower, this is Gulfstream Romeo Bravo Delta Victor One; we are fifteen kilometers west-northwest, requesting permission to land on runway three-two-zero. Over."

"Gulfstream Romeo Bravo Delta Victor One, this is Maiquetía Tower. You are cleared third to land on runway three-two-zero. Follow the FedEx jumbo at a two-kilometer interval. Acknowledge."

"Roger, Maiquetía Tower. Gulfstream Romeo Bravo Delta Victor One to land on runway three-two-zero, two kilometers behind FedEx jumbo. Over."

■   ■   ■

Captain Donnel yelled to Wendy, Michael, and Thomas from the cockpit. "We're cleared to land in Caracas, folks. Time to strap on your dancing shoes."

"That's better," Wendy thought. "There's a human behind those dark eyes."

Swenson and Wendy were both wearing blue short-sleeved button downs sporting the Drummond logo and creased navy-blue khakis, proper attire for oil company flight stewards. Both shirts were a bit tight across the chest. Michael thought Wendy looked gorgeous for fifty while Thomas looked dangerous for forty-one. Michael was dressed in a polo and creased tan khakis, proper golf attire for an oil executive offering a free jet to a despot.

Three self-contained oxygen packs, along with Swenson's Sig, were stowed in an upper galley cabinet.

Moments after the tires chirped, a flashing guide car raced alongside the plane and swooped in front. Donnel braked to the speed of the car and followed it to a large hangar away from the terminal that proudly displayed "República Bolivariana de Venezuela" on its facade.

She braked solid and shut down the engines as a ground technician gave her the "full stop" signal with crossed arms and two neon flashlights.

Wendy stuck her head into the cockpit. "Rocky, I'm thinking this goes smoothly. After a security inspection, we'll invite President Maduro and his entourage to board and marvel at his new acquisition. I believe he'll willingly agree to go for a spin, at which point I'll signal you to wind up the engines. My intent is for Maduro himself to make the call to the tower via the wireless mic. That singular voluntary act keeps you and me out of jail if things go to hell."

Captain Donnel stared at Wendy for several seconds, and then said, "Roger."

"Once we're wheels up, you'll decompress the cabin, which will activate the oxygen drop-downs. Will, I'll signal you when all the masks are on, and you'll hit the servo toggle for the switch to the halothane-oxygen mix. Got it?" She looked at Donnel, then at Butters.

"Got it," they both said.

Swenson had pulled the front cabin door open and secured it as two ground techs pushed a rolling ladder into place. The scene outside the plane was very different from that in Pyongyang. There were no attack helicopters, no armored personnel carriers, and no Chinese limousines. Two black Cadillac Escalades pulled up within a few feet of the ladder, and one man in civilian attire exited the front passenger door.

He climbed the ladder, stopped at the entrance, and saluted everyone. Michael stepped forward, and the man said in Venezuelan-accented Spanish, "Permission to board for inspection, sir?"

Definitely Navy, Michael thought. You can take the man off the ship, but . . .

Michael responded in his Minnesota-taught Spanish. "Permission granted, señor," he said, and he waved the man in with a flourish.

The security man nodded at Wendy, spent an extra moment registering that Swenson, even scrunched down in his seat as he was, did not look like any flight steward he'd ever seen, and walked slowly aft, inspecting overheads and map pockets and taking in the incredible luxury of his boss's new ride. He only took five minutes, which told Wendy that no one was expecting a Trojan horse. As he left the plane, he turned and saluted again.

Much like the officer had done in Pyongyang, the security man went to the front passenger door of the second Escalade and bent to speak to a man for maybe twenty seconds. As he stood back up, all the doors of the two Escalades except the drivers' opened, and six more men got out. Two appeared to be generals, and one, from the rear SUV, was obviously Nicolás Maduro. He wore a dark business suit, dark sunglasses, and his Saddam Hussein moustache.

There were no armed soldiers, and there was no paranoid exterior inspection of the Gulfstream. These men were all casual, several of them smiling. Maduro had a smirk on his face that said, with no need for an interpreter, "Dumbass Yankees want to give me an airplane, I'll take their airplane."

The security man went back up first, followed by Maduro and then the others. The security man took up the responsibility of a proud tour guide, gesturing to this and that as they walked to the rear and back.

Wendy approached President Maduro and took his right hand in both of hers. Maduro smiled, apparently believing the tingling he felt was mutual attraction. Michael winced. She did look damn good in that shirt.

She said to Maduro in English, "Would you like to take a spin in your new plane, Mr. President?" She then looked at Michael, who translated into Spanish.

Maduro nodded, still smiling at Wendy. "Si! Excelente!" Michael handed him an ornate, official looking document headed with "Certificate of Title of Gulfstream G700-001." The header was repeated beneath that in Spanish, along with "Gifted to President Nicolás Maduro by Drummond Petroleum SA."

Maduro's smile grew still broader. Michael laughed to himself, knowing that airplanes don't have certificates of title like a used car. They had bills of sale.

Wendy gestured for the group to take their seats. Swenson remained scrunched in his, still reading the table of contents of the G700 operation manual. She went through the galley to the cockpit, looked Donnel in the eye, and twirled her finger. Fire 'em up. The engines roared to life.

Walking back through the galley, Wendy unlocked an upper cabinet and took down the handheld wireless mic. She handed it to Maduro, who, still smiling, looked at her curiously. Wearing the biggest smile she owned, she said in English, "Mr. President, it would be appropriate if you announced this short presentation flight to the tower." Michael repeated the suggestion in his Minnesotan accent–tinged Spanish, and Maduro nodded vigorously. His entourage seemed to expect the flight and registered no protests to their president.

He pressed the mic key and said, "Tower, Maduro." He released the key and looked over at his men while laughing like a ride operator on the midway collecting loose change below the Zipper carnival ride. "Please clear Venezuelan Air Force One for an immediate test flight. Over." The men applauded, and Maduro beamed.

The Maiquetía Tower responded through the pilots' headsets. "Gulfstream Romeo Bravo Delta Victor One, you are cleared for immediate takeoff on runway three-two-zero. Traffic in front of you has been cleared."

Donnel looked back at Wendy, and she nodded. The twin Rolls-Royce engines revved to taxi speed as the ground crew pulled away the ladder. Michael closed and secured the front cabin door like a pro. Swenson remained scrunched in his seat.

In less than a minute, Donnel had turned the plane from the taxiway onto three-two-zero and applied full power. The Gulfstream sprinted down the runway and elegantly lifted into the air. The captain activated "gear up" and climbed at thirty degrees, heading outbound from Caracas to the Caribbean. The Venezuelan passengers were animated and jabbering among themselves and looking out the windows. While the plane was still climbing, Wendy came forward and tapped Rocky on the shoulder. She nodded and deactivated the cabin pressure system.

Immediately, a klaxon began blaring from the open cockpit, the cabin oxygen compartments popped open, and the masks dropped down in front of the startled passengers. Wendy and Thomas put on their oxygen masks, and Michael stepped in front of their guests. In Spanish, and with concern in his voice, he yelled, "We've lost cabin pressure! No need to panic, but we all need to have our oxygen masks on."

While the passengers fumbled with the task, Wendy calmly went from person to person, making sure their masks were secure. Then she walked back to the cockpit, and this time tapped Butters on the shoulder. He toggled the halothane servo, and moments later the ruling government of Venezuela was asleep.

Wendy leaned into Will Butters. "Okay, Will, go ahead and re-pressurize the cabin, but keep the passengers on the halothane mix until our approach to Ekman." She turned to Donnel. "Rocky, set a course for Ekman Island. We're in a hurry—we've got one more phase to complete before Admiral Brown can signal the cleanup."

"Roger that," Donnel responded.

■ ■ ■

Wendy plopped into the seat next to Michael and let out a breath. "Great job, my dear. You're a natural!"

Michael looked at her. His hands were shaking a bit. "I've never kidnapped anyone before. Can you believe that?"

She nodded. "Technically, they agreed to be on this flight. It's when we left Venezuelan airspace that the issue became more technical. You hang in. I need to update Hiram."

He was still staring at her. "The secretary of the Navy."

"Yeah, that Hiram," she said as she dialed the number.

At the same time, Thomas Swenson went from passenger to passenger, searching for weapons. He found three semiautomatic nine-millimeter Berettas and thought to himself, "This is a much classier group of thugs."

CHAPTER TWENTY

The trip back to Ekman Island was uneventful. Everyone except the pilot and copilot got plenty of sleep. When they were about a half hour out, Wendy headed back up to the cockpit to update the pilots.

"The airstrip is fifteen hundred feet long, and we take thirteen hundred. The surface is patched asphalt, but adequate. We'll be landing in darkness, which is good. The Koreans don't know we're coming, so hopefully they won't be near enough to be a bother. But just in case, let's do this. Position the plane for takeoff before we unload our passengers. That way you can be full throttle as the last Venezuelan steps off the ladder. Time on the ground: two minutes, max. Questions?"

Donnel was as succinct as Cliff Mattern. "No, ma'am."

"Will, go ahead and toggle off the mix. We'll pull their masks now and try not to interrupt their beauty sleep."

"Yes, ma'am," he said. Wendy thought he'd make a good captain one day.

She turned her attention to corralling Michael and Thomas. "Guys, we're about thirty minutes out. Rocky will position us for takeoff before we boot these guys." She looked at Swenson. "Figure of speech, Thomas. We can communicate with this group verbally."

"Damn it." He was SAS, for goodness' sake. He wasn't trained to blow kisses.

"And Michael, it will be up to you again to communicate to our guests. In the last go, Thomas's good manners and Korean language skills evaded him at the same time, and one of the Koreans was forced into a double somersault as he left the plane." She paused and turned to Swenson. "By the way, how was his landing?"

Swenson smiled. "Only a three point two. He landed hard on his arse."

Michael didn't speak. He just stared at them both.

■　■　■

All the passengers were awake when the captain keyed Sir Richard's landing lights to "on," and they were visibly agitated by the time the wheels touched down. The three who had been armed were searching themselves like they'd just walked naked through a poison ivy patch. Maduro was scowling at them as if to say, "Find your guns and shoot these people." No such luck.

Swenson retrieved the folding ladder from the galley cabinet and stood by the door until Donnel gave him a nod. The engines were powered down but still running. He opened the hatch, unfolded the ladder, and said to Michael, "You're up. Make sure to throw in a couple 'ándales' and 'arribas.'"

Michael rolled his eyes and turned to the Venezuelans. "¡Salid, salid!" he yelled. And then, "¡Ándale! ¡Arriba!" Swenson smiled.

The men stood, all of them cursing Michael in Spanish and, even under stress, cursing him again for his insolent use of the words *ándale* and *arriba*, which were of Mexican origin and definitely *not* proper Spanish. Swenson took three quick steps from the forward door to the cabin, revealing his full girth and intensity to the men. They stepped forward toward the door, now just complaining among themselves.

The first at the ladder stopped and looked around at Michael, with a question. Michael yelled, "¡Salga!" and the man climbed down. Michael yelled this way at each of them, and each man climbed down.

Thomas smiled again. Definitely a more refined group of thugs, he thought. He pulled up the ladder and rapped twice on the cockpit wall. Donnel pushed the throttle to the stops and let off the brakes, and the Gulfstream jumped forward. He latched the door, stowed the ladder, and headed aft.

Wendy leaned into the cockpit again and said only, "Honolulu." Donnel nodded. "Got it."

Because of the darkness, they didn't get a chance to see how well the two groups of marooned louts might play together. Wendy thought again, "Oh, to be a fly on their wall . . ."

■ ■ ■

Nigel Miller shook Wendy's hand. "This might be the last time we see each other, ma'am. I must tell you, meeting you has been the biggest honor of my life. The stories I'll be able to tell my grandkids!"

"Ah, about that, Nigel." Wendy put her arm around his shoulder and walked him to a corner of the conference room.

Captain Cliff Mattern and his copilot Eric Coventry had taken over for Rocky and Will on phase three and were seated on one side of the table. Michael, Swenson, and Crowley were seated across from them. Mattern was talking softly to Crowley. "Sir Richard, Syria is too far without refueling at least once. There is zero chance of getting there and back to Honolulu with the onboard fuel, even with the extra bladders."

Crowley nodded. "I agree, Cliff, and Admiral Brown has come up with a disastrous plan to resolve that."

Wendy and Miller came back from the corner and sat in while Crowley continued. "Admiral Brown has positioned the USS *Abraham Lincoln* to rendezvous with us at this point in the Atlantic." He slid a laminated map over to Mattern.

Mattern looked at the coordinates and quickly figured out what was going on. "No way, sir. I mean, respectfully, no way, sir. I mean, goddammit! No way!"

Wendy looked at him with concern. "Cliff?"

He leaned in toward her, face flushed and bulges on the sides of his neck. "The *Abraham Lincoln*, ma'am?"

Wendy nodded, a question in her eyes. "So?"

Mattern yelled loud enough to rattle the conference room windows. "It's a fucking aircraft carrier! This is a Gulfstream, not a taildragger. This plane takes thirteen hundred feet to land, and the *Lincoln* is eleven hundred feet long! And I'm—I've never—"

Crowley calmly interrupted. "I have, Cliff."

Mattern was now angry *and* confused. "What?"

"I think it's a terrible idea, Cliff, and I said so to Hira—Admiral Brown. When he was commander of the *Forrestal* maybe eighteen years ago, he buggered up some orders, at great risk to his career, and put me into an A-6, which I'd flown a couple of times previously. Keep in mind, I was neither in the Navy nor a US citizen. But he put me into an A-6 on the deck of the *Forrestal*, hooked me up to the catapult, and had his crew throw me and that A-6 off the end of the bloody deck, turning six Gs."

Mattern was in shock. "No fucking way." He looked over at Wendy and said, "Sorry, ma'am," then looked back at Crowley and repeated, "No fucking way."

"He bloody did!" Crowley was shaking his head. "I thought he was pulling my chain, having me take front seat, full uniform, pretending to hook us up to the slingshot. And then by god if he didn't wave at the 'shooter' and they threw me off the ship! It was little consolation that Hiram was in the rear seat.

"So first I pissed my trousers, I kid you not, only minutes after downing a day's worth of tea, and then I got hold of the plane and kept it out of the water. Only then did Hiram tell me, 'Richard, I'm gonna get you certified, you show-off thrill seeker.' And I say, 'No way in hell, cap,' and he says, 'Richard, you're either going to put this Intruder back on that deck, or we're both gonna drown.' So I did it. He guided me in, and I put it back on the deck. Bounced four feet in the air and missed the first cable, but I did it."

"Unbelievable!" Captain Mattern was shaking his head.

"No, Cliff, it gets worse. After we landed, Hiram says, 'Again.' I'm shaking my head like the little hula doll on the back shelf of a '63 Chevy, and he says, 'Again.' He says, 'Certification is five drops, not one. Again.' So the deck crew pulls us up to the slingshot, hooks us in, and we go again. By this time, the pee has leaked down into my boots . . ."

The whole room was now rolling in tears, laughing so hard they could barely breathe.

Crowley kept going. "Five times I put that A-6 back on the deck. And after the fifth, Hiram said to me, he says, 'Three things, Richard,' and I'm thinking he's going to do a debrief before we even pull back the canopy. He says, 'Three things. First, you're certified. Second, I've never been so scared in my life! And third, this cockpit is starting to stink really, really, bad. Let's get the hell out of here.' And that was that."

The room was quiet for a minute. Then Mattern said, "So you're flying this trip?"

Crowley shook his head. "No such luck, Cliff. I'm just putting it down on the *Abraham Lincoln*. You get the rest."

"You put it on the *Forrestal*—and back off, correct?" Mattern was a stickler for details.

Crowley smiled at him. "Yeah, but taking off is a piece of cake. You've got that." He turned to Miller. "Nigel, to that end, put new brakes on my bird, will you? We won't be able to slow down with a cable."

■ ■ ■

Barely forty-five minutes later, Miller was back in the conference room. "Sir, your pit crew handled the job in record time. Tail number has been changed again, fuel and halothane have been topped off, and the brakes are new. Also, the crew recovered three Beretta semiautos from the galley and were wondering—"

Crowley cut him off. "Spoils of war, Nigel. Distribute them as you see fit."

"Thank you, sir. Your bird is ready when you are."

Crowley took charge. "Okay, folks, here's the plan. Michael, you'll stay at Pac-Comm to manage communications. By the way, I heard your accented Spanish was . . . highly entertaining."

Michael looked over at Swenson and flipped him off. Swenson grinned.

"Cliff and Eric are up front. Wendy and Thomas will provide 'guest service'"—he winked at them—"and I"—he shook his head— "will be providing the midflight entertainment. Questions?"

Mattern asked, "SOP is for the *Lincoln* to video all landings, correct?"

Crowley responded warily, "I believe so."

Now it was Mattern's turn to smile. "I want a copy."

■ ■ ■

Having received one final application of adhesive-backed vinyl, the Gulfstream's new tail number was SAR 1, for Syrian Arab Republic One.

Bashar al-Assad had taken over control of the country, succeeding his father. He was intelligent, educated, and considered at the time to be an agent of change and modernization. However, his "new world order" leanings dissolved with the challenges of staying in power in a Muslim nation, and it became clear that his faith and worship were focused more directly on himself.

Assad accepted the gift of the Gulfstream as Crowley's appreciation for Assad's assignment of six gates at the Damascus terminal to Crowley Airlines and their appointment as the management company for Syria's only private fixed-base operator. Flyover permission was granted for the G700, and landing approval was assured.

After a long and uneventful ride, Wendy leaned into the cockpit as they began their final approach to Damascus International Airport. "Cliff, Eric, the landing in Damascus should be easier than Pyongyang, and we likely won't encounter the demonstration of military power, either. Our challenge will be when Assad enters the aircraft. He's not as childlike as Kim, nor as buffoonish as Maduro. He's a smart, conniving mass murderer, and getting him to announce a 'spin' to the tower isn't a sure thing. We'll be punting and holding our breath—though one positive is that Assad speaks passable English.

"Cliff, should we get to 'wheels up' with guests, I'll give you the nod for loss of cabin pressure, and Eric, you'll work the halothane toggle. Got it?"

"Same as Pyongyang, ma'am?"

"Exactly. Thanks, guys."

■ ■ ■

Wendy was correct. There were no issues with the flyover or permission to land, and the runway was smooth as silk. As at Maiquetía, a guide car raced up beside the Gulfstream. It led them to a military terminal away from the civilian version. As the plane rolled to a stop, a rolling ladder was brought up, and Swenson opened the forward door. A single Mercedes C-Class sedan pulled up beside the ladder, and two men got out, one from each of the front doors, both dressed in Western business suits and ties. They immediately climbed the ladder.

Sir Richard and Wendy greeted them, while Swenson slouched off to the side. Both security men gave each of the cabin occupants a considered study but did not acknowledge the greeting. They were serious, lithe, and deadly bodyguards who regarded the five crew members as either threats or nonthreats.

One turned to the cockpit, inspected the two pilots, and instructed them to stand to be searched. Standing in the cockpit of a Gulfstream was not possible, but Cliff and Eric gamely wiggled up to the maximum height available and allowed the man to massage them without protest.

The second security man started with Wendy, and then Crowley, doing a thorough search without apology or deference to gender. When he told Swenson to stand, he stood, much to the alarm of the five-foot-nine bodyguard. The guard called to his partner and spoke quickly in Arabic. The partner gracefully pulled out what appeared to be a Colt 1911 .45-caliber semiautomatic, which was, until recently, the same sidearm issued to all officers of the US Army since 1911.

Swenson acknowledged two things. One, as he towered over the security men and outweighed each by fifty pounds, he understood their concern. And two, he was intrigued by the Colt. It was a distinctly American weapon, and much heavier than even his Sig Sauer. Maybe the guy was just a cowboy, which prompted Swenson to behave and be careful.

With the body searches completed, the lead Syrian carefully worked his way aft. The other kept his Colt out and visible. The entire search took fifteen minutes and was thoroughly professional. The Syrians spoke only to each other and left the plane without another look at the crew.

Crowley let out a sigh, exhaled heavily, and said, "I have something of a reputation for appreciating excitement. But some days"— he gazed down the ladder at the Mercedes—"not so much as other days."

The lead Syrian talked into a lapel mic and had his second move the car away from the plane. A minute later, a large black Mercedes

S-Class sedan pulled up to the ladder, braking hard. Three men got out, and the driver remained in the car. One of the men was in military dress; the second was carrying a briefcase and might have been a chief of staff. The third was Bashar al-Assad.

Assad was six foot two, trim, and fifty-five years old. He came to power in 2000, after his father's death, unopposed in an election in which he received 97 percent of the vote. There was a quietly passed joke in Syria that the other 3 percent of the electorate were never seen again. He was known to have been importing nerve gas from North Korea since 2012 and had made use of the poison via barrel bombs on Syria's civilian population on at least several occasions.

He took in the plane from thirty feet, neither smiling nor scowling. The lead security agent led the way into the Gulfstream, followed by Assad, then the general, then the chief of staff, and finally the second security officer.

Wendy stepped toward Assad with a big smile and wide eyes. She clasped his right hand in both of hers. "President Assad! Welcome aboard!"

Assad stared at her, not smiling or giving any acknowledgment of her greeting. Swenson looked over from his G700 operator's manual and thought, "Awkward. That's not a good start."

She finally released his hand, and Sir Richard Crowley stepped in, hand outstretched and all thirty-two teeth on display. "Mr. President, I'm Richard Crowley, and I'm so happy to finally meet you." They shook, and Assad finally showed signs of life.

"Mr. Crowley, I have followed your career and exploits with great interest. I am pleased to meet you as well. Please call me Bashar." And he smiled.

Wendy took note, confirming to herself that Sir Richard would be the lead dog in this hunt.

Crowley, too, knew that he was going to have to make this sale. "Mr. President—Bashar—let me show you the state-of-the-art avionics on your new Gulfstream," he said, and he gestured toward the cockpit. Assad was fully engaged and asked several questions about the impressive array of flat screens and computer modules.

As Crowley guided Assad aft, the general took a quick look into the cockpit and stepped back out. The other three Syrians stood where they were like potted plants.

Crowley and Assad eventually came forward from the sleeping quarters. Crowley had apparently just finished a joke, and Assad was laughing heartily and responded with his own rejoinder. Wendy smiled and thought, "BFFs. Sir Richard may be the eighth wonder of the world."

"Bashar," Crowley now said, one arm on the man's shoulder, "I would love to take you for a spin in your new plane. May I?"

Assad looked at his chief of staff and his general, who both shrugged and nodded. Assad sat in the first cabin chair, leaned back, pointed to the cockpit, and said, "Make it so, Number One!" Crowley literally burst into laughter, and several of the others did as well. Swenson, Security One, and Security Two, remained stone-faced.

Wendy stepped to the cabin and said quietly, "Light 'em up, Cliff." The engines whirred into action. Wendy was holding the wireless microphone, and Crowley took it from her. He handed it to Assad and said, "Mr. President, it would be an honor if you would inform the tower that your new Gulfstream G700 is going on its first flight as Syrian Air Force One." Assad smiled, nodded, and took the mic. As a former army colonel, he knew the drill.

He keyed the mic. "Tower, this is Assad. Clear the runway. I'm taking my new plane for a ride."

A moment later, the tower responded, registering only in the headgear of the two pilots. "Gulfstream Sierra Alpha Romeo One, you are cleared for takeoff on runway three-two-zero. We have cleared all other ground traffic. Over."

Cliff responded, "Roger, Damascus Tower. Gulfstream Sierra

Alpha Romeo One taxiing to runway three-two-zero and will take off when in position. Over."

At the end of runway three-two-zero, Captain Mattern pushed the throttle to the stops, and the Gulfstream G700, momentarily of indeterminate ownership, sprinted down the airfield. With wheels up, the Mediterranean was only fifty-one miles away.

Thomas Swenson thought, "Note to world: If you don't want your leader abducted, don't build your capital fifty miles from the ocean."

As the plane gained altitude, Wendy, one last time, leaned into the cockpit and tapped Mattern on the shoulder.

The captain deactivated the cabin pressurization system, and the klaxon again bellowed and the oxygen masks again dropped from the overhead panels in the cabin. Swenson and Crowley strapped on their breathing apparatuses as Wendy held hers and gave an agitated yell. "Listen up! We've lost cabin pressure, and we need to put on our oxygen masks—now!" She moved toward President Assad to adjust his breather.

However, the plane was not yet above ten thousand feet, which was the point in the atmosphere that cabin pressurization was required. Oxygen was still plentiful in the cabin.

All passengers except the lead security agent continued to put on their masks. Wendy moved to the seat behind Assad to help with the next man's mask. The security man was in a front seat to Assad's right. He stood and pulled out his Colt. Swenson saw it first and took a step closer. Wendy took in the scene in alarm. Crowley remained in his seat, never having faced this predicament before.

The Syrian pointed the .45 directly at Thomas Swenson and growled, "There is no emergency. I can breathe, and your pilot can simply stay below ten thousand feet. What in the name of Allah are you trying to do?"

Eric was looking back from the cockpit, and Wendy gave him a nod. The halothane started flowing one second later.

The Syrian bodyguard put both hands on his pistol grip and assumed the classic shooting stance. Assad's eyes were wide and wild, but he seemed to be getting groggy. Swenson didn't move and continued to stare directly into the eyes of the Syrian. Wendy darted to her left, between Swenson and the shooter, as he squeezed the trigger. Twice.

Thomas Swenson knew he was dead, but he didn't feel dead. Sir Richard Crowley knew Thomas was dead, but he didn't look dead. The Syrian couldn't see Swenson but was damn sure Wendy was dead. Wendy knew she was dead, but that was old news. For a moment, she felt bad. Her whole goal, her apparent mission in coming back, was to make people's lives better. In that process, she'd now been shot five times. That made her feel disappointed. But she recovered quickly.

Mattern was yelling from the cockpit, "Thomas, what the hell's going on?"

Swenson turned his head back to the pilot and simply said, "Keep flying, Cliff."

Wendy held her hand out to the Syrian, asking silently for the pistol. He was literally in shock, from the noise, from the adrenaline, and from disbelief. He had just killed this infidel standing in front of him, with two .45-caliber rounds that should have put two holes in her chest and two exit wounds the size of a baseball out her back. But she was still upright, holding out her hand for his gun.

In the shooter's moment of confusion, Wendy leaned closer and put her right hand over the pair of Syrian hands still wrapped around the Colt. He lowered his hands and let Wendy ease the pistol away. Assad and the rest of his crew were out. Crowley was wide-eyed, trying to digest what he had just seen.

Wendy quietly said to Swenson, "Thomas, will you ask Eric to repressurize the cabin but keep the halothane flowing?" Swenson did so without responding. As he stepped back into the cabin, she handed him the Colt, which he immediately relieved of its clip and the live round in the chamber.

The Syrian was back in his seat, as confused as any human could possibly be. Wendy turned to Swenson, then to Crowley, and said, "We'll talk about this later. Thomas, will you make this man comfortable and assist him with his oxygen mask?"

Swenson looked from her to Crowley to the Syrian and said, "Yes, ma'am." The man did not resist and was soon napping with the rest of his team.

Captain Mattern yelled back again. "Thomas, for god's sake. What's going on?"

"Captain, in a nutshell, a Syrian didn't like his situation, he drew down on me, Ms. Halstad stepped over, he fired twice, she deflected the shots, and all our passengers are now asleep."

Crowley was coming out of his stupor, though not with any comprehension. Almost to himself, he added, "And there are no holes in her . . . or my airplane."

■ ■ ■

It was a three-hour flight to the rendezvous point with the *Abraham Lincoln*. The three cabin crew members were all seated, pondering life. After an hour in which no words were spoken, Crowley finally looked at Wendy and said, "Who are you?"

She looked at him for a moment, then sighed. "It's quite complicated, actually, Richard. I'm really not sure myself." She didn't speak for several minutes, and they didn't press.

"Michael knows about this, and my kids know. None of us understand, but we're . . . dealing with it. Now you both know," she said, as she glanced over to Thomas. "I had a massive heart attack three years ago and I died."

Both men's eyes grew large but quickly settled back down.

They'd both known that Wendy had some unusual vibe, almost a hypnotic thing. But she definitely wasn't dead. Most likely definitely.

"It was my mistake with the shooter. I was attending to the others, hands-on and all that, and I forgot to calm the guys with guns first. I'm still learning, I guess. Fortunately, he was a trained professional, and hesitated just enough before shooting a high-caliber weapon point-blank in a small aircraft."

"You saved my life, Wendy," Thomas said quietly. "I—I don't know whether I should ponder that or ponder you."

She hesitated. "I'll tell you what I know. What my kids and my husband know as well. I remember dying, but I don't remember being dead. I'm hoping that's normal." Sir Richard got the first glimmer of humor in his eyes since the shots were fired.

"I showed up back at home one day, Michael took me in, and we just started fixing things. Like, well, the recent religious rush from hatred to community involvement?" Both men nodded, with questioning looks on their faces.

"Well, I was involved in that a little bit at the start."

"A little bit," Thomas interrupted.

Wendy added, "Oh, and a young man shot me there as well, in front of the Al Hakeem Mosque in Minneapolis. It turned out that he was a caring fellow who was somewhat confused."

Crowley chimed in, "And this 'caring young fellow' shot you."

"Three times, actually, but he apologized, and I helped him with an alibi." And she shrugged. "What can I say? It's not about me. It's about humans rejecting nonsense, dogma, and their self-imposed limitations. Killing each other in the name of God. It's about intellectual growth after thousands of years of near stagnation.

"The 'new' churches are donating facilities to their communities; partnering with parks and rec departments; sponsoring AA meetings, homeless shelters, and battered women's shelters; and serving meals to seniors and shut-ins. They've cut their need for income by 50 percent and reduced their hosting communities' social service expenses by 25 percent.

"There are still some in India who believe that cows are sacred and some in Yorba Linda who swear that smoking peyote is inhaling the essence of God, but for the most part, churches are changed, but still vital and relevant.

"I don't know why I'm here. I have no plan, and then, one day, I have a plan. And like, four days ago, I woke up thinking, 'Well, I've met the secretary of the Navy, and we seemed to get along, so maybe I should leverage that.'"

Crowley smiled and nodded. "Marketing one-oh-one."

Wendy laughed, then asked, "So . . . does any of that make any sense?"

Swenson replied immediately. "No, ma'am."

She smiled. "Well, now we're all in the same place, up to the same speed. Oh, except, well, Melinda—you know Melinda Vanderbilt?"

"Melinda Vanderbilt," Thomas repeated.

Crowley smiled. "I know Melinda very well. We've worked on some projects together."

"Well, we came up with a scheme, and she's implementing it. Based on a new but shockingly simple invention, she is in the process of buying coal-fired power plants relatively cheaply and converting them to burning highly pressurized cardboard-based spheres until the plants can be replaced altogether."

Crowley chuckled. "And you're involved . . ."

"Just a little bit," Wendy said.

Swenson had another thought. "Uh, about the bullets . . ."

Wendy nodded. "I can't explain it. It happened, you saw it, there's no way that was real, and here we are."

Thomas pondered for a moment, and said, "I'm choosing to

focus on me being alive. With that resolved, I can deal with the rest as time goes on."

Wendy nodded again. "That's the only option, Thomas, other than maybe shooting yourself and ending it all—but that would have wasted a lot of effort on my part."

They all smiled and fell into silence. After a few minutes, Wendy started to make her calls.

CHAPTER TWENTY-ONE

"Admiral? This is Wendy Halstad. We're wheels up on phase three. Assad and his team are in dreamland in the Gulfstream, and we're about two hours out from our rendezvous with the *Abraham Lincoln.*"

"That's great news, Wendy! And everything went okay?"

"Well, no, actually. There were some issues, but everyone who was alive when the shooting started is still alive."

Wendy heard Brown jolt forward in his chair. "Shooting?"

"Yes, sir. One of Assad's bodyguards did some quick math when the oxygen masks dropped down and pulled out his sidearm."

"And?"

"We must have hit some turbulence. He fired twice, and no one was hit. The sound of his own gun must have stunned him for a moment, and we were able to . . . subdue him. The halothane mix did the rest."

"My god," Admiral Brown replied, and then went silent.

Wendy jumped in. "So we're finally ready for the cleanup phase. You've got things ready in Korea for your signal?"

Brown came around to the task at hand. "Just waiting for the green light. The president will send an immediate dispatch to North Korea through the Swiss embassy, and our ambassador to China will meet with his counterpart there to prod them into letting history take its course. President Park is on call to board a plane from Seoul to Pyongyang, and the caravan waiting at the DMZ is fueled and ready. Are you giving us the green light?

"Yes, Admiral. Please proceed."

"Excellent. Wendy, please hold while I inform Ambassador Vanderbrink in Seoul." There was background chatter as Brown apparently used another phone to call the ambassador, and then the sound picked back up. "Thank you, Charles, and good luck. Wendy, I'm back with you."

"Okay. As planned, Sir Richard will contact Juan Guaidó in Cúcuta, Colombia, and green-light him to cross into Venezuela via the Simón Bolívar International Bridge. And now is the appropriate time to inform the officials that remain in Caracas that Maduro has decided to defect. Richard will release the same information on social media, so I suspect that Guaidó's entrance into Caracas will be something of a celebration."

Admiral Brown was nodding. "The US Special Envoy to Venezuela has been briefed by President Gallagher and has his statement ready to go."

"And as far as Syria," Wendy said tentatively, "you're still comfortable with that plan? It seems dangerous to me."

"Wendy, the Middle East has offered no easy answers for two thousand years, but thankfully, I'm on the sidelines on that one. When we hang up, the president and secretary of state will notify the Palestinian unity government that Assad has abdicated and that Syria has agreed to become the permanent Palestinian homeland. Frankly, there is no such agreement, but there also is no one in Damascus with the power to disagree. And our ambassador to Russia will suggest to *his* counterpart that Russia, as well, should let history take its course."

Wendy was pleased. It was a complex plan, involving three simultaneous abdications of three hard-line adversaries and international bad actors. "And as far as the United States government's perceived involvement?"

"From everything we know," Brown said with a chuckle, "all three abdicated of their own volition, with no known hostilities and no direct involvement of the United States government. Is that understanding still correct?

"Yes, Hiram. The three 'bad actors' might disagree, but their words and actions are very clear. Even Assad, whom we were a bit nervous about, gladly announced his departure to Damascus air traffic control. He and Sir Richard even became best of friends—until he wakes up, I would think."

Admiral Brown laughed loudly. "Anything else, Wendy?"

"No, Hiram, it's all working out as well as we could have hoped. Ah, by the way, did Richard actually soil his flight suit when you two were tossed off the *Forrestal* by catapult?"

Brown began laughing even louder. "Yes indeed. I believe he had drunk about a quart of foul-smelling English tea before I loaded him in that A-6, and the smell was much worse by the time he dumped it all into his trousers. Goodbye, Wendy." The admiral was still laughing hard when she disconnected.

CHAPTER TWENTY-TWO

An hour before they reached the USS *Abraham Lincoln*, Sir Richard took the left seat up front, and Captain Mattern switched to the right. Mattern said to his copilot, "Eric, you have the job of saving the sleeping Syrians should Sir Richard not nail the landing and dump us in the drink." Crowley smiled, but didn't look away from the control array. "On second thought, Eric—just try to save Wendy and Thomas. I wouldn't want to strap you with too much responsibility."

Several minutes later, Crowley called to the carrier, "*Abraham Lincoln*, this is Gulfstream Sierra Alpha Romeo One, requesting permission to land, low power drop, no cables. Over."

"Gulfstream Sierra Alpha Romeo One, you are cleared for landing. The deck is empty and arresting cables have been removed. What is your rated distance from wheels-down to full stop? Over."

"Two hundred feet beyond the end or your deck, *Lincoln*. Over."

"Roger that, Gulfstream. Our 'no-wave-around' protocol will be in place. An angel and a dive team will be standing by. Over."

"Ah, sir?" Captain Mattern was looking at Crowley, talking on the cockpit intercom.

Sir Richard glanced at him and saw genuine concern on Mattern's face. "Well, Cliff, as you know, the arresting cables are designed to catch an A-6, or nowadays an F-35, and yank it to a stop in about fifty feet."

"Right . . ."

"And you know that the Gulfstream G700 needs thirteen hundred feet of runway to land."

"Right…"

"What you may not know is that the *Lincoln* deck is one thousand one hundred ten feet long. An angel is a rescue helicopter."

"Ah, no, I did not know that." Crowley thought Captain Mattern sounded somewhat sarcastic.

"Carrier aircraft land at 80 percent full throttle, so if they miss all three cables with their hook, they can be at 100 percent power in an instant, nail their afterburners, and stay in the air when they run out of ship."

"Right…"

"But because we don't have a hook, we can't use the cables, and thus we have to hit the deck around two hundred miles an hour slower than a fighter does."

"Right…"

"And thus, should we run out of deck, we can't build speed fast enough to remain in the air." Crowley looked over at Mattern. "That's why I had new brakes installed in Honolulu."

"And will that allow us to stop in time?"

Crowley was glued to the flight controls. "We're going to find out in three minutes, Cliff."

The landing was not nearly as exciting as it could have been. The Gulfstream was guided in not only by the traditional landing officer waving large fluorescent 'paddles' but also by a lighted guidance system on the deck itself, which prodded the pilot to remain in the green for level and altitude.

Even though the ship was in forward *and* side-to-side *and* fore-to-aft motion, Richard Crowley kissed the deck like a pro. He cut power and hit the brakes with everything he had. By midship, the brake housings were red hot, but they didn't burst. Toward the end of the deck, the pilots now saw that two motorized equipment tugs had been chained down about twenty feet apart, and there was no getting around them. Crowley and Mattern both had a WTF moment, and they braced for the collision. And then the plane stopped, with the nose gear one foot from falling off the foredeck, and each wing one foot from hitting the tugs.

Neither man breathed for several moments. They stared at the Atlantic Ocean, sixty feet below and as far as they could see out the windshield. They finally let out a collective breath. Mattern looked over at Crowley. "Did you wet your shorts?"

"No. You?"

"No. Based on your warning, I haven't drunk a drop of anything since Damascus."

Crowley replied, "Me either." He smiled at Cliff, and they both unstrapped from their seats.

■   ■   ■

While the *Abraham Lincoln*'s fuel team gassed up the Gulfstream, all five crew members deplaned, joining up ten minutes later in the pilots' ready room. Four poured themselves hot coffee, and Crowley found a stinky tea. They were standing, chattering quietly, when the ship's commander, Captain John Delaney, walked in and headed toward the coffee urn. He turned, took a sip, and introduced himself, shaking hands with each. When shaking Wendy's hand, his eyes popped wide open. Thomas and Sir Richard looked at each other and smiled.

Crowley broke the moment. "Captain, with all due respect, why in the hell were two tugs chained to the flight deck with the obvious purpose of destroying my new Gulfstream?"

Delaney stared back, but he was smiling. "Let me answer that question with several of my own. How much fuel was in your wing tanks?

Mattern answered for Richard, who still seemed to be carrying a bit of a blush. "They were both bingo, sir. We had eight thousand pounds left in our belly tank."

Delaney continued, still addressing Crowley. "Would your plane have exploded if those empty wing tanks had hit my tugs?"

Mattern answered for Crowley again. "No, sir."

Delaney lost his smile. "How close did your plane come from falling off the front of my ship?"

Still agitated, Crowley stepped in front of Cliff Mattern. "One bloody foot, sir."

"And, Mr. Crowley," Delaney growled, "if you had traveled one more 'bloody' foot, what would have kept your fancy plane from falling off my fancy ship?"

Sir Richard figured it out and softened considerably. "Why, your bloody tugs, sir!" He finally smiled. "And I thank you for your efforts to maintain my net worth!"

Captain Delaney fought to keep a smile at bay. "Mr. Crowley, I don't give a 'bloody' damn,"—he was now mocking one of the richest and most eclectic men on earth—"about your net worth. It costs me five thousand dollars in fuel to fire up that twirly, and it would force me to put a number of highly trained sailors in harm's way to fish you and your crew out of the drink. At that point, I'd have to make the gut-wrenching decision about whether to save your sorry ass or save five thousand dollars and the cost of drying my divers' gear. I chose a more sensible path."

Crowley looked down at the floor. "I apologize, Captain."

Delaney was on a roll. "And besides that, Hiram told me that if I didn't give you a wheelbarrow full of shit, he'd demote me to yeoman!"

After a momentary pause, Delaney and Crowley broke into laughter at exactly the same time that the others in the room let out their collective breath.

■　■　■

The team loaded back into the G700, and the deck crew unchained the two tugs, one of which pulled the plane back 1,109 feet, to the stern of the ship and the aft end of the flight deck. The Syrians were still napping.

Sir Richard insisted that Captain Mattern take the left seat. "Cliff, you have one chance in your life to fly a plane, any plane, off a carrier—in this case, a plane not designed for a carrier, a plane that needs two hundred more feet to take off than this deck has."

Mattern was scared, which made him surly. "Sir, you're detailing the reasons I *should* fly this plane off this deck?"

"Yes, Cliff, I am. Are you a better pilot than I am?"

"Well, sir, in a Gulfstream, yes. I'm the best in the world."

Crowley was nodding. "So why in bloody hell would we elect a lesser pilot to make this jump? Look, this plane should not be able to take off from this deck, correct?"

"Agreed."

"And if I handle the takeoff, there's a good chance we'll all die, correct?"

"Agreed."

"So, Cliff, what's the worst that could happen if *you* handle the takeoff?"

"We all die."

"Exactly! You've just proved the point. And there's a smaller chance that we all die if you're in the left seat than if I'm in the left seat. Correct?"

Mattern refused to respond.

"So what's your plan?"

Mattern growled at Richard Crowley. "I'm going to wind the twin Rolls-Royces up as high as the hot brakes will handle. I'm going to release the brakes and push the throttle to the stops. I'm going to roll this plane down this deck as fast as God will allow it to go."

Crowley nodded, listening intently.

"Then I'm going to roll past the end of the deck and kiss my ass goodbye." Mattern wouldn't look at Crowley.

Richard pumped up some false British optimism. "Well then, let's try everything but that last part and see how things turn out, shall we?"

Mattern did not notify flight control. Every spare eye on this boat was watching the Gulfstream. He gently increased the engine rpms until the brakes were bouncing at 81 percent full power. Then he released the brakes and pushed the throttle to the stops in a single motion, and the G700 quickly accelerated.

As the Gulfstream slipped over the fore edge of the *Abraham Lincoln*'s flight deck, it sank fifty feet—ten feet less than Mattern's stomach. Every sailor's eyes, from the captain's on down, were stuck on the spot where Gulfstream G700, tail number SAR 1, disappeared from sight.

But it leveled off ten feet above the water and quickly gained altitude. At four hundred feet in front of the carrier, the plane came back into view, and every sailor cheered. Captain Delaney did not. He simply nodded his head and turned the bridge over to his executive officer.

Captain John Delaney was too young to remember Doolittle's raid on Tokyo, but he'd seen it on film a dozen times. Sixteen B-25 medium bombers were launched without fighter escort from the USS *Hornet* on April 18, 1942. They were too heavy to take off from an aircraft carrier and had no capacity to land back on one. Each of the sixteen bombers dropped from sight upon leaving the *Hornet*, but each reappeared moments later, flew their mission, and released their bombs over Tokyo. They were the first American planes to do so in World War II, and all crash-landed in China or Russia.

Delaney was confident the Gulfstream would get off safely. He watched and nodded but did not cheer. He had no doubt. No visible doubt.

CHAPTER TWENTY-THREE

The long flight to Ekman Island was uneventful. Mattern and Coventry twice exchanged control duties, to both rest and stay alert. They bypassed Honolulu, as Ekman was beyond Hawaii to the west.

This drop was a day approach, which raised the adrenaline of all the crew members. Half an hour out, Wendy had Eric changed the halothane-oxygen mix back to pure oxygen, and she and Thomas removed the masks from the passengers. Over the next fifteen minutes, the Syrians woke, groggy and confused. The shooter was the first to come to full consciousness, and he made an effort to stand. Swenson was standing in front of him, as high as the airplane and nearly as wide, and shook his head, left, right, and back to center. The Syrian dropped back down.

At Wendy's direction, Mattern landed and taxied the remaining length of the runway, turned the aircraft around, and wound the engines down to idle. There were two groups of men several hundred yards away, near the collapsed hangar, apparently having remained in packs according to nationality. The larger group, which had to be the North Koreans, had erected some type of shelter or hut made from detritus galvanized panels salvaged from the rubble.

Wendy counted and confirmed that all the North Koreans and all the Venezuelans we still there, still alive, and thus still playing nice. Their dynamic was soon to change.

Swenson pulled the cabin door open while Sir Richard retrieved the folding ladder from the galley for the last time. As Thomas positioned the ladder, Wendy went from guest to guest, putting a hand on each shoulder and urging each to stand and move forward.

Thomas Swenson was no Seaman Ortega, and so he glared at each man, flexed his pecs, and pointed to the ladder. There were no disputes and no kicks required.

When the Gulfstream had turned around and stopped its forward motion, several of the men near the old hangar had started running toward it, but as new island inhabitants started coming down the ladder, the runners stopped and just watched.

Once all the Syrians were off, Swenson kicked the ladder toward them. It was no further use to the mission, and he figured maybe the men could build a jungle gym or something. "Maybe Ortega gave me a tiny little lesson in humanity," he thought. But he shook his head and chuckled to himself. He knew he just hadn't wanted to lift the ladder again.

■ ■ ■

Back at the Pac-Comm FBO in Honolulu, Nigel Miller had his crew fuel the Gulfstream, pull the belly tanks and spare oxygen canisters, and switch out the tail numbers one last time, back to those that came from the Derby factory. As the crew worked, he approached Captain Mattern and asked, "What happened to the new brakes? There's nothing left of them. I mean, they're disintegrated."

Sir Richard's head popped up, and he looked expectantly at Mattern as well. The captain shrugged his shoulders. "We burned them up on the *Abraham Lincoln*, precisely one foot from the end of their lives. After we landed on Ekman, I knew we had nothing left. But at that point, our choices were to take off or to be eaten by the local cannibals. I chose the less culinary path. When we landed here, I just coasted. If I'd miscalculated, I would have wrecked your plane *and* your FBO, but I'm the best Gulfstream pilot in the world. Nigel, did I tell you that I flew this baby off an aircraft carrier? Piece o' cake!"

Miller turned to Crowley. "I put on a new set, sir."

Sir Richard then addressed the Halstads. "Wendy, Michael, can we give you a lift to the Twin Cities?"

Wendy fluttered her eyeslashes and put on a bit of a drawl. "Why, Sir Richard, Ah'd fly with you anywhere!"

Michael rolled his eyes. "Twin Cities are good for me, Richard."

CHAPTER TWENTY-FOUR

The "cannibals" on Ekman Island weren't actually at that stage yet. Thomas Swenson had been correct: before noon on their first full day on Ekman, Kim Jong-un was no longer the leader of their pack. Between the ranking general and the lead security officer, the pecking order was still being sorted out, but they were functioning more as equals than as competitors.

The first thing to give way to wilderness living was Kim's pompadour. He had no clue what to do with it, and his hairdresser couldn't be found. In less than twenty-four hours, he looked like a very short, fat Elvis right after a shower. He refused to forage for himself, and all his team would give him were bananas, because bananas didn't require much effort. Thus, at the end of the first twenty-four hours, on a diet of nothing but bananas, Kim Jong-un had the shits like he'd never had in his life. The silver lining was that it appeared he might be down a few pounds already.

The rest of the North Korean team prioritized their dilemma with military precision. Food seemed abundant. Water was a concern until one of them found the spring-fed stream. Shelter became their focus, and the raw materials were readily available. They decided they initially needed protection from sun and rain, but there were no tools, no knives, no machetes with which to build it.

They decided that the logical location would be next to the collapsed hangar, thus keeping the trip hauling in the galvanized panels short. They found a partial panel with a jagged edge, and two of the men, using palm leaves wrapped around their hands for protection, were able to down a half dozen eight-foot-tall by three-inch-diameter bamboo stalks. They rigged the stalks up as posts and placed two galvanized panels on top. The contraption stood for around twelve seconds.

They decided to make it a lean-to. The panels were curved to the oval shape of the former hangar, so they only needed three front posts and two crossbars. The rear of the lean-to would slope to the ground, and the front would have an overhang in front of and above the posts. They built the corner supports as tripods, with three stalks leaning together like tepee poles, supporting each other. With vines and their long-ago-learned boy-soldier skills, they tied the apparatus together and secured the metal panels over the supports. No protection from storms, snakes, or wild boars, but for the moment, they had food, water, and shelter.

The Venezuelans were deposited the next day, and they kept their distance but watched as the North Koreans gathered food and improved their comparatively cozy home. It rained the first full day the Venezuelans were there, which encouraged them to be more industrious in the construction of their own home.

Venezuela is a country of vast resources, beauty, rivers, and jungles, but none of these men had spent any time appreciating or living in any of that. Nicolás Maduro was far more capable than Kim Jong-un. While substantial in girth, he was also strong as an ox, modestly intelligent, and a born leader. He remained king of their pack but learned quickly that he would need to earn that right all over again every day. And unlike he had in his life to this point, he would also need to work as hard as his team to keep their respect.

As self-appointed enemies to pretty much everyone, the North Koreans offered no advice or assistance. They did not, however, claim ownership of the hundreds of remaining roof panels of the old hangar. The Venezuelans, seeing the prehistoric quality of the North Korean estate and knowing that, to a man, they were more civilized and intelligent than any North Korean, set out to build a more fitting structure.

Beneath the roof panels of the hangar were steel girders. The hangar was a Quonset design, first developed at the Quonset Point Navy shipyard in Kingstown, Rhode Island, as barracks to house the expanding number of soldiers and seamen who needed housing during their training at the start of World War II. The half-oval design was self-supporting, but larger Quonset structures, like this huge hangar, required additional basic bracing for structural integrity.

The girders were made of steel rods the diameter of a broom handle welded together in X patterns to span the width of the hangar. After seventy-five years, the last thirty of them spent as collapsed rubble, the girders were very rusty, but the South American team scavenged enough solid pieces to construct a steel framework for the castle they envisioned. To get the remnants to conform to the shapes required, they used a stout tree at the edge of the jungle as a center fulcrum, and two men on each end of the metal remnant would bend the truss into the proper shape. If they needed a cut, they would bend the piece back and forth, using the fulcrum tree as the center point of their cut or break. It was time-consuming, sweaty, backbreaking work, but the frame took shape with interlocking joints.

The framework was assembled to conform to the bend of the galvanized roof panels, and the final structure came together in a day after the frame was completed. The result was a steel-sided, steel-roofed round building, ten feet tall and thirty feet across, resembling a corn storage bin. It was animal-proof, rainproof, and around 140 degrees during the day.

After several days on the island, one of the North Koreans walked over to the new home of the most recent occupants sharing their island. He stopped about thirty feet from the new structure (likely close enough to feel the heat emanating from within) and waved at the nearest Venezuelan. The Latin man waved back, and they looked at each other for a full minute. The Korean then turned and ambled back to their lean-to. First contact.

And then the plane returned. Both groups assumed they were being picked up after a short but uncomfortable nature lesson, and several men started running to the Gulfstream.

The Koreans all pondered the same thing. If they were rescued, they would need to kill and dispose of Kim Jong-un, or they themselves would be shot upon their return to North Korea. The Venezuelans all pondered their own private dilemma—who was monitoring their stolen money if they weren't there? The Syrians began walking slowly toward the two other distinct and separate groups. Bashar al-Assad was pondering that the man with a gun would own this island.

CHAPTER TWENTY-FIVE

A small caravan of nonmilitary South Korean cargo trucks, some open and some enclosed, received a call and began slowly driving the two miles from their temporary camp of the past twenty-four hours and toward the only gate through the demilitarized zone between South and North Korea. There were no soldiers and no weapons in the ten-truck convoy, though one of them was outfitted with a modern array of satellite dishes on its roof.

As the first truck approached the closed gate, two North Korean soldiers, sporting AK-47s at port arms, walked forward. The South Korean driver stepped down and greeted the soldiers in Korean. There was a short conversation, and then the driver handed each soldier a new Samsung smartphone. The phones were set to an internet site that was repeating a two-minute message, which stated that North Korean leader Kim Jong-un had defected in order to more smoothly effect the reunification of North and South Korea. The video showed Kim entering a luxury private jet with a smile from ear to ear and strapping into a leather seat. The driver told the soldiers that the trucks were loaded with gifts from the people of South Korea to the people of North Korea in celebration of the reunification.

One of the soldiers handed the phone back to the driver, saying he had to call his superiors. The driver held up both hands, palms out, and told the soldier that the phone was now his to keep, with its current international internet connection and no-cost unlimited calling to anywhere in the world. The soldier stared at him for a moment, pocketed the phone, and trotted back to his guard station to make his call. A moment later, he emerged, raised the gate, and waved at the driver to bring his trucks through.

The progress through the DMZ was slow. Every North Korean within sight of the trucks was handed a new Samsung phone, and the back half of the convoy was presenting each person with a new boxed thirty-two-inch Samsung flat screen TV. Every person in sight got one of each.

The interior of the convoy's communications truck lit up like a Christmas tree as more and more of the five thousand phones were handed out and activated, connecting to family and friends in the north and the south. It was like a rainy warm front advancing across a parched prairie at the speed of sound. And every single person touched by that warm front was happy.

■ ■ ■

Anticipating Sir Richard Crowley's call, Juan Guaidó was poised at the Colombia–Venezuela border with his advisors and expatriate cabinet members. An hour before the call, Crowley had sent a news release and video to CNN that was similar to the one running in South Korea. However, there was much freer access to broadcast and telecommunication messages in Venezuela, and the country was alive with the news that Maduro had abdicated, proven by the dictator's smiling face inside an airplane at Simón Bolívar International Airport near Caracas.

The Guaidó caravan was not accompanied by any armed protection, which put them at great risk should the Venezuelan Army be on alert. But they were not. The checkpoint on the Venezuelan side of the bridge was abandoned, and the rest of the drive to the capital was fast and uninterrupted.

Juan Guaidó had already been chosen as leader of the country's National Assembly, a governing body that was authenticated by free elections, as opposed to the rigged plebiscites that kept Maduro in power. In January 2019, the National Assembly announced its vote to install Guaidó as the legitimate president of Venezuela, and the bulk of the governments of the world recognized him as such.

Entering Caracas, the caravan was surrounded by cheering, flag-waving residents, slowing the caravan's travel to the Federal Legislative Palace to a crawl. There was still no sign of the military, which only a day ago had been visible on nearly every street corner. The vehicles pulled up to the front steps of the palace, and Guaidó stepped out, immediately surrounded by a scrum of his cabinet ministers.

His communications director had set up a press gathering halfway up the grand staircase to the building, and Guaidó stopped at the gaggle of cameras and microphones positioned there. He stood silently, gazing over the crowd and looking each and every reporter in the eye. As the hubbub settled, Juan Guaidó cleared his throat.

"My friends and countrymen," he announced in Venezuelan Spanish. "Today is a new day in our country. Maduro has left without even saying goodbye." He paused and smiled, and the crowd on the steps cheered. "That gives us an opportunity to fix what is broken, starting today. I have been elected by the people of Venezuela, and recognized by most countries around the world, as your president." The cheering again overwhelmed the microphones, and he waited until the noise subsided again.

"However, I am an engineer, not a politician. I will serve in this position only until you elect my replacement. To that end, I am announcing a presidential election to be held ninety days from today. I am encouraging anyone—anyone—who believes they have the capacity to lead this country to become a candidate. That person may be me, or it may be someone better. That question will be decided in a free, open, and internationally monitored election." Thunderous cheering and applause followed.

"Until then, we will be making immediate and dramatic improvements to your lives, and they start today. First, I am disbanding the Venezuelan military. We are surrounded by friendly nations. There is no threat from outside our borders. Until today, our military was used to control you"—he pointed—"and you, and you! No longer. We will reconstitute our National Guard to respond to emergencies and natural disasters. And we will save two billion dollars a year!

"Next, I will *not* issue an amnesty to the thugs posing as generals in Maduro's army. To them I say: If you have not committed any crimes against your country or its citizens, I welcome you to stay in your homeland. But if you have engaged in bribery, thievery, money laundering, drug trafficking, false imprisonment, or other illegal activity, you are not welcome, and I give you two options.

"We will guarantee safe passage to any person choosing to leave Venezuela and not come back. If you are a crook, you may leave without fear. But if you stay, you will be investigated, possibly charged, and possibly convicted. This is the best deal you will ever get, and I implore you to leave now.

"Next, at this moment I officially disband the Supreme Court of Venezuela and declare new elections for those positions during the presidential elections. And those judges have the same option as our former generals. Get out now, or face investigation. One cannot imagine a group more corrupt than these thirty-two individuals, and I hope you all make the correct choice and leave, hopefully today.

"Next, by the end of today, we will have fired the management cabal of our national oil company, PDVSA, and installed a new, capable, and honest group of engineers and managers. Our oil production is down 80 percent, and our refining capacity is down even further, mostly due to corruption and mismanagement, but also due to international blockades. However, on my drive into the city, I spoke to the presidents of numerous countries, including the president of the United States, and every one of them assured me that the embargos will be ended by the end of this press conference." The cheering erupted once again and carried on for several minutes.

"And finally, I encourage you to embrace democracy and reject the failed vestiges of corrupt socialism. That will involve a dramatic change in your everyday lives and in what you expect from your government. But I will promise you, right here, right now, that because Venezuela has some of the most substantial and valuable natural resources on the planet, you will never be poor again." The cheering began again and didn't end. The press conference was over, and Venezuela was on a new path.

■　■　■

In Syria, the replacement of Bashar al-Assad was more challenging. There was no regional player like the Republic of South Korea, no Juan Guaidó with the respect of the Syrian population or its neighbors. There were some obvious and very bad options, like occupation by the United States or by Russia.

The Palestinian unity government, also known as the "consensus government" of Palestine, was the eighteenth Palestinian government for the region since 2004. However, as that entity's decision-making had very recently and vary rapidly become secular rather than religion-based, it was the choice to fill the vacuum.

The six-hundred-pound fly in the ointment, of course, was the extremely capable, experienced, and ruthless Syrian military. It was the military that forced the parties supporting the change to be less ceremonial than in North Korea or Venezuela. There was no parade or grand procession, no flags waved or flowers thrown.

The "play" was multifaceted and complex. Involvement of the United States could not be acknowledged. The power and reaction time of the Syrian military had to be blunted. And the new unity government needed assurance that they weren't walking into a trap in Damascus.

It was widely believed that in addition to having sole access to the treasury of the Syrian Arab Republic, Assad had stashed away a hundred million or more for his eventual retirement, allowing him to run at any time—a rumor that lent credence to his abdication. The obvious solution was to get the NSA involved, but that couldn't happen. So President Gallagher got the NSA involved.

The previous tracking of Syria's purchase of chemical nerve agents from North Korea had been fairly straightforward. Syria had dozens of barrels of the stuff. It was manufactured, clandestinely, at only three plants in the world, and one was known to be in North Korea. But there was no evidence that North Korea was stockpiling, or had ever used, nerve agents. Their focus was on a nuclear apocalypse.

The tie to nerve agent sales to Syria was substantial but circumstantial. However, there was now an opportunity, through South Korean President Park, to take the next step. President Gallagher asked the secretary of state to make immediate contact with Park and request his assistance to confirm the trail of the gas and the payment for it. Permission was granted immediately, and the process was actually easier than expected.

President Park directed the Reconnaissance General Bureau, the benignly named agency that managed North Korea's clandestine operations, to provide the NSA access to the agency's top secret—until yesterday—computer storage facility. The director of that agency refused and was fired and replaced within an hour. The new director took it one step further. Instead of allowing the NSA access to the facility, she simply initiated a remote connection, allowing access to the Pyongyang system from the NSA's Cray supercomputers in Fort Meade, Maryland.

The rest was child's play. With remote access and all required passwords, the NSA technicians downloaded the entire contents of the North Korean computers and promptly identified the full scope and provenance of their nerve gas production, sales, and shipments. The alarming discovery that several years ago Israel was one of the buyers would need to be addressed separately.

The money trail, however, did not lead back to the Syrian Arab Republic. Instead, it led to a series of Panamanian accounts that were subaccounts of cutouts of subaccounts owned by Bashar al-Assad containing $11.4 billion.

But the money could not be transferred without a password, which in hindsight was easy. President Gallagher herself called her counterpart in Panama and explained the situation: The new government of Korea had asked the United States to help track the production and sale of North Korean nerve gas to Syria. The path led through an account owned by Bashar al-Assad held in a Panamanian bank. Assad had abdicated, and the new government of Syria, the Palestinian Unity Government, needed immediate access to the account in order to force the Syrian military to stand down, as well as to legitimize the new government's authority.

The president of Panama said there was no way in hell he would allow that transfer. President Gallagher then calmly explained, in perfect Spanish, that she would be forced to accuse the Panamanian government of aiding and abetting the sale *and use* of internationally outlawed nerve gas. She also explained that the USS *Ronald Reagan* strike force just coincidentally, happened to be one hundred miles west of Panama, and that the United States just coincidentally happened to be looking around for a fifty-first state. There was no other sound on the line until the Panamanian president said the funds would be released within the hour.

The man did have a sense of humor, though. His last words before disconnecting were, "Ah, Angela, who should we make the check out to?" Gallagher was laughing as the line went dead.

■ ■ ■

The discussion between President Hallam of the Palestinian unity government and General Amed al-Hamed of the Syrian Arab Republic lasted nineteen minutes. Hallam was able to demonstrate ownership of Assad's private accounts, which, he said, Assad had willingly transferred to the new Syrian government as a gesture of goodwill. And he was able to demonstrate to Amed the path of North Korean nerve gas through Amed's own hands and onto the heads of his countrymen in Arepa.

Hallam offered the general the options of taking the next flight out of Damascus International or just being turned over to the citizens of Arepa, where it was assumed Amed would be hanged upside down by piano wire and dismembered. The order those physical insults would take was unclear.

CHAPTER TWENTY-SIX

Finally arriving back in Stillwater, Michael and Wendy both plopped down on their couch. Michael was reflective. "What do you suppose Sir Richard is going to do now?"

Wendy furrowed her brow. "What do you mean?"

"Well, he just engineered and participated in the peaceful overthrow of three despotic dictators, marooned them on a secret abandoned island in the Pacific, and ostensibly orchestrated the stunning installation of three new governments, all of which were up and running on day one."

"Yeah, it was all pretty cool, I guess," she said.

Michael paused for a minute before asking, "You think he'll reveal your involvement?"

"Not a chance. We discussed the situation at length, and he understands. Understands that I was not there. Understands that people cannot look to me as some kind of symbol. Plus, I might have told him that if he does spill the beans, I'll give his fancy airplane away for real."

"Ha! Nothing works better than threatening to take away a guy's toys. But my point is, he's an excitement junky, and he just engineered one of the most amazing world transformations in history. How could he possibly top that?"

"Well, Michael, let's just say that Sir Richard has this new vibe."

"Yes, I'm well aware of that *vibe*."

Wendy continued, "And he now knows that, for the rest of his life, he'll be looked at as a catalyst, as an 'empowered' instigator of worthwhile humanitarian projects. He literally has the reputation, the résumé, and the ability—the vibe—to authenticate whatever he feels are worthy improvements."

Michael sat for another minute. "Is that what this is all about, Wen?"

"Michael, I truly don't have a clue. But if that's the case—if that's what this is all about—it's not a bad thing, right?"

"No, Wen. It's not a bad thing."

■　■　■

The next morning, Wendy and Michael sat at their kitchen table, Michael sipping coffee and Wendy reading a technical manual. Michael peered at the manual and asked, "What are you cooking up for today, Mrs. Twenty-Four Seven?"

"Well, it seems that we're focusing our efforts on eliminating reasons for war, right?"

Michael smiled. "Yes?"

"So, I'm thinking we haven't addressed the whole 'oil' thing well enough yet. The coal plants fall into that category, eliminating reliance on fossil fuels, but renewable sources of energy are the future, and a lot of places settle down when people aren't fighting over oil."

"Agreed. And a couple of weeks ago, I would have said, 'But Wendy, what can we do from Stillwater, Minnesota?' But I would never be that naive today. What are you plotting?"

Wendy smiled. "I'm plotting solar energy production. Huge volumes of solar energy."

"Ah, Wen, I hate the look of those giant fields of solar panels. I appreciate the intent, but they aren't easy on the eyes."

"Agreed." She looked up at him. "We're singing from the same hymnal. But there are huge advances in solar application and economics just waiting to be commercialized, capitalized, and put into mass production. More efficient and inexpensive solar collectors, amazing new power storage technology, and even near-invisible ways to convert the sun's free heat into electricity. The opportunity is to mainstream solar power—immediately."

Michael was nodding in agreement but stopped as an obstacle occurred to him. "Which will involve huge amounts of money," he said.

"Correct, but look what else is going on. By switching to the compressed cardboard, 'coal-generated' electricity is becoming 46 percent more efficient while we sit here. As in 46 percent less expensive. The money spent on defense in the United States alone could drop by half a trillion dollars a year in the next eighteen months. The governmental and community expenses for social services may be cut in half thanks to the partnership between cities and churches.

"So, if killing for oil was eliminated and the cost of power were to drop by, say, 50 percent, the money would be there to make geometric improvements in energy production, which would drop costs even more. That would create a higher standard of living for six billion people!"

Wendy and Michael were both excited about the prospects. They looked at each other, knowing the bugger was in the details—details like, "Which comes first, the chicken or the egg?"

Michael was the first to speak. "I have a friend from engineering school..."

Wendy raised an eyebrow.

"He's a genius. Specifically, a solar energy genius. I shit you not. Used to teach at the U of M."

"Used to?" Wendy had always sensed that Michael's college friends all shared a common theme of workplace disruption.

"Well, yeah. Phred might have staged a sit-in or two—or three—involving the University's use of their private coal-fired power plant."

"Wait. Is this the P-H-R-E-D Fred?"

"That's him. When he got his PhD in bioengineering, he

changed the spelling of his name to include 'PhD' so that he wouldn't have to bother putting the designator behind his name. Anyway, we've kept in touch, and he's passionate about solar energy."

"Let's invite him over, Michael. We could use his expertise, and we might enjoy his worldview." Wendy totally loved dorks.

She started to fill in the blanks. "I want to convince power companies to be the catalyst. It costs a billion dollars to build a new gas-fired power plant. A new nuclear plant costs eight to ten billion, but none are being built, and it takes years to make one happen. I want to convince power companies that rather than putting huge amounts of money aside for their next plant, they should put all of that money into solar incentives, no-interest loans, and seeding new research."

Michael nodded along, still able to follow her thinking out loud for the time being.

"I'm also thinking that the macro-approach might be too much for us mere mortals to deal with, so I've done some Wendy math. Let's take solar shingles."

"Let's!" Michael said.

"There are several new shingle products that are sturdy, good looking, relatively easy to install, and have the capacity to handle all the power needs for an average home, plus 20 percent."

Michael nodded. "A no-brainer—except?"

"They're more expensive than asphalt shingles."

"And the 'plus 20 percent?'"

"That part's easy. There's already a process in place to sell excess electricity produced back to the power companies. For instance, a wind farm produces a substantial amount of power that is metered and sold to utility companies. A home system could do the same thing by using an inexpensive power inverter. So a home shingle system can produce all the power the home needs while the sun is up, plus enough electricity to sell that it would pay for the system."

"But no sun, no power," Michael prodded.

"Not true! You hear that nonsense all the time from people who refuse to consider solar power out of hand. But a solar-powered home is selling power back to the utility, right?" She didn't wait for an answer. "Which means that home continues to be connected to the existing power grid, right? When the sun doesn't shine, the home can either use stored electricity or buy it from the utility company. The naysayers want people to believe that when the sun doesn't shine, they're in the dark. And frankly, I'd like to shove that logic somewhere the sun doesn't shine!"

Michael was beaming. "As Oprah would say, you go, girl!"

"By the utility company funding, say, a no-interest loan to a homeowner to cover the installation of a solar shingle system, the payments on that loan will come from the homeowner's energy savings *and* the 20 percent they sell back. It costs the homeowner no additional money and is eventually paid off. And the utility company meets its state-required renewable energy mandates."

"But the efficiency comes from mass implementation, right?" Michael asked.

"Right! We just need to come up with a way to ensure that every new home and every new roof on an existing home will be built with power-generating shingles."

Michael leaned back and stared at Wendy. "Through the prudent use of 'Wendy vibe,' correct?"

"Correct . . . and hopefully sprinkled with some Phred Peterson additives."

■　■　■

Phred didn't drive, what with the failure of Detroit to develop solar-powered cars. He'd considered an electric car, but they were expensive, and while there were substantial tax incentives available for purchasing an electric car, he'd never actually made enough money to pay taxes, so the tax incentive was a nonstarter.

So he showed up at the Halstad home on a bicycle even though he lived twenty miles away in St. Paul. Phred was the same age as Michael, was beanstalk-thin, and had a ponytail down his back. There was no hair on top, however—his pate was as smooth as a compressed-cardboard fuel pellet. He had no sense of humor, couldn't get a joke if it slapped him in the face. And he spouted sayings constantly. The sayings were relatively enjoyable for three or four minutes, but after that, people generally wanted to duct-tape his mouth shut—which had actually been done a couple of times.

Michael met him at the door. "Phred! Good to see you! But damn it, if I'd known you were biking, I could have given you a ride."

"Michael, I'd be a hypocrite if, instead of biking to reduce my carbon footprint, I accepted a ride from you, thus expanding my carbon footprint. Why take the buggy when the buggy's got bugs?"

Michael laughed. "You haven't changed!"

Peterson shook his head. "Of course I have. I've got no hair, I have three dental crowns, I have scars on my right leg from some asshole who used the bike lane as a passing lane, I've had—"

Michael broke in. "Phred, this is my wife, Wendy. I'm pretty sure you two met back in college."

As Wendy held out her hand, Phred stepped back with alarm. "I thought you were, like, dead." He was a gifted wordsmith.

She didn't miss a beat. "Yeah, I had a heart attack a few years ago, but here I am, no worse for wear." She shook his hand, and his ponytail curled up several inches from its dormant position.

Peterson was surprised, but not dumbstruck. He said, "Michael, is it okay if I fall in love with your wife?"

"No."

"Hmm. Can I be 'in like' with her?"

"That's up to Wendy. Wen?"

She pondered the question. "We'll play that by ear. Phred, come on in and let us fill you in on our little scheme."

Wendy began without preamble. "We want to immediately—like, starting today—get homeowners, local governments, and construction companies to commit to using solar shingles on every new project. We're hoping you might have some ideas."

"Ideas are the mother of invention, but my mother was run over by a Metro Transit bus."

"Bummer." Wendy was not to be distracted. "We obviously need to start with one house, then one neighborhood, one city, one state . . ."

"I worked for a solar installer a couple years ago, and we did several solar shingle projects."

Michael jumped in. "Wow! How'd that go?"

"We had a disagreement about adhesive placement, and I kicked him off the roof."

Michael hesitated, then asked, "As in told him to leave the worksite?"

"No, I physically kicked him off the roof. Not sure how that project turned out."

Wendy jumped back in the fray. "If we set you up with a crew and some funding, do you think you could be the installer on our first project?"

"Um. Would I have to get permits and all that?"

"I'm sure. We'd want to do this right," Wendy said.

Peterson thought for a moment. "I suggest you put the permits in Michael's name. I've had some issues with the permitting authorities."

Wendy was surprised. "In Stillwater?"

"Uh, pretty much statewide. But I'd love to take on this project."

■ ■ ■

"Okay, so, let's sort this out. Let's use our house as the guinea pig. One, we get to practice without getting sued if the end product sucks. Two, Michael, as the homeowner, you're allowed to do your own roofing, as long as you get the permit and have the Stillwater Building Inspections department do their progress inspections. Can you come up with a crew for Phred?"

Phred interrupted. "I can do that—I already know a crew. They're hard workers, they're pros at shingling, and they leave their phones in the car."

Wendy nodded. "Okay, make it happen. Also, you'll need to source the materials. Is that a problem?"

"Nah, I've got all my old contacts, and I know what I'm looking for."

"Perfect. So, Michael, you're the permit guy. And by the way, I'll get hold of Melinda and see if I can talk her into funding the local roofs through the newfound profit in her power plant efficiencies. However . . ."

"Uh-oh. I hate 'but' and 'however.'"

Wendy ignored him. "This first project should be transparent. As such, it would be best if we did our house with our money. Do we have any?"

Phred looked up curiously. Michael answered a bit too quickly. "Sure. I tucked away your life insurance and your 401(k) as a rainy-day fund." He glanced over at Phred and continued. "A new roof seems like the definition of a rainy-day need."

"That works," Wendy said. "And that allows me to pitch this to Melinda without it looking like we're trying to play a game with her."

Phred raised an eyebrow at Michael. "Melinda?"

"Friend of Wendy's," Michael said. "Melinda recently bought the Alan King Power Plant in Bayport and has modified its process to the point that it's generating not only electricity but money."

"Must be nice to have rich friends," Phred said. "If at first you don't succeed, give up and call someone with money."

Michael looked away. If he only knew, he thought to himself.

■　■　■

The permitting went fine, to Michael's surprise. The city would indeed allow him to reroof his own home for a 150-dollar permit fee and 40 dollars per inspection. Work would need to stop for inspection after installation of the frost shield, after the flashing and shingles were installed, and after the site was cleaned up.

The building department manager, Julia, noticed Michael's surprise and explained that the permit process is actually pretty straightforward, other than two common roadblocks. One, people want to do things that are illegal, at which point the permitting process becomes contentious. And two, once someone lies to her, they really have a hard time getting their permit. At that point, the manager smiled at him benignly, and he got the message. Don't cheat. Don't lie.

Phred had his crew lined up by noon. While he was the first to acknowledge that he had issues with authority figures telling him what to do, he'd never had problems with people who worked for a living. For some reason, though, he did not accept that people who told him what to do were actually working.

The crew included four men. Miguel, the foreman or lead was a US citizen, having been born in the country. Luis, Ronny, and Hector each claimed they had green cards, but kept their hands in their pockets. They were to show up the next morning and prep the roof, which caused Michael a moment's distress—not because they'd show up, but because the insurance company had replaced the roof only two years ago after a hailstorm. In effect, they'd be operating on a healthy patient.

The materials weren't available in Stillwater but were on hand at a distribution warehouse in Minneapolis. On the phone, Phred checked off each item as the city desk clerk at Under One Roof filled the order, then gave the man Michael's credit card number. Everything they needed would be delivered the next day. He thought to himself, butchering Ben Franklin in the process, "Using another man's money makes a person healthy, wealthy, and wise."

■ ■ ■

Wendy's discussion with Melinda went very well. The cardboard pellets were working as advertised, the cost savings were real, and Melinda's general manager had canceled all upcoming coal deliveries, much to the frustration of the supplier and the rail line.

Plus, as they'd discussed, the plant needed all of the increased efficiencies of the pellets to come close to replacing the energy from the huge amounts of coal it had previously burned every day. Making a noticeable dent in usage by way of home-generated electricity would ensure constant power availability, even during peak demand.

■ ■ ■

The crew arrived the following morning at seven and began tearing off the nearly new shingles and tossing them over the roof's edge into a ten-yard dump trailer that Miguel had brought with them. Phred showed up on his bike at eight, panting and sweating and pondering his carbon footprint. His crew came to work in a late-model four-door Silverado pulling a ten-thousand-dollar trailer, and he got here late on a bike.

The materials showed up at nine, along with several neighbors. Their roofs had been replaced two years ago as well, and they were all aghast at the wastefulness of Michael Halstad. One of them said in an aside to Phred, "I've never witnessed such a stupid thing in all my life!"

Phred turned, looked the fellow up and down, and said, "When a less-than-honest man searches the world for stupid, it's usually because he has no reflective surfaces in his own home." The neighbor looked at Phred with no comprehension whatsoever and turned to further kibbutz with his friends.

By noon, the roof was bare, and by two, the frost-shield layer was on. Michael called the city building department. Within twenty minutes, Julia, the department's manager, was there for an inspection.

Michael said, "Wow! That's fast service!"

Julia responded while walking the perimeter. "Like I said, everybody's on my good side until they break a law or lie to me. On my good days, I take it in stride. Contractors are always men, and they are of the unanimous belief that a woman can't understand permitting and shouldn't even be allowed to do inspections just on principle."

"And on your bad days?"

"I want to pull out their entrails with a meat hook and watch 'em bleed out." She looked at Michael. "I try to have more good days than bad."

Michael didn't respond but was immediately convinced that no one lied to Julia twice.

The inspection took all of ten minutes. When she climbed the ladder to the roof, Miguel said, "Hey, Julia," and Julia said, "Hey, Miguel."

Michael walked her back to her truck, and as she opened the door, she turned to him and said, "When you applied for your permit, I saw a guy with no roofing experience and no clue how to install solar shingles. Then today, I see you're at least smart enough to hire a pro. You'll have no problems with me. Miguel is 'good people.'" She hopped in the truck, closed the door, and drove away without another look.

■ ■ ■

While Miguel and his crew worked the roof, Phred organized the materials according to what would go up next, moving the pieces over to the ladder. Michael helped him load and carry. "Julia said you hired the right guy as your foreman."

Without breaking stride, Phred said, "When I saw her drive up, I suddenly realized I needed to pee."

Michael wasn't surprised. "You two have had words?"

"You got to know when to walk away and know when to run."

"That's not original, Phred."

"It is when used out of the original context—or as a double entendre."

Michael shook his head but didn't respond.

"I'm a genius, okay? But unlike most geniuses, I'm smart enough to recognize my weaker traits."

"Which include . . .?"

"I treat everyone else like they're stupid. Which they are, compared to me. But even though I'm smart enough to know that, I fail at corrective implementation. In Julia's case, I might have once told her that she didn't know shit from sagebrush."

"Sagebrush?" Michael said.

"Yes."

Michael set down a box of shingles with a sigh. "So why don't you just—"

"So why don't you just stop drinking, you say to the alcoholic? Or just eat more, you say to the anorexic? There is no 'just,' dude. As Popeye once said, 'I am what I am and that's all what I am.'"

"Another stolen saying."

"I'm branching out. Over the centuries, there have been several people whose quotes rival mine." As a genius, Phred was naturally pretty much always right.

Peterson yelled up to the roof. "Miguel, you know any Mexican electricians?"

"Other than my brother? No. But I told him we need him."

"Well then why the hell didn't you bring him along?" Phred asked. Michael thought he saw a smirk on his ordinarily humorless friend's face.

"He's waiting for you to call him, assholio." The other three roofers got a laugh out of that but didn't slow down.

Phred called Leo, who was at the Halstad's an hour later. "Leonardo, how they hanging?" Phred said, reaching his hand out to welcome.

"A lot lower than yours, you bald-headed hippie gringo." Leo grinned and shook Phred's hand. Phred and Leo had a history, all good.

"The crew will work from the roof down. You can start from the bottom up. I've got the power inverter and all the supplies you'll need to make the reverse hookup into the house's electrical box. Your brother said you aren't as sharp as you used to be, so I've got an installation manual for you too."

Leo inspected the inverter. "Already with the insults, Phredo? Well, I have an old Mexican saying for you. 'Never pull a knife on a knife fighter.' What do you think of that?"

Phred chuckled. "Ah, Leo. You think you're as good at insults as the master?"

Leo responded in a fake Mexican accent. "No, señor. I no say I ees good with insult. I say I ees good with knife." He held up an eight-inch military-issue KA-BAR and angled it with practiced ease to get the sun to shine off the blade and into Phred's eyes.

"I yield to your expertise, Leo. You need an electrical permit?"

"Si, señor. A permit and a Gatorade. I had to rush to get over here."

"Michael, get this man a permit and a Gatorade, will you? I have no issue with authority figures, as long as I'm the authority figure," Phred said and returned to his inventory duties.

■ ■ ■

Solar roofing was substantially more work than asphalt shingling. Instead of nailing in the pliable old-style shingles, they had to install glassine-composite marvels that sandwiched a newly perfected solar collection film. Clips had to be installed on the roof for each row, and an electrical connection had to be maintained between each shingle. Wendy and Michael's house faced east, which meant it would collect sunlight on the east-facing and west-facing gables. That meant more material cost and more work but also more energy produced by the system.

Once the work was completed, the entire project team gathered together, and when Leo turned the inverter to the "on" position, they all high-fived each other as the electrical meter stopped turning. Any electricity reverse-fed into the utility grid after the house used all the solar-produced power it required would be tracked and uploaded to Xcel Energy by the inverter's computer.

Wendy turned to Phred and Miguel. "Congratulations! You did it. The total cost is reasonable, the process works, and you have a professional team. I propose that we incorporate you into a new business, line up as many installs as we can, make you all wealthy, and do our part to save the world."

Phred never, ever missed an opportunity to pontificate. "What do you call a man who does a good deed and gets rich?"

Michael grimaced. "I'll bite. What?"

"A Republican. Am I going to have to wear a tie?"

■ ■ ■

The butterfly effect was staggering. The Vanderbilt Foundation was buying a power plant every day and partnering with utility companies for conversion on as many more. The day after completion of the Halstads' test project, Phred Peterson secured eight more solar roofing projects. That same day, he, Miguel, and Leo incorporated as equal partners into Free Juice LLC. Each of their new projects involved homes that actually needed new roofs, and the foundation's Free Juice Initiative funded half the project costs for all, with no-interest payback tied to the electrical savings generated by each home.

Without a boss telling him what to do, Phred found his calling and was selling new projects by the hour. The Free Juice Initiative expanded to the locality of each coal plant purchased or partnered with.

Luis, Ronny, and Hector immediately became foremen, each managing a new crew. They were very proud of Miguel's brainstorm to staff the new crews with white guys. Capable Mexican roofers were a valuable commodity, and each one hired was brought on as a foreman or supervisor. Miguel explained the new dynamic to Michael one morning. "The white guys seem capable and smart enough. They just need a lot of training and supervision." He wore a modest smile as he headed off to the next install.

Leonardo became the company's director of connectivity and was tasked with hiring a Mexican electrician and Mexican foreman in each locality that had a Free Juice Initiative plant sponsor. It was not necessarily a requirement that each of his electricians be of Mexican heritage, but his logic was "if it ain't broke, don't fix it," and their business plan was definitely not broke.

Phred set up a fund for Luis, Ronny, and Hector. In the current political environment, it was nearly impossible for a Mexican to get a permanent resident green card, especially by one who might have inadvertently overstayed their "visitor" status. However, federal law allowed an immigrant to buy a green card by investing $500,000 in an existing US company. Phred's fund was built through bonuses to the three founding crew members of Free Juice LLC and would be rolled into ownership stock in the company.

Phred met with Wendy and Michael to update them on how shockingly fast this had all come together. "We're going to have to franchise to keep up with demand. The 'free roof' concept is fool-proof, and it's sweeping the country. While it's not technically *free*, the whole thing pays for itself in a circular process where each component enhances the viability of the other."

Michael nodded in agreement. "Wendy, you keep saying that you don't have 'plans,' just concepts. Do you still claim that this phenomenally successful venture is accidental?"

"Let's call it a theory of hoped-for but unintended consequences that just needed a catalyst, good karma, the right people, and some vibes." She winked at Michael.

"I believe it's a little more profound than that, oh ye of limited height," Phred said. He began to wax philosophical. "You know, the first person to eat an omelet was also the first person who ate what fell out the ass of a chicken."

Both Wendy and Michael grimaced, then pondered, and then shrugged their shoulders. Phred was probably right.

CHAPTER TWENTY-SEVEN

As Wendy was learning in her reading, the conversion from coal to compressed pellets was simply a transition from lots of contaminants and waste to fewer contaminants and less waste. Solar power was the zero, the logical goal. Converting every home in the United States to being energy neutral—and possibly energy negative— was a win in every regard, not only environmentally and economically but also in emergency and disaster situations. It was even a win for national security: if the power grid was destroyed by calamity or skullduggery, America would not be shut down.

But energy gained from capturing the heat of the sun on solar panels and turning that into electricity was still inefficient. Obviously, it was more efficient than burning coal or gas, but it was not the holy grail.

The holy grail was nuclear fusion.

For most people, hearing the word *nuclear* created an immediate negative mental picture of the mushroom cloud from a nuclear bomb or *The China Syndrome*—the fear that a wayward nuclear power plant could burn right through the core of the earth with nothing to stop it. Add to that the need to dispose of spent nuclear fuel rods, which remain radioactive for thousands of years, nuclear power based on existing fission reactors became synonymous in the minds of everyday folks with bad planning for our future.

Nuclear fusion, while technically still a nuclear explosion, was nearly the opposite of the nuclear fission process typically used in nuclear power plants. In fact, it was so shockingly different—and shockingly better—that it became the focus of all of Wendy's efforts.

Nuclear fusion was the process of joining two hydrogen atoms at an extremely high speed and temperature. The source of those hydrogen atoms is H_2O—water. Once commercially developed, a gallon of fusion fuel derived from water could provide the same energy as ten million gallons of fossil fuel, or, as it was commonly called, oil.

Now, water was a finite resource, but via nuclear fusion, there was enough water on earth to provide 100 percent of the earth's current power needs for many millions of years. The byproduct would be minimal—and minimally radioactive.

And while Wendy was learning that the process to create nuclear fusion was highly difficult, complex, and expensive, she also learned that there were only marginal amounts of money funding the research and development of the most mind-boggling opportunity in the history of mankind—sad as that history was, in terms of "advancement."

For instance, the United States allocated fourteen million dollars to fusion research in 2019 while spending nearly one trillion dollars on "defense." The math was ridiculous. One trillion is one thousand billion. One billion is one thousand million. So: while oil was the source of so much war, hoarding, and price gouging and could arguably end up being the root cause of the expiration of life on earth, the replacement of oil as a fuel was being funded by fourteen thousandths of one percent of the money spent in a year to protect one country from war.

Wendy was consumed with the thought. Eliminating faith-based war was a good start. Repurposing military hardware was a logical next step. Sidelining warmongering dictators produced some positive and satisfying results. Shutting down coal production was a worthy goal. But online nuclear fusion would free up trillions of dollars a year that was currently spent on war, energy, pollution mitigation, and on and on.

So she pondered. How could Wendy Halstad, the girl with the vibe, with highly placed new friends, and an unknown amount of time, make this happen. The thought wasn't a question. It was merely another challenge.

■   ■   ■

She pondered until three in the morning, and then it struck her like a two-by-four across the back of her head. She struggled to wait for a reasonable hour, and finally called Andie and Andy and invited them over to plot a strategy.

They showed up separately this time, having both come from home before getting a chance to inject their day-brightening shots of caffeine. Wendy did the honors while Michael, Andrea, and Andrew all sat around the kitchen table, clueless and a bit wary. Wendy had a recent propensity to suggest crazy, unreasonable, outlandish, dangerous, and quasi-legal solutions to age-old problems.

Once the coffee was served, she got right to it. "I want to set up a stock offering."

Andie, the attorney, interrupted right away. "For what company?"

"It doesn't exist yet. I was thinking that maybe you could make that happen."

Andy, the investment counselor, was next. "What kind of company?"

"We'll finish the research, proof of concept, development, and construction of the world's first nuclear fusion power plant."

Michael's head dropped to the table, where his forehead met the surface with a fairly loud thud. Wendy ignored him. Both of their kids looked much like Michael had after he'd been incapacitated with a Taser.

Andy was the first to recover, but talked very slowly, as if trying to communicate with a four-year-old. "An initial public offering for a company that doesn't exist, to invent a technology that doesn't exist, in order to build a power plant that's never been built before."

"Exactly! What do you think?"

Michael raised his head. There was a flat area on his forehead, but no blood. He stared but did not speak. What he wanted to say was, "What do we think? What do we *think*? Like we're supposed to say, 'Wow, what a grand idea. I wish I'd come up with that!'" But he couldn't say that, so instead he said, "Wow! What a grand idea! I wish I'd come up with that!"

She was excited. "I know! You might have, but you sleep a lot."

Andy stumbled back into the conversation. "Um, what sort of valuation are you thinking?"

"My back-of-the-envelope math says five million shares at ten thousand per share. Do you think that's enough?"

Andie felt as if she'd fallen through a wall and was floating somewhere above the kitchen table. "Mom," Andie said, her voice much firmer than Andy's. "You're asking us if fifty billion dollars is enough to build a nuclear fusion power plant."

"Bingo! But it's not just building the plant. The facility itself will cost around thirty billion."

"Give or take," Michael said.

"Agreed," Wendy said, not seeming to notice Michael's sarcastic tone. "Give or take. The rest is to fund the final development of the process."

It was back to Andy. "And you think there are enough investors out there who will spend ten thousand dollars a share to raise fifty billion dollars to fund a new company to invent a new power source to . . .?"

"Save the world. And yes, I'm pretty sure there are. In fact, I know several like-minded people who might buy the first million shares with seed money to make sure the IPO takes off."

"Mom," Andie said again, "forgive us if we keep repeating what you're saying, but . . . you know people who will put up the first five billion as . . . seed money?"

"Sure. I'm confident that savvy investors will look at this as a huge opportunity rather than a risk. Imagine replacing all fossil fuels with a clean, safe, economical, and nearly inexhaustible source of power. The stock might be worth ten times more than the original offering by the time the plant goes online."

Andie stepped in out of turn in the round-robin of incredulous questions. "Mom, I've never heard the words *nuclear* and *safe* used in the same sentence."

Wendy smiled and straightened up, clearly prepared for this particular concern. "That's because what people know about nuclear power is about nuclear *fission*—the splitting of atoms that causes an explosion that generates extreme heat to produce steam to turn turbines to create electricity. If a fission plant loses its cooling capacity, a meltdown is uncontrollable. But to create nuclear *fusion*, the particles are combined or fused at extreme speed and in extreme heat to produce the 'explosion' of energy. To stop the process, you merely turn off the heat that's applied to the particles, and the reaction ends."

There was a whole lot of staring going on, so Wendy decided to just continue and assume the sale.

"So, Andie, if you agree to come on board, I'll need you to file articles of incorporation ASAP. You'd be a full-time employee of the corporation as general counsel."

"Um, I'm really sorry for repeating everything, okay? But you're saying I'd be general counsel of one of the largest corporations in the world, stepping up from small-claims court filings and fence disputes."

"Yes. Starting today, if possible. And Andy, I'd need you to get the IPO filed with the Securities and Exchange Commission and do all the yada yada involved with going public. Oh, and you'd be the chief financial officer."

Andy mimicked Andie. "Chief financial officer for one of the largest corporations in the world."

Wendy smiled at him. "Correct." And then, raising an eyebrow at each of them she said, "You know, you two have a bit of your father's sarcastic streak in you, don't you?"

Michael took the bait. "Andie, Andy, you can set up shop in our garage for now, if you'd like."

■ ■ ■

The University of Minnesota had its own fusion laboratory, including the beginnings of a tokamak reactor on a sprawling site thirty miles north of the Twin Cities in Wyoming, Minnesota. Wendy had always thought the city's name a strange choice, but then the state also had Nowthen, Climax, Blue Earth, White Bear Lake, and Mahtomedi, so Wyoming felt right at home in Minnesota. Wendy asked Phred Peterson to make some calls, and they quickly learned that the experimental campus was closed down in 2014 due to lack of funding. Phred located the former director of the facility, Walter Asabi, an American of Japanese ancestry, who was still actively working on fusion physics at a private laboratory.

■ ■ ■

Phred called Wendy. Before she could get a word out, he said, "A smart man once said, 'Leave me the hell alone.'"

Wendy was confused. "Random thought, or do I need to play twenty questions?"

"I talked to Walt Asabi this morning. He was the director of the U of M project to advance the research on fusion reactors. He's still pissed that the feds stopped funding the work a few years ago, and he told me to drop dead. Actually, he was less discreet. He suggested that I impregnate myself. But then the weirdest thing happened."

"What was that?"

"He didn't hang up. He wanted to talk physics, and after falling victim to my unrivaled charm, he agreed to meet with us at two."

"What—today?"

Phred's unrivaled charm had, of course, "gone fishing" back when Carter was president. "No, Wendy, he wants to meet with us at two on the Doomsday clock—which, by the way, is already at eleven fifty-nine and twelve seconds. Of course today!"

She ignored his faux exasperation and said, "Super. Can you pick me up?"

"Earth to Wendy. I ride a bike."

"Oh, right. I'll ask Michael to take us. We'll pick you up."

Phred paused. "What kind of mileage does his car get again?"

Wendy didn't have a clue, but said, "Thirty-six."

He nodded. "That's adequate. I'll be out front."

■　■　■

Michael dropped Wendy and Phred off in Walt Asabi's parking lot, then drove off to find a coffee shop. Phred found the door they were looking for.

Walt Asabi's laboratory was in a section of a warehouse in Hugo, Minnesota, about fifteen miles from Stillwater. Hugo was named after its founding father, Sven Hugo, and there was actually a statue of him in the city park. No one knew if it was a good likeness of him. Sven had been dead for ninety-three years, and the face of the statue was missing due to a lightning strike.

Walt was sixty, short, and compact, and he elicited a double take from Wendy, as he was the clone of the mentor in *The Karate Kid*. He greeted Phred by nodding once and saying, "Peterson." Wendy felt a twinge of dread: it appeared that Asabi was at one time in a supervisory position over Phred Peterson.

Phred very formally did the honors. "Dr. Walter Asabi, Wendy Halstad."

The doctor of physics held out his hand. "It's nice to meet you, Ms. Halstad." And without missing a beat, he said, "Either I'm having a stroke, or you have a biokinetic aura about you."

Wendy smiled but said nothing.

Walt tipped his head toward Phred. "Are you aware that you're traveling with trouble?" he asked.

"Ah, c'mon, Walt. It wasn't that big a deal."

Asabi ignored him. "When he was terminated from the university—"

"It was a mutual parting," Phred said.

Asabi responded to Peterson by way of an explanation to Wendy. "The parting was mutual because when the police were called, he agreed to leave of his own accord."

Wendy glanced over at Phred with an eyebrow cocked. Phred simply shrugged his shoulders, which was evidence enough for Wendy that Walt was probably telling the truth.

Asabi continued, "Mr. Peterson here found the time after the termination of his employment to rig a bomb to my car."

Wendy jerked her head toward Phred. "What?"

"Ah, c'mon, Walt, it wasn't a bomb." He looked at Wendy, shaking his head. "It was actually very ingenious, if childish. I shorted the cigarette lighter in his car so that when turned it on, the lighter would activate on its own. Then I put a little M-80 firecracker—"

Asabi broke in. "The most powerful explosive publicly sold in the United States without a permit."

"—I put a little M-80 firecracker into the lighter socket so that when the lighter coil got red hot, it lit the fuse, which produced a loud but harmless noise—"

"An explosion, amplified by the tight confines of my car, that blew the lighter itself through my rear window."

"Which I paid for, Walt. The lighter was kind of an unintended consequence. Plus, I said I was sorry."

"What? When?"

"Three seconds ago, okay? Look, that was a long time ago, man. You need to let the past stay in the past."

Walt looked at Wendy and smiled. "What Phred doesn't know is that every time I tell that story, my wife and I both start laughing like we're drunk." And he nearly doubled over laughing.

Phred stared at Asabi in horror. "Wha—why—you jackass!" he stammered. "You were never mad?"

"Phred, that was the most exciting thing that has ever happened to me in my life. I was scared to death for a moment. Then the police wanted to arrest you, but I pulled them aside and told them that creativity should not be against the law."

Wendy was momentarily pleased that, for once, Phred Peterson would be speechless. But she had no such luck.

"When one reacts in anger, the penalty is often a lifetime of guilt."

Wendy looked at him. "Phred, that was actually pretty profound. Are you feeling all right?"

He shook his head. "No ma'am. Might have a touch of bursitis." Walt and Wendy chuckled as they walked into Walt's office. Phred had no clue what they were laughing about.

Phred and Wendy sat in comfortable leather chairs, which were the only uncluttered surfaces within sight, while Asabi wound his way through additional piles on the floor to the well-worn chair behind his desk. Wendy dove right in as usual. "Walt, we've started a new enterprise to put fusion development back on track—in fact, on a fast track."

Asabi's eyes widened in an instant. "You gotta be shitting me!" he blurted out. "For real?"

"For real. In fact, my husband is on the phone in a coffee shop trying to negotiate for the rights to take over the old fusion facility up in Wyoming. We'd like to make it operational again, and Phred tells me that you used to manage that project."

"Wendy, I'll be blunt. The Fusion Development Campus was the culmination of my life's work, and I hoped to die in this chair, which I stole when they shut me down. I'll do anything within my power to help you, including lighting an M-80 or two to wake people up."

Wendy smiled. "I've read your bio, and believe it or not, you've received a glowing endorsement from the idiot savant sitting next to me—"

Phred cut in. "There are better descriptors available."

"—and I'd like to offer you the position of managing director of Star Power Development."

Walt Asabi's eyes went glassy as he stared at her.

Phred cut in again, softly. "Love the name."

Wendy leaned toward him and said, "I had also been thinking of Fusion-R-Us."

Phred nodded. "I like that one too."

Wendy decided not to explain that Fusion-R-Us was a joke. Besides, Asabi was coming out of his trance.

"Please excuse my initial emotional response. When would I start?"

Wendy pretended to look at a watch that was not on her wrist. "How about . . . in twenty minutes?"

Phred shook his head and turned to her. "Wendy, that's not enough advance notice. Why not give him an hour?" He was dead serious.

She buried the laugh as far down as she could and deadpanned to Asabi, "How about you start in an hour?"

■ ■ ■

When Michael picked Wendy and Phred up from the lab, all three were wearing smiles—even Phred, who never thought anything was funny. Michael went first. "They bumped me up three times until I was talking to the president of the university. He confirmed what we thought: that the site was owned by the State of Minnesota and selling it would require an affirmative vote by the state legislature, as well as a whole lot of posturing before that."

Wendy nodded. "So far, so good."

"I told him that we'd prefer to lease the property anyway to preserve capital and that we already have an agreement in principle."

Phred was surprised. "Just like that?"

"Yep. The president said the site was a financial drain on the university, in that it needs twenty-four seven security across three hundred acres and all the buildings need to be heated to keep them from freezing up. They have to keep the plant insured and maintain liability coverage as well. So we'll take over those expenses and make a lease payment of—ready for this?"

"A million a year?" Wendy said. Phred nodded.

Michael shook his head, the smile on his face growing wider. "One. Dollar."

"What?" Wendy and Phred said in unison.

"Yessir. One dollar a year. The president explained that the U of M is a research institution, not a for-profit enterprise, and having the fusion campus operational again—at no cost to the U, no less—was a win for them. There was one little glitch, however."

Phred exhaled. "Damn. Glitches have cost me numerous jobs."

"Any improvements we make on the property become property of the university," Michael said.

Wendy probed a little. "So if we added, say, a thirty-billion-dollar fusion reactor . . ."

"Would become property of the U, correct."

Wendy probed some more. "How long of a lease?"

Michael smiled his biggest smile yet, knowing his answer was the right answer. "One hundred years."

Wendy high-fived him. "We're golden."

■   ■   ■

The incorporation process only took a day. Michael would be president and CEO, Andie General Counsel, Andy CFO, and Walt managing director. They were all sitting around the kitchen table—a table that had witnessed the hatching of an exciting number of improvements over the past couple months.

Andie questioned Wendy's plans for the corporate structure with concern. "You mean you're not going to be involved in any capacity?"

Wendy took her hand and glanced at Walt Asabi, who had been made aware of her status. Then she lowered a serious gaze at her daughter's eyes. "Honey, when I came back, I didn't have a green card."

Andie blinked and shook her head, not understanding.

"I'm not a permanent resident."

"Oh," Andie said. She managed to keep it together but couldn't stop the tears rolling quietly down her cheeks. Wendy was the only one able to keep a dry eye.

■   ■   ■

Setting up the initial public offering wasn't nearly as difficult as Andy imagined. On its day of inception, the company would have only four employees, no tax structure to audit, no history to authenticate, and no liabilities needing due diligence. The company was set up as a for-profit corporation, acknowledging that a fifty billion dollar capitalization would not pass muster as a charity. But the intent was, in fact, to function as a nonprofit—cover all expenses and establish a cash reserve, but otherwise sell electricity to the utility companies at cost. The value of owning stock would not be in the profitability of the company but in the increasing value of the company, and thus its stock.

Wendy made sure that Richard Crowley, Melinda Vanderbilt, and several other recent friends were on board, and on a Monday morning in June, the stock offering of Star Power Development Corporation hit the market. The day began with a number of huge purchases in billion-dollar increments, and as anticipated, the remaining shares were sold nearly as fast as the orders could be written. All ten million shares were sold on the first day of offering, and by the market close on the second day, the shares were trading at 7 percent higher than the initial $10,000 offering price. One of the most interesting purchases was when Dr. Walter Asabi bought ten shares.

In short, millions of committed investors were determined that the world was ready for fusion power *now*.

CHAPTER TWENTY-EIGHT

Wendy answered her phone and was immediately told, "Please hold for Admiral Brown." Half a minute later, Brown indeed came on the line. "Wendy?"

"Good morning, Admiral. Nice to hear from you. I'm betting you have some news."

"As a matter of fact, I do." His tone was serious. "Yesterday, there was a volcanic eruption on Pico Island, in the Azores chain in the Mid-Atlantic, and it was devastating."

"Oh no, Hiram. Is the *Gerald R. Ford* ready to go?"

"That's why I'm calling. The refitting was complete several weeks ago, and the five-ship task force is fully staffed and en route. Are you familiar with the Azores?"

"Admiral, I could only identify twelve of the US states in high school. The Azores have never blipped my radar screen."

Brown chuckled. "They're a chain of a dozen or so islands about fifteen hundred miles west of Portugal and are a protectorate of that country. Pico is a modest island of a bit less than five hundred square miles and a population of fifteen thousand.

"The volcano blew its top. Ash and debris covered the island pretty quickly. The airport is out of commission, and the small port on the island was all but destroyed by volcanic rock. We do have sat-phone connections with the emergency services there, and they've asked for our help."

Wendy was completely focused. "How far out are the ships?"

"That's the good news. The task force was steaming toward the Mediterranean when the volcano erupted, and it's just pulling into the harbor as we speak. I've been speaking with the commander of the *Ford* every half hour or so, and we're going to be in a perfect spot to do some good. You recall how the retrofitting reduced the weight of the carrier to the point of substantially reducing the draft of the ship?"

"Absolutely. From a fully loaded carrier draft of thirty-nine feet, to a 30 percent lighter rescue ship draft of twenty-eight feet."

"Correct. And guess how deep the Pico Island harbor is?"

"Hiram, remember, I don't know where the state of Illinois is . . ."

"Oh yeah. Well, the harbor is smooth bottomed at thirty feet. The *Ford* is being pulled into position by tugs and will be the largest ship ever to dock in the Azores. The new 'air wing' on the ship is a fleet of six King Stallion heavy-lift helicopters, which can carry up to fifty-five passengers or a smaller but still impressive number of injured. The aircraft were in flight even before the *Ford* entered the harbor."

"Do you have an idea of the number of injured yet?"

"Only that it's horrific. The debris from the volcano spread in all directions from the crater, and apparently no surface on the island was spared. The material came down as dust, pebbles, rocks— even some boulders weighing a thousand pounds or more. There are several hundred dead, Wendy. The very modern Pico hospital has no power, and we, the *Gerald R. Ford* and its staff and crew, are the dividing line between living and dying."

"Oh my!"

"Oh my is right, Wendy. But the fact is, we're there! We have the capacity, right this minute, to save hundreds of lives. We'll possibly be transporting several thousand people to the ship for treatment. Our kitchens might be feeding *all* of the survivors. We'll be providing shelter for thousands, along with communications, fresh water, and security.

"But Wendy, the real purpose of my call was just to let you know that, while I was personally devastated to be responsible for the disemboweling of one of the most magnificent warships ever built, I am as proud as a person can be that we had an emergency response flotilla under steam to come to the rescue. At the moment, we are this island's *only* rescue option. And maybe, just maybe, this is what the United States Navy will be, going forward."

"Hiram, thank you. I'm so happy our paths crossed!"

"Don't be a stranger, kid," Brown said before clicking off.

CHAPTER TWENTY-NINE

Life on Ekman Island had settled into a hierarchy and a routine. Darwin was in charge of the hierarchy. The North Koreans, not by genetics but by Pavlovian conditioning, were not good decision makers. They took direction and they completed the tasks assigned.

The Venezuelans, in spite of their boorish behavior when in power, were nurturers. And the Syrians, having lived generations of lifetimes fighting to survive, ruled the island.

After several months celebrating nature, they were all still alive, even Kim Jong-un. Arguably, however, he had not acclimated well. His entire life experience had been as a spoiled, self-serving, self-impressed, daddy-appointed monarch. None of those traits were of value when stranded on the proverbial desert island.

In three months, Kim had lost one hundred pounds. Jenny Craig would have given him a medal and an endorsement contract—if he could only have found Jenny Craig. But Kim's was not a healthy transformation. Having had no skills, no friends, no subjects, and only a limited grasp on reality when he got there—he'd been building offensive nuclear weapons while ruling one of the most impoverished countries in the world, for goodness' sake—he very quickly became unstable. Let's just say this was an example of how to go from supreme leader to lost dog in one little plane ride.

No one brought him food. He survived only on bananas and the food waste of the others. He spoke to no one except himself, and he didn't seem to get along with himself too well. Time was not a friend of Kim Jong-un.

The three "abdicated" groups maintained their separate packs, but all built, lived, and comingled in the landing strip area around the old hangar. They kept their separate languages, but more or less adopted Spanish for intergroup communication, mostly as a practical compromise of sorts. Arabic and Korean seemed useful only to those immersed in them for a lifetime. Spanish emerged as more teachable and understandable. Only the Venezuelans were fluent, but the others were able to pick up the basics: "Don't pee in my doorway"; "Don't steal my food or I will kill you"; "Not tonight, I've got a headache."

Which brings us to the age-old jailhouse dilemma. The sponsors of this free vacation in paradise had neglected to drop off any women. Several of the inhabitants fantasized that another plane was on its way, filled with brutal dictator-type females like, say, Madonna or Mariah Carey. But there were no more planes.

And, to the good fortune of sheep everywhere, there were no sheep on the island, either.

Bashar al-Assad was their communal leader, but in a watered-down way, as leadership goes (read: he didn't have a gun). He would settle a dispute before two residents killed each other and would investigate the few instances of theft, all found to be by Kim Jong-un. The punishment for thievery was that the thief was forced to remain Kim Jong-un.

As time went on, clothing became an issue, in that several of the men decided not to wear any. That inflamed the sensibilities of most of the residents and made a couple of them too randy to be manageable. Assad made one of his few decrees: In public, everyone would at least cover their vitals with underwear, or a loincloth, or a leaf, or otherwise stay away from the others. The penalty was decreed to be a "snip-snip" with Kim handling the knife. There were no further infractions.

They invented fire by way of one of the Koreans' eyeglasses and some dried grass, and with that, they were eventually able to cook some food. One of them actually caught a wild boar when one curiously walked up to him while he was doing his business squatting against a tree. Assad assigned his trusted lieutenant, the man who did most of the "wet work" for him back in Damascus, to gut and prepare the beast.

Several of the men learned how to fish, and those three became very popular with the rest of the residents. One day, a ten-foot shark made the mistake of being too close to shore as the tide was going out, and in spite of aggressive twisting and turning, it was unable to avoid becoming a donation to the Ekman Island food shelf. Assad's blade man was again assigned to partition the fish, and he creatively served up some shark fillets, shark tenders, and shark kabobs. As an unexpected bonus, the stomach of the beast also contained the bony remains of a human foot and a nicely preserved rubber boot. The blade man claimed it as his own, discarded the foot, and wore the single boot from that moment on. The North Koreans called him "resourceful," the Venezuelans still called him "Hey you," and the Syrians from then on called him "Bootleg."

They also became adept at preparing chicken-fried snake, which had the side benefit of making it safer to get up at night to go pee.

Early on, they ran across the oversized coolers that the Seabees had abandoned, which, to their disappointment, proved a timeless sailor's oath, "No beer shall be left behind." But the coolers did become useful, as the men would fill them with coconut milk and then place them out on the runway in the relentless heat for several days. The result was the foulest smelling, foulest tasting intoxicant ever to touch the lips of mankind. The brew was also an excellent laxative.

All in all, it wasn't a terrible existence, and it was actually a step up for the two lower-ranking North Koreans. The food was better, and they were no longer in fear of being shot for thinking.

CHAPTER THIRTY

The general counsel and chief financial officer of Star Power Development Corporation never actually set up offices in the Halstads' garage. Within twenty-four hours of Michael's agreement with the university and the ceremonial payment of the dollar, they were able to assume control of the remote fusion campus, and they moved into the musty-smelling but fairly modern administration building.

It was huge. Three stories, covering half a block, with the square footage represented to be 100,000 feet—for four employees. The four followed the strict and time-proven process of starting a corporation. First, they picked their respective offices. Next, they each investigated their paths to the restrooms. And finally, they convened a meeting in the conference room.

Michael started it off. "Where in hell do we start?" The other three just stared at him, so he kept talking. "I have a suggestion. Let's start by agreeing on some ground rules, okay?" They continued to stare at their new CEO. "I'm thinking that we need a power structure. We've all got our titles, and thus some specific responsibilities, but I suggest we step back and set up the golden rule of Star Power Development." Three pairs of eyes blinked back at him. "I would like to suggest two things. We need to agree to let each other do our jobs and to not second-guess the decisions of the other three. Agreed?"

Walt, Andie, and Andy looked at each other, then back at Michael, and said in unison, "Agreed."

"And second, I suggest that no major decisions are made, and no major actions are taken, without the four of us agreeing to it in advance."

Andy responded without much conviction. "Agreed?"

He looked each of them in the eye, one by one. Walt was the first to speak. "That's pretty . . . unconventional. Why?"

"You just nailed it, Walter. Why? I've worked at several corporations where the CEO was a tyrant. No one was allowed to disagree with him, because he figured he couldn't have become CEO if he weren't smarter than all the others. But, in fact, he wasn't smarter than any of them. He may have been educated more than some, but not smarter.

"I heard Phred say once, 'Decisions made in a vacuum always suck.' And have you ever noticed a house that has had some additions added on to it that make the house look like a monstrosity? I've always claimed that those houses were missing two things—an architect and a wife to filter some of the husband's dumb ideas."

Andie tried to coach him along. "This is very complex."

"What I'm trying to suggest is that we need to have each other's backs, fact-check each other's conclusions, and all be on the same page when we make the larger decisions."

Walt was nodding. "That makes sense, Michael, and I, for one, will love the opportunity to make the daily decisions in my area without taking each little thing to committee. That drove me nuts during the first iteration of this facility. But what, ah . . . *level* are you thinking warrants a 'larger' decision?"

"Ten million."

The CFO's jaw was the first to drop. "Your suggestion is that each of us might be making ten-million-dollar decisions without consensus?" Andy asked.

Michael nodded. "Exactly. Look, we're on a fast track. We've got a budget of fifty billion dollars, and this thing needs to come together at the speed of . . . a particle accelerator, not a freight train. Walt, you need to hire a couple hundred highly specialized people, including scientists, and quality control engineers, and geniuses at multiple levels in your development and implementation process. Ten million only buys you that staff for six months. You need the authority and flexibility to make that happen—like, say, by tomorrow afternoon?

"And Andy, with that much money physically sitting in the bank, you need to be able to maximize the unused portion of that little nest egg to make sure we've got enough left when we're ready to throw the switch."

Andy gave one perfunctory nod. "Can do."

"But at the same time, no one should be so independent as to think their larger ideas don't need consensus, right? Speed of decision-making dictates this ten-million-dollar 'rapid response' capacity. And responsible due diligence dictates that we should all be in agreement above that. What do you think?"

He looked at Walt. "I like it."

He turned to Andy. "I like it."

And he turned to Andie. "I like it."

And then Andy said, "Whew! "We solved the old 'asshole prima donna CEO' conundrum in less than fifteen minutes!"

They continued on with Michael's mental agenda. "Andie, what do you think you'll need for staff?"

"We'll obviously need to grow as we progress, but for now I'm looking for one associate attorney and two paralegals. And, a little off topic, but I'm amazed at the volume of equipment that was sitting idle in here for, what, six years? Copiers, lithography machines, CAD stations—there's even a laptop on basically every desk in the building."

Walt chimed in. "None of them are usable."

Andie was surprised. "What? Why not?"

"They were brand new when we lost funding, the latest and greatest. But that was 2014. They're obsolete, like a Model T Ford truck—good for parades, but worthless for hauling."

"Nuts. Bummer. Maybe I'll take one home for my kids to play games on."

Asabi shook his head. "Good luck with that, Andie. If your kids are into *PAC-MAN* and *Asteroids*, then you're golden. But if you load the current *Man O' War* or Madden 2020, the machine will just lie there like an old dog on a porch."

Michael pulled the conversation back to the present. "Walt, have you thought about engaging some of your old vendors?"

"Like maybe Western Magnetics? Pace-Gordon Electronics? Sure, they might be a help." Asabi started writing a new list as he spoke.

"Great. Here's what I'm thinking. What was the biggest issue back when you were operational?"

"Ha!" Walt didn't hesitate. "Funding."

"Right," Michael replied. "And what was your second biggest issue?"

Asabi rolled his hand in a "duh" gesture. "Running out of funding before we got anything done."

"Exactly," Michael said. "So, in this current go-around, the biggest two challenges to progress have already been solved. Which leads us to our next priority—racing to the finish line. What I'm thinking is, rather than approaching those firms as suppliers, maybe we should try to include them as partners? Give them a seat at the gaming table and incentivize the hell out of them if they meet our deadlines."

Walt broke in. "Deadlines that they'll all say can't be met."

"Exactly. We need to get everybody off the 'la-di-da, this is a big-money, long-term gravy train' and into a mindset of them begging us to speed up the project. Make sense?"

"Makes sense—and you hired the right guy, Michael. I lost my career when this project shut down because we weren't in a hurry, and we all thought that no one would pull the plug on what was sure to be one of the greatest achievements of humankind."

"I love you, man," Michael said. "And here's the thing. This is fusion, right? We're not colliding atoms to create massive explosions. We're fusing particles in a process that cannot explode. Speeding up won't kill us. Hire the best in the world, and make sure they come to work wearing their track shoes."

■　■　■

Wendy had been walking the development campus, inspecting what they were getting for a dollar a year. And she was being followed.

The follower wasn't dodging between buildings or pretending to read a newspaper when she glanced his way. He was just trying to keep up with her aggressive pace. So she stopped and leaned up against a building bearing a sign that said "Campus Cart Storage." Peeking in through the door glass, she saw fifteen or so golf carts lined up in two neat rows, apparently for transportation around the several-hundred-acre property. She chuckled at the irony. For a dollar a year, Star Power got a world-class research facility, equipped as if everybody just went to lunch, yet they'd be spending fifty billion to get to the point of actually producing electricity.

The stalker finally caught up, breathing heavily. He was a tad plump, sporting disheveled hair; boots; jeans; a "We Are the World" T-shirt; and a beard that announced, "Yes, I'm a writer."

"Hi, I'm Micha McGuire, a writer with the *Star Tribune*. Would you mind if I asked you a few questions?"

Wendy pondered that for a moment. While confession was good for the soul, it was generally not a good idea when talking to the FBI or a newspaper reporter. She decided to stay anonymous and have some fun.

"Yes," she said.

"Hmm—yes, you'd mind if I asked you some questions?"

"Yes."

"Ah, why's that?"

Wendy responded as seriously as she could manage. "That sounds like a question."

"Well, yes, it was a question. Is that a problem?"

She was getting into it. "That also sounds like a question."

"I . . . I don't understand." He was the Religion and Faith editor and wasn't experienced at grilling people.

"You asked if I minded if you asked some questions. I said yes, and then you asked me two questions. Why would you do that?"

"Well, I just . . . oh my. I'm sorry."

This was working out well. Step one with a reporter, get them on the defensive. Actually, she had no clue what step one with a reporter actually was, but she was going to ride that horse to the buzzer. "Sir, this is a secure private facility. I suggest you make an appointment with the communications director if you have questions."

"Ah, sure. I can do that. Do you have their name?"

Wendy immediately wondered if she wasn't that good at this after all. The company had no communications director. But she forged ahead. "Sir, I assume you're aware that this is a nuclear fusion experimental facility and extremely important to the security of the United States."

"Yes, I guess I know that."

"Then you must also know that answers are on a need-to-know basis, and it seems obvious to me that you don't need to know."

"You're shitting me! I thought this was a commercial enterprise. This is actually the—the—" He was afraid to say letters, afraid "they" might decide he knew too much.

Wendy simply nodded, and then turned her head to speak into a nonexistent lapel mic. "Tango Charlie, I might need a housekeeping team over at the cart shed, copy?" She lifted her eyes as if listening to her nonexistent earpiece, then said, "Roger that, Tango Charlie. Foxtrot out." She was ready to explode with laughter but channeled that into false aggression.

"Now, I'm going to tell you what you're going to do, reporter boy. You're going to answer some questions for *me*, and then if you're lucky, I'll let you walk out of here and not look back. We know who you are, Mr. McGuire, and we know every word you've written. You've been flitting around, asking questions about things that don't concern you, like your unknown, unnamed 'concept guru,' right?"

"Y-yes, ma'am. I was just—"

"What else do you know? Right now. What else do you know?"

"Nothing . . . really! Just snippets and rumors, you know?"

This guy was actually scared! Wendy couldn't help but take it to the limit. "Tell me now, or I'll get 'housekeeping' over here to clean up your mess with a garden hose." She had no idea what that meant.

"Okay, okay! Please! There were just stories—unverified, right?—of a person sort of instigating the upheaval of local religious institutions, and then it went global, and I . . ."

"Tell me something I don't already know, *Micha*." She emphasized his name like she was taunting a schoolkid.

"There were . . . reports—just rumors, really—that the same woman might have been seen in the cabin of an airplane that might have—"

"We know all that. What else?"

"Power plants?" He was hoping that he knew something, anything that might calm her down.

"Yeah, yeah. Conspiracy one-oh-one. We've disproved each of those fairy tales. Now, here's the deal. You're a religion writer, correct?"

"Y-yes, ma'am."

She pointed at him like she was Uncle Sam selling war bonds. "Stick to religion. And never, ever talk about any of this again. Are we clear?"

"I'm, well, that's fine—"

Wendy grabbed his shoulder and yelled, "Are we clear?" Mc-

Guire screamed as if someone had just hit the switch on his electric chair. She wondered if her vibe maybe intensified with emotion.

"Clear! We're clear!" he screamed. "I need to go!"

Wendy nodded, and pointed to the campus gate.

McGuire shook his head. "No! I need to *go*! I need a—a restroom!"

She let him pee in the men's room of the cart shed.

■ ■ ■

Back in the admin building, Wendy sauntered into Michael's office. "Remember that religion writer for the *Star Tribune*?"

"Yeah . . ." Michael said, eyeing Wendy in anticipation.

"He just got religion. I don't think he'll be snooping around any further."

■ ■ ■

The activity and the excitement at Star Power Development seemed to grow by the hour. The labs were filling with scientists. The cafeteria was an opera of voices in several languages. Trucks rolled in and out in a near-constant stream. And even as the experiments were ongoing, the fusion reactor was being built.

The reactor had been under construction when the facility was shuttered in 2014 and was 20 percent complete. The foundations down to bedrock were in place, and hardened concrete had been poured for the base of the huge structure. There were numerous particle accelerators around the world, though the skeleton of this one was larger than most. Fusing hydrogen isotopes had to be done at great speed and extreme heat, in a reactor large enough to allow the intense heat of the reaction to propel steam through giant turbines to produce commercially significant amounts of electricity. And the process needed to produce more energy than was required to create the fusion.

The devil in the details wasn't specifically the science. That was a matter of math and physics that had been established for decades. The challenge was coming up with a system to isolate the speeding, fusing particles to prevent them from touching anything, and the solution was thousand-pound magnets, like the ones on-site from Western Magnetics. These were to be installed in the reactor to keep the isotopes suspended. There was no structural entity that could maintain its form when subjected to the million-degree heat of a fusion reaction, but by having the process suspended within the accelerator through magnetic force, fusion was achievable.

So the combining of structural steel and hardened concrete had begun, or rather, had been restarted. Twenty-four hours a day, crews were erecting, pouring, measuring, testing, consulting, and repeating. And creating a thirty-billion-dollar reactor from scratch pressed the designers, engineers, constructors, and installers to the extremes of their abilities. No one had done this before, and nearly every device within the confines of the growing reactor had to be custom designed and custom manufactured. A cooling control panel that could monitor and manage the extreme heat cost a million dollars and would take a year. But, interestingly, with an incentive of another four million dollars, Dr. Asabi was able to have it designed, built, and delivered in thirty days. So it went with most of the equipment.

Phred Peterson was a frequent visitor at the fusion campus. While his expertise was focused on solar, and the bulk of his time allocated to those efforts, he was beyond the ability to control his craving to be involved in the reactor design. And Walt appreciated his input, sometimes just as a sounding board. As the smartest guy in the room most of the time, he found that conversations were often banal or nonexistent. Phred filled that void and had actually been the instigator convincing Asabi to discard one of his theories in favor of a more logical approach.

This particular afternoon, Phred and Walt were sitting in Walt's office, discussing the problems with start-up and shutdown, and Walt was frustrated. "We can't create electricity until the isotopes fuse, and at great speed and heat, right?"

"Duh." Phred was smart, but not terribly polite.

"And it takes three hours to ramp the system up to the speed and temps that allow fusion, right?"

"Your clock still works, that's a plus." Be impolite, but creative—that was Phred's motto.

Asabi was ignoring Phred's sophomoric responses. "And an hour and twelve minutes to shut the process down. That leaves a four-hour gap between when we've met current demand and when we can be online again."

"Four hours and twelve minutes," Phred corrected.

Walt looked at him for a moment. "If I wanted a smart-ass answer for each question, I'd have my brother-in-law sitting over there."

Phred shot back, "When the truth causes diarrhea, either change your diet or buy more duct tape."

Asabi was shaking his head. "My god, you're annoying, not helpful, *and* disgusting. You've hit the trifecta."

"You were saying?" Phred tried to get him back on track.

"If we shut it down, we lose productivity, and if we keep it running, we overheat."

Phred was now more serious. "And there's just "on" and "off" as the options?"

Walt nodded. "Correct."

"Then you change the rules, Walt. Throw out the 'start module'—the software and the hardware."

Walt shook his head. "That system cost six million dollars."

Phred ignored him. "Throw it out and start from scratch. Your ramp-up goes from zero to 100 percent, correct?"

"Right . . ."

"So you need a variable governor system to enable you to hold the ramp-up at, say, 20 percent. Comparatively low speed and low heat. Hold it there forever *or* until the grid calls for more juice."

"You mean don't shut it down?"

"Exactly. Have the process run at idle, if you will, and you cut, what, an hour off the ramp-up?"

"More than that." Asabi was liking the idea. "The acceleration process is geometric. The initiation process takes an hour all by itself, and then the ramp-up is substantially slower at the front end than when it's approaching full acceleration. We'd probably save two hours."

Asabi stood and started marking it up on a whiteboard. Then he paused, turned halfway around, and said, "You know, Phred, you're still annoying and disgusting, but occasionally, you *are* helpful." He pivoted back to the board.

In his fifty years, Phred Peterson had never, ever allowed anyone else to have the last word. "Walter, I took a one-credit course from the old bandleader Lawrence Welk back in the day. It was a business class, believe it or not, as he was very successful with the money. And one of his lines I remember as clearly now as then. He said, 'I never hired a musician unless he was better than me.'"

Asabi didn't turn around. "You're not on the payroll."

"But I should be."

"Not gonna happen. Ever."

"Yeah, yeah. Well, I now recall another of that old German's classroom quotes. He pitched us to keep ego out of our decision-making. He said, 'The bandleader is complimented when the band plays in tune.'"

Dr. Asabi still refused to turn around. "You're not the bandleader. I'm the bandleader."

"Any other challenges I can help you with today, Walter?"

CHAPTER THIRTY-ONE

Wendy and Michael's evenings had evolved into a pattern of sharing updates on their various projects, he working production statistics on his computer and she studying books on even more outlandish theoretical treatises—*Space Travel at Light Speed, New Worlds—Explore, not Conquer,* and *Aspirational Intelligence: How to Make Humanity Want to be Smarter.*

He broke in on her studies. "Wendy, exciting news. The lab rats at Star Power have solved the particle suspension roadblock with a combination of magnetic force and extreme high pressure."

"Oh, Michael," she gushed, fluttering her eyelids. "No one has ever said anything like that to me before!" She closed her book and plopped down on the couch beside the man and his laptop, an inseparable combination as of late.

He ignored her sarcasm. "They've completed thirty test runs in the 'baby reactor,' and each test produced the same result. They've got it solved."

"That's amazing," Wendy said, serious this time.

He folded up his laptop. "You know," he said. "I loved driving bus, listening to kids laugh and yell and show off. But working at the fusion campus, I get a daily—an hourly—satisfaction that no other job has ever come close to providing. We're truly doing something important. We're changing the world."

"Like Steve Jobs?" she asked.

Michael shook his head. "Nah, he was a prick."

Wendy laughed. "Speaking of, have you talked to Phred lately?"

"Sure. He's over there a couple times a week. And hey, he's not a prick."

She laughed again. "I know, I know. He's just . . . eccentric."

"Walt would add 'annoying and disgusting' and then follow it up with 'but a hell of a mind.' I haven't talked to Phred at length for a while, though. What's up?"

"Two pretty interesting things. One, they ran the country out of solar shingles. The previous demand was modest at best, and now they're pretty much the only roofs being installed."

"Wow! That's awesome, Wen. So, what does he do when they're out of shingles?"

"Ready for this? He bought the company that makes them, kept their management team in place, and doubled the size of the plant. In two weeks!"

"Doubled? In two weeks? We're talking about Phred Peterson, right? The guy who would disagree with the pope on the color of his white hat? That Phred?"

"Ah, c'mon. You know, he's found his place in the world, just like you. Despite him being such a strange duck, people listen when he quacks."

"And the other interesting thing?" Michael asked.

"Their company got sued yesterday by the US government for antitrust."

"What? How could I not have heard about that, or at least the lead-up to it?"

Wendy was cozied up to him on the couch, displaying no anxiety about a little old antitrust lawsuit. "I'm telling you, Phred is a changed man. He knew it was coming—actually thought it was inevitable, due to the success of Free Juice LLC. He's been putting a process together for several months now to expand Free Juice nationwide beyond the half dozen cities that the company is doing business in now."

Michael nodded. "Yessir, that sounds like antitrust to me. And that's his solution?"

"No, silly. The success of Free Juice has put hundreds of other roofing companies on the ropes. That, along with the fact that Free Juice is using 100 percent of the solar shingles produced in the country, has gotten the attention of antitrust watchdogs. His expansion plan includes franchising as many of those roofing companies as are willing to sign up. But he's waiving the franchise fee and providing supervisors to train crews on installation. His only stipulation is that the franchisee pay the Free Juice trainer."

Michael pondered that. "It's a decent plan, but what does the parent company get out of it? He's basically giving away any future growth opportunity."

"Have you ever played Phred at chess?"

"Um, no. That was a curious sharp left turn from the antitrust topic."

She shook her head in exasperation. "Michael, you are a world-class checkers player, but Phred would eat your lunch and turn it into compost before you'd beat him at chess."

"Well, yeah. He's a genius, and I'm ... somewhere in the middle."

Wendy smiled. "I'll grant you upper middle, okay? Phred knew that Free Juice's unexpected takeover of the entire residential roofing market in the United States was leading to trouble—not only for the company but for the industry. So he developed the no-cost franchising plan while buying up the only supplier of the product."

"Ah, I see where you're going."

"Yeah, in a checkers sort of way, you do. So he buys the manufacturer, including its patents, and immediately doubles solar shingle production. The expected antitrust suit comes down the pike, and he'll settle it immediately by giving away the franchises. And all the while, Free Juice owns the product being installed."

"But ..."

"But now Free Juice is in antitrust violation as the only solar shingle supplier? Not so, oh one of lateral thinking. No one else was making solar shingles before, due to the limited market. Free Juice put no manufacturer out of business. No antitrust. The company will license its patents to any and all comers who will agree to meet the manufacturing standards, and product competition will spring up on its own. And because of the phenomenal recent popularity of the shingles, some inventor will patent a new and improved version, and away they go."

"Damn, that guy is good! I still think I could beat him at checkers, though."

Wendy nodded. "Phred's heart wouldn't be in a checkers game. You might be able to sneak up on him."

Michael prodded. "That isn't the end of the story, though, right?"

"Not quite. After telling me all of the above, he looked me in the eye, put on this Darth Vader look—"

Michael interrupted. "Vader wore a mask."

"Argh. He got this *Angry Birds* look on his face—"

"Better."

"—and said, 'Think like a devil, act like a saint, and don't let a little tsunami tip your kayak.'"

Michael shook his head. "Oh my god. If that guy had a twin brother, I'd have to shoot one of them."

Wendy nodded. "For sure."

CHAPTER THIRTY-TWO

The next day was a Saturday, and the Halstads had invited the Star Power team over for a celebratory lunch—Andie, Andy, and Walt Asabi, plus Phred Peterson, their ad-hoc advisor and confidant. By mutual request, they were having pizza delivered.

Whop-whop-whop. A polite rapping at the front door. Michael answered. It was Chirpy. "Hi, I'm—"

"Don't say it! Please, no slogans. I'll reduce your tip a dollar for each slogan."

Chirpy stared at him, confused and out of place in his presentation.

Michael asked, "Are you, like, Paul's only delivery driver?"

Chirpy perked up. "Oh, no, sir. He's got seven, but I call dibs on this house just in case."

"Just in case we pay you and then give you the pizza?"

Chirpy shrugged. "Never know."

"Okay, so how much? And remember, every slogan costs a dollar."

Chirpy struggled. His pattern was all messed up. "Um, twenty-five?"

"That's fine," he said crisply, handing over thirty dollars. "Keep the change. You did a good job following directions." He reached for the pizzas, and Chirpy looked disappointed. "Sorry, bud, we're hungry."

Chirpy reluctantly handed over the pizzas and was again on his phone before he even left the stoop. "Hey, Gordo?" Michael heard him say. "Bad news, man. They kept the pie."

■ ■ ■

The table conversation was brisk and happy. The reactor was complete, and Star Power Development was about to go live with its first full-system test. And then there was another knock at the front door.

Whop-whop-whop. Polite but firm. Michael pulled the door open and found not two but three men in black this time, two of whom he recognized. "Well! Asshole and Buzz! What brings you here in the middle of our lunch?" He was being snide, but he didn't push too hard. He still remembered his inability to stand during the last time they were here.

Bertinucci glanced at the third man when Michael addressed him as Asshole but quickly regained his composure. "Sir, this is the special agent in charge of the FBI regional office in Minneapolis. He's here to arrest Ms. Wendy Halstad for conspiracy to commit sedition, plus another"—he looked at his notebook—"eleven charges. May we speak to her?" He nodded to the kitchen, where the group had jumped to their feet, and yet another pizza went uneaten.

Wendy put on a big smile and strode into the living room, grabbing Bertinucci's free hand to shake it. He felt the jolt, and she quickly reached for the FBI agent.

"Don't shake her hand!" Bertinucci bellowed. "She's a human joy buzzer. Let's just do what we're here to do. Read her her rights, Finkelstein."

Michael stepped in front of her and let out his own bellow. "Whoa! Let's settle down here for a minute." The lighted fuse in the room was, at least temporarily, pinched out. "I've got two concerns we need to address. First is what the hell this is all about. But let's go from second to first, like a baseball double play."

The FBI agent looked at Bertinucci for guidance. Bertinucci rolled his eyes at Michael. Buzz kept quiet and off to the side.

Michael continued, "So, second of all, you said 'Read her her rights, Finkelstein,' correct?"

The NSA man nodded, and Michael, being uncharacteristically polite, said, "Azolé . . . you said, 'Read her her rights, Finkelstein,' and without looking, I know that the big bald hippie behind me started laughing and is probably still laughing." Michael turned, and they all looked at Phred, who had a big-ass smile on his face. He quickly wiped it clean.

"Agent Finkelstein, what's your first name?"

The agent again looked at Bertinucci for guidance, but then said to Michael, "It's Chad, sir."

Michael nodded. "Much better. Azolé, when you're in a tense situation and the FBI guy is named Finkelstein, you never, ever address him as Finkelstein. You know why?"

Bertinucci wouldn't respond, but he was curious enough to lift an eyebrow.

"Because when you say, 'Read her her rights, Finkelstein,' big bald hippies have no option but to laugh at you. It's in their DNA. And everybody else in the room wanted to laugh too, but they have more self-control than the genius hippie in the kitchen."

Michael looked back at Phred, who just shrugged in agreement.

"You need to own the room, Azolé. Project power and authority. Did you ever hear Efrem Zimbalist Jr. on *Hawaii Five-0* say, 'Book him, Ogelthorp'? No! He said, 'Book him, Danno.' That had style and elegance. 'Read her her rights, Finkelstein' undermines your whole *Men in Black* theme. But if you say, 'Read her her rights, Chad,' you're still in control."

Bertinucci looked over his shoulder. "Tase him, Chad." And he did.

■   ■   ■

Wendy put a couch pillow under Michael's head, then said to Berti-nucci, "Azolé, let's slow down a bit. I'll waive my right to an attorney and answer all your questions if you'll agree to do it at the kitchen table, rather than in a holding cell."

Andie choked out, "Mom!" but Wendy held up her hand to signal her to stop, focusing on the NSA man.

He pondered a moment, then said, "I see no problem with that." As they settled around the table, Phred looked over at Michael on the floor in the living room. His left foot was shaking, but he otherwise looked comfortable, so Phred, and Walter and Andy backed off to lean on the counter and watch.

The FBI man started the interview, speaking into a recorder. "My name is Chad Finkelstein, special agent in charge of the FBI regional office in Minneapolis, doing a precustody interview with . . . please state your name, ma'am."

Before Wendy could respond, Andie cut in. "Mom, give me a dollar." Wendy looked at her, and Andie again said, "Give me a dollar." Wendy reached into her clutch purse and pulled out a dollar. It was easy to find, as it was the only other thing in the purse except for a mini pack of moist towelettes.

Andie spotted the towelettes and gave Wendy a quizzical look.

"I shake a lot of hands," Wendy said with a shrug.

Andie refocused. "Mr. Finkelstein, I have been retained as Mrs. Halstad's attorney," she said as she held up the dollar, "and I'm advising her to not answer any questions."

Wendy smiled. "Honey, I appreciate your help, but I've got this. If you'd like, you can object to each question and advise me not to answer, so it'll all be on the tape, but I made a deal just now so that they could do the preliminaries right here." To Agent Finkelstein, she said, "My name is Wendy Halstad."

Michael was again cognizant and was listening intently from his reclining position.

The FBI man cleared his throat. "Let's start with allegation one: conspiracy to circumvent the power and authority of the United States Government." All eyes widened, except for Wendy's. "We are in possession of a signed affidavit from a North Korean army driver that you were seen in the cabin of a Gulfstream G700 in April of this year, in consultation with the former supreme leader of the Democratic People's Republic of Korea. As you may know, it is illegal for a private citizen to negotiate with another nation without the direct approval of the president of the United States."

Michael yelled from the living room, "That's bullshit."

Bertinucci turned to Buzz. "Gag him." And he did.

"Now, in conjunction with that episode, you are also alleged to have entered North Korean airspace, and in fact landed there, without a valid US passport; kidnapped said supreme leader of North Korea; and murdered him and his security detail by dumping their bodies at sea."

Phred couldn't help himself and made up a parable. "If you're convinced you're a representative of God almighty, just make shit up and call it gospel." Phred was not an appreciator of government power.

Michael was nodding quietly.

Finkelstein continued, "How do you respond to that, Mrs. Halstad?"

Andie said, "Don't answer, Mom."

Wendy patted Andie's hand and said to the agent, "Wow. That's pretty complex. Let me go from the easy answers to the more challenging ones." She smiled at the agent. "Challenging for you, I mean. I'm thinking that you won't understand. So let's see. Murder. No, I didn't kill anyone, didn't witness anyone being killed, didn't throw anyone out of an airplane at sea or witness it, didn't kidnap anyone or witness it. I'm confident that those charges are all a bluff, because none of it happened, and there is no evidence to even hint that it happened." She looked across at Andie. "How'd I do, sweetie?"

"That was great, Mom. You have my permission to continue."

"Whew! We got that murder stuff out of the way quick. Now let's see . . . I was, in fact, a guest on a Gulfstream that did, in fact, land in Pyongyang, North Korea. However, the plane had permission to land *and* take off, and I never left the aircraft, never touched North Korean soil, and was never approached by a customs or immigration agent. So, by law—" She paused and giggled. "I do a lot of reading. Anyway, by law, I didn't actually enter the country, and a passport was not required.

"Now, the sedition thing. Does anyone you spoke to claim to know what I said that was seditious?"

"Um . . ."

"I didn't think so. Do you have a statement from anyone who actually heard me negotiate with Kim Jong-un?

"Um . . ."

"I didn't think so. Hmm. In hindsight, it's good we're doing this interview in my kitchen, because if you had actually arrested me, my daughter would be forced to sue for false arrest. What a mess that would have been. Now, do you think you could ungag my husband?"

Bertinucci answered the question with a question. "Do you think he can stay quiet?"

Wendy shrugged. "Probably not."

Bertinucci remained in his chair.

Finkelstein tried to regain his footing. "I'm not saying we agree with any of your statements, but let's move on. This next one would be a state charge, but I've been asked to address all of them. Filing a false death certificate."

"Interesting! Did I do that?"

"We allege that you're aware of it, ma'am."

"Well, I didn't sign it, so I obviously didn't file it. You might need to take that one up with the guy you tased and gagged, lying over there on the floor."

Phred started applauding, and Bertinucci nodded to Buzz and pointed to Phred. The quiet NSA man started walking toward him, and Phred climbed up on the kitchen counter, hoping that maybe a leg electrocution might be better than a full-body shot. Buzz looked at his boss, and Bertinucci shook his head. "Never mind."

Phred breathed out a big sigh, and Bertinucci added, "For now."

Phred remained standing on the counter.

Finkelstein took control again. "Impersonating a federal agent."

She laughed. "Let me guess—CIA?"

"Correct."

"Well, Chad, look at the transcript again. Your witness, Micha McGuire, is a newspaper reporter. He gets his facts straight. He never actually told you I identified myself as a CIA agent, did he?"

The man went back through his notes for a full minute. "Ah, no, ma'am, he didn't. He said you were 'pretending to be a CIA agent.'"

"What else?"

"Insurance fraud."

Wendy nodded. "That one's pretty good, though you'd have to prove several things."

Finkelstein cocked his head. "Such as?"

"For starters, who am I?"

"Ma'am, you're Wendy Halstad." He smirked.

Wendy replied, "Can you prove it?"

Finkelstein laughed. "Don't have to. You admitted to it."

"I did. But you're claiming that I'm a seditious, kidnapping, murdering, conniving fraudster. Your position is also that I'm not a liar?"

Phred, from his oversight position, gave a single clap, but as soon as Bertinucci turned his head, Phred's right hand shot over to itch his left shoulder, and he quietly said, "Sorry." Andy took several precautionary steps away from him.

Wendy continued, "And assuming I am who I am—a line Popeye would be proud of, by the way—who would then be in that jar?" She pointed to the urn on the mantel.

"That's not our issue, ma'am."

"Oh, it most definitely is, Chad. You've got a first-degree mess here. No provable facts, holes in every little thing you've alleged, and hundreds of hours of legwork to do before you're ready to sit back down in my kitchen and try for a redo. Who am I? Who's in the jar? Who did the funeral home incinerate? Where is Kim Jong-un? Three Taser assaults on my husband, who has not threatened you or Asshole Bertinucci in any way, and then ignoring his injuries while he lay on the floor, spittle running down his chin." Michael wiped his face with his shirtsleeve. Wendy went on, "Threatening to tase an internationally acclaimed doctor and national hero"— she tossed her thumb over her shoulder at Phred—"for clapping his hands. Have I forgotten anything, Andie?"

"No, Mom. I'd be proud to have *you* represent *me*, any time."

Finkelstein tried one more time. "Inciting a riot."

Wendy looked over to Bertinucci. "You didn't explain that one to him, Azolé?"

Bertinucci looked away, declining to meet Wendy's or Finkelstein's eyes.

"I think we're done here, guys, unless you can make some more stuff up real fast. That reminds me. Would you care to share some cold stuffed-crust pizza with us?"

Finkelstein said softly, "Thank you, ma'am, no. I think we're done here." Everyone stood, except for Michael.

As the feds migrated toward the door, Buzz kneeled down beside Michael and said, "Hey, I'm sorry man. I got seven kids to feed, you know?" Michael nodded, but didn't say anything. He was still gagged.

■ ■ ■

Phred smiled at Wendy. "I liked the 'national hero' part."

"Sorry, Phred. I was grasping at straws." Everybody laughed but Phred.

They were eating cold pizza like it was sizzling prime rib, decompressing, and laughing and shaking their heads. Michael looked up from the several remaining crusts, staring at Phred until the stare was returned. "You knew?"

"For god's sake, Michael, one doesn't have to be a genius. I've been working alongside Wendy for months. When she shook my hand on that first day, I truly thought it was love." He winked at her. "But I came to my senses within moments. What I felt rolling up my arm wasn't love. It was purpose, overwhelming purpose."

He looked again at Wendy. "And I was at your funeral. Michael didn't see me. He didn't see anyone. He was on Neptune." He turned back to Michael. "Standing in your front hall, greeting Wendy—I was hit by two competing freight trains: the addictive, pulse-raising touch of Wendy and the inconsolable grief on your face at her funeral. And I understood."

Michael was still staring. "But you didn't say anything? For all this time?"

Phred laughed. "Look, I'm the smartest guy in this room, all right?"

Dr. Walter Asabi coughed loudly.

"Dang, Walt, are you catching a cold?" Phred asked. Everybody laughed except Phred. "I figured it out, but so what? It is what it is. You," he said, gesturing to the whole group of his friends sitting around him, "gave me new life and focus, and together we've accomplished what decades of blood and guts and heart given by thousands of people could not. My motto is 'Don't look a gift horse in the ass.'"

Dr. Asabi smiled. "That's your only motto?"

"Yessir," Phred replied. "At this moment in time."

Michael simply said, "Thank god," and started silently counting on his fingers.

"However," Phred continued, "as soon as you think you've got a woman figured out, you might as well stick your head up that horse's ass, because you've got shit for brains."

The noise of the laughter made the neighbors' dogs bark. Michael was trying to catch a breath. "I—I counted—" He took one more deep breath between laughs and then said, "I counted to four! His 'only' motto was replaced in four seconds!" Tears were running into his boots.

■　■　■

After the group quieted down, Wendy turned to Michael. "When you told Agent Bertinucci that you had two things to discuss, you started with the second thing, which somehow produced a baseball metaphor—"

Phred interrupted. "Even I didn't get that, and I'm—"

The entire group finished his sentence in unison: "the smartest guy in the room." Walt coughed again, and Phred again looked at him with concern.

Wendy said, "Shut up, Phred." Turning back to Michael, she said, "You never got to the first thing."

"Which," Phred said, "based on the order of presentation, was actually the second thing."

"Shut up, Phred. What was the first . . . ah . . . the other thing again?"

Michael said, "I wasn't able to make my first point—"

Wendy looked sternly at Phred and shook her head.

"—because I was tased and incapacitated after making the 'Finkelstein' point."

"Which you made at length, surely knowing that the FBI and the NSA would not respond well to a history lesson on sixties television combined with a semantics lesson on agency protocol."

Michael nodded. "Yeah, I figured that might activate a Taser, but I sacrificed myself to slow events down."

Wendy smiled at him. "Really?"

Michael looked down at the table, sheepishly hiding his blush from the rest of the team. "Yeah."

"I'd marry you all over again, Michael."

"Hell, I'd marry him for that!" Phred said. Then he, too, actually blushed. "Well, you know, in a platonic sort of way," he added, then paused and looked at Wendy. "Assuming, of course, that you're still unavailable."

CHAPTER THIRTY-THREE

The following Monday morning felt like a national holiday inside the Star Power Development Company campus. There were half a dozen TV trucks sprouting satellite antennas and several thousand people wandering the streets of the facility—it was the first time the public had been invited to explore what had become the most high-tech and highly anticipated undertaking in anyone's memory.

One wing of the admin building housed a 200-seat lecture hall, which was filling with people. The excitement in the room was palpable. There was a presentation area up front with a lectern and six chairs, three on either side. The back of the presentation area was filled with a huge screen the width and height of the pie-shaped auditorium.

There actually wasn't much to see of starting up a nuclear power plant, but the team had designed a rolling video format of five stationary live-action cameras at various vital points around the facility. The cameras would feed into a production room at the raised rear of the auditorium, where the feeds would be rotated to create a little more action.

The first camera was positioned in front of the control panel that would "start" the reactor. In reality, it had been ramped up to the 20 percent "idle" speed earlier in the day, but the "live" activation would spin the accelerator to full speed and heat over the course of an hour.

The second camera was showing the accelerator itself, even though there would be nothing to see. The particles were densely enclosed and invisible to the human eye, but the camera was positioned so that the foot traffic in that area would be visible.

The third camera was placed up and behind the large set of LED gauges. One displayed the current percentages of maximum speed and heat achieved and, when fusion was actually in process, the amount of kiloton energy produced. Another gauge displayed the temperature of the steam being produced by the reactor, and yet another showed the speed of the turbine generators, from zero to peak.

A fourth camera was positioned in front of the readout registering current kilowatts of electricity being produced at that moment—the whole purpose of this amazing, expensive structure.

And the fifth camera, manned by a seated operator to facilitate various people shots, was placed within the auditorium itself to record, in essence, the reactions to the reactor. The entire management team would be in the auditorium, along with the governor of Minnesota and several of the major investors, including Sir Richard Crowley and Melinda Vanderbilt. Admiral Hiram Brown was also there, dressed in civvies to avoid attention.

The startup was scheduled for noon, and the room settled down about ten minutes before, as the principals entered the stage from the side. Wendy was in the wing, hugging family members and friends as they walked out. She avoided contact with the governor, who was pretty wrapped up with her own entourage, anyway.

Michael was the last to leave the wing, and Wendy gave him a hug and a kiss before he walked on stage. "Michael, you are an amazing man," she said.

"And Wendy, you are . . ." he began, and he stopped. They both smiled into each other's eyes, raised their hands, palms up, shrugged, and laughed hard.

Perching nervously on her chair stage right was Andie Wiberg, whose husband, Chris, was back from his National Guard deployment and waving to her from the rear of the hall. Next up front was

Andy Halstad, whose wife, Caroline, stood next to Chris, chatting softly. Next, and closest to the lectern, was Phred Peterson, president of Free Juice, LLC, and identified in the event program as a Star Power senior consultant.

Michael had pondered the placement of Phred. Seating him that close to a microphone was a danger, but putting him at the end was putting him too far away from Michael's control. He had arranged with the production booth that if Phred grabbed the mic and started spouting cosmic—or profane—platitudes, they would cut the sound.

To Michael's left, next to the lectern, was Governor Allison Newberry. She wanted to be a senator and therefore never missed a grand opening, whether it was of a nuclear power plant or a day care center in Bayport. Next to the governor was Dr. Walter Asabi, vice president of Star Power and Director of Operations. Next to Walt was an empty chair.

Michael tapped the microphone. "Ladies and gentlemen, thank you for coming to the startup of the world's first nuclear fusion power plant!"

The room broke into immediate applause. Everyone there knew they were in the midst of a truly historic event.

Michael turned toward Asabi and said into the mic, "Walt, it's going to start, right?" Walt pointed to a jury-rigged metal box the size of a coffee can, nodded, and gave a thumbs-up. The crowd laughed at Michael's joke and applauded at Walter's thumbs-up. In fact, the start sequence was controlled by an app on his iPhone, which was inside the dummy box.

Michael then looked at a watch he hadn't worn in twenty years. "Folks, we've got six minutes before Walt hits the switch. My team insisted on the tight timing, claiming that if given the chance, I'd talk until next Wednesday." Another solid laugh from out front.

"But I wanted to introduce you to the team that brought today from theory into reality." He looked at Asabi again, feigning concern. "Reality, right, Walt?" Asabi gave another thumbs-up.

Michael gestured to his right. "My daughter, Andrea Wiberg, is the general counsel for Star Power and was a key decision-maker as this facility went from concept to completion." Andrea waved modestly. She didn't like the spotlight, and even a small-claims court appearance would force her to skip lunch.

"Next is my son, Andrew Halstad, the chief financial officer. Andy set up the public stock offering and has managed the fifty-billion-dollar development and construction budget. Andy, how far under budget was the entire project?"

Andy remained seated and held up three fingers. Michael responded in mock surprise, "Three dollars? Well, I guess under budget is under budget."

There was a smattering of laughter as Andy signaled "billion" to his father. Michael obviously knew the budget down to the cost of toilet paper but, pretending to still be talking to Andy, said, "Oh, you mean three *billion* under budget?" He turned back to the audience, "Now we're starting to talk real money!" And they applauded at the prompt. Again, Michael quizzed his son. "Andy, what do you think we should do with that surplus?"

As they'd set up earlier, Andy pointed to himself and put on a hopeful look. "Give it to you as a bonus?" Michael asked. He shook his head at the audience and said, "To paraphrase Dana Carvey quoting President George Herbert Walker Bush, 'Read my lips! Not gonna do it.'"

There was polite applause, and an eye roll from every person in the room who had heard him do that schtick before.

"To my right is Dr. Phred Peterson, genius, rocket scientist, hippie, and lead consultant on our development of fusion energy. He's also the president of Free Juice Corporation, and that company's solar roofing achievements have taken the country by storm.

He spells his name P-H-R-E-D so that the letters P-H-D will never be missing from any introduction. Phred, would you like to say a few words?"

Phred was surprised but started to get up. Michael looked at his fake watch again, and said to Phred, on mic, "Ah, Phred, I guess we're short on time." Then to the audience, Michael said, conspiratorially, "There is no chance in hell that I'll let that hippie have my microphone." There was laughter, clapping, and some hooting from the back row.

"To my left is the governor of Minnesota, Allison Newberry, who has been an ardent and rock-solid supporter of this project since day one. But because it's rumored she's running for our open Senate seat, she doesn't get the microphone either." Adequate laugher from a captive audience.

"And to Governor Newberry's left is Dr. Walter Asabi, vice president and director of operations of Star Power. Dr. Asabi has been managing this project since the first day, and I think it's safe to say it couldn't have been done without him." Walt gave a nod of his head. The appreciation from the attendees was gratifying to Walt and the entire Star Power team.

Michael's smile then faded, and he looked across the two hundred people in front of him, and then directly into the numerous TV cameras. "I'm sure you've noticed there's one more chair up here. My wife"—he gestured to his right—"and Andrea and Andrew's mother, Wendy Halstad, died almost four years ago." The room was soundless. "She was the creator, the instigator, the brains, and the passion behind this project. Her degree was in social science, not rocket science, yet she learned everything there was to learn about nuclear fusion, and this amazing achievement is due to one thing: she said, 'Why not?'" The applause was thunderous, and in the wing, for the first time since Michael found Wendy leaning against his car all those months ago, there were tears running down her face.

Eventually, the room quieted down, and Michael turned to Dr. Asabi, "Walt," he said into the mic, "what time is it?"

Walter actually did still wear a watch. He looked at it and nearly yelled back to Michael, "It's noon, boss!"

And Michael said simply, "Let's fire this thing up and see what happens."

Asabi reached into the contraption on his lap, activated his iPhone, and hit "Engage" on the Star Power app. "Engage" was his unnoticed salute to Captain Picard that he'd designed into the program.

And nothing happened. At least nothing immediately noticeable. But servos spun, and the inertia governor released, and second by second, the subatomic isotopes in the accelerator were moving faster and heating up.

The screen behind the platform came to life, and the images from the five cameras slowly floated across the massive screen from right to left. In each live shot, team members were seen cheering, slapping backs, and high-fiving. The fifth camera featured close-ups of the management group on the stage, documenting their joy and sense of accomplishment.

The program that had been handed to the attendees as they entered the hall explained the process and that it would take some time for the reactor to ramp up, but nobody left. Some stood and chatted. Others sat and stared at the images on the screen as the counters worked their way up, by a degree, a minute, and a kilometer.

■　■　■

Immediately after Walt pushed 'Engage,' Michael walked over to the wing to find Wendy, who had obviously stepped away. But Phred was there, and he was unusually happy, sporting a large smile like he'd just been laughing at a joke. Which was impossible.

"How you doing, big guy? Did I mess you up when I wouldn't hand you the mic?"

"Nah, but I was waxing poetic there for a moment."

"So then, what's got you so happy?"

"Just life, man. I'm so friggin' charged up about Free Juice and Star Power and the future! And it didn't hurt that Wendy just gave me a hug with a supercharged jolt to it. I love you all, man." And he gave Michael a hug. A long, emotional, uncomfortable embrace. When he didn't let go, Michael said, "You can kiss me, but no tongue, okay?"

Phred let go immediately, but he was crying, and he said, "I'm just so happy, man. I feel like the goose laid a golden egg in my lap and then crapped all over my former mother-in-law. Like a twofer, you know? God, I hated that woman."

Admiral Brown walked up and shook Michael's hand. "Michael, congratulations. What an achievement! If we were still building warships, I'd make the next one fusion powered. But we've scrapped all future builds. No reason to keep building museums, you know?"

"Thanks, Admiral. And, you know, I've been wondering—and if it's classified, I understand—but what were the ramifications of your coordination of the events surrounding the missing bad guys? I mean, people all over the world were suggesting that the United States orchestrated the whole thing."

The admiral looked left, then right, and then leaned in a little closer and smiled. "It *is* classified, Michael, but you were in the thick of it, so I'll let you in on a secret. In a private ceremony, President Gallager awarded me the Medal of Honor. Can you believe it? The whole thing was Wendy's scheme, if you will, but she insisted on being, well, invisible, so the president saw me as the instigator."

Michael was thrilled. "That's fantastic, sir! The highest military award—"

Brown shushed him. "Yeah, yeah, it is. But it's top secret for obvious reasons. My grandkids will be told some day, and that's all I need."

Michael shook his hand again. "Well, thank you for coming, Admiral. It means a lot to both me and Wendy. By the way, have you seen her since Walt hit the button?"

"I have. She gave me a hug about ten minutes ago. She's floating around here somewhere." The admiral spotted Sir Richard Crowley and excused himself.

■　■　■

At 1:03 p.m., the system was at full speed and heat, and fusion began. Again, it was invisible to the human eye, but the bank of readouts told the story. The heat in the reactor mushroomed to one million degrees. The heat was instantly routed to three huge water boilers, which produced steam within several seconds. Within several seconds more, the massive turbines were turning, gearing up to operating speed within one minute.

The most enjoyable gauge to watch, at least for the Star Power team members, was the KP readout—kilowatts produced. As the production increased, it was fed immediately and seamlessly into the transformer station on the campus and then onto high-voltage wires before going out to the regional electrical grid.

Nuclear fusion was live. Cheers erupted from the crowd as people watched the KP digits, but the scientists and technicians at Star Power Development simply nodded, exchanged a few fist bumps, and then went about their business. They knew they had designed and built the most important device in human history, with machining and tolerances more precise than any creation ever imagined, and they were already confident it was going to work.

■　■　■

As the Star Power turbines charged the wires, the Alan King Power station turned off the conveyor that, until the changeover to compressed cardboard, had fed the thousands of tons of coal into the furnaces each day to produce the area's electricity. At one point, every home in Minnesota was heated with coal, and every light bulb and phonograph functioned through the burning of coal. And just like that, with the flick of a switch—or rather, the tap of an iPhone—coal was as obsolete in Minnesota as beaver hats and public hangings.

■   ■   ■

As things settled down and the honored guests and visitors filtered out, Michael began a more diligent search for Wendy, but he had a bad feeling.

CHAPTER THIRTY-FOUR

Michael soon enlisted Andie and Andy in the search. They walked the entire campus, every street and path and shortcut. They entered every building, shed, and hiding place, and they could not find her. Andie suggested, with false optimism, "She must have gone home."

Michael shook his head. "She doesn't drive, she has no license—and our car is still in the lot."

Andie looked over at him. "Ever heard of Uber, Dad?"

And Michael grabbed onto the thought. "That must be it. Why don't you two grab your significant others and meet me there." He was jogging to his car before either could respond.

There was no evidence that Wendy had been at home recently, either. No books spread on the couch, no new scribblings in her notepads. But as the kids and their spouses pulled into the driveway, he spotted a handwritten letter on the kitchen table. His heart sank.

As the four of them walked through the front door, Andy saw the look on his father's face and stopped. "Oh no," he said.

Michael didn't speak; he just pointed to the table. As his kids approached the table, Chris and Caroline stayed back. The letter, which was addressed to Michael, Andie, and Andy, was several pages long. Andie dropped into a chair, a sad look on her face. Michael boosted himself up on the counter, and with his legs dangling, he said, "Andy, it's addressed to the three of us. Why don't you read it aloud." As he said that, he motioned for Chris and Caroline to join them.

Andy read through the first paragraph to himself, then decided he'd need the comfort of a chair as well.

Dearest Michael, Andie, and Andy,

What a wonderful day we had today! I'm so proud of all of you! You built in a year what no one else thought was possible in a lifetime, and you made the world a better place. And Michael, whether Steve Jobs was a prick or not, you're now in his league!

Andy looked up at Michael, who gave a hint of a smile and said, "Inside joke." Andy continued.

I had no idea what the remainder of the day would be, but once I was credited with . . . fostering the Star Power concept, it was obvious that I could no longer be flitting around the edges. And Michael, I'm NOT saying that you should not have done that! It was indescribably touching . . . but today was definitely going to be "the day."

And our amazing new friends and confidants were here to share the day. Melinda Vanderbilt, who has done so much to further our efforts. And Sir Richard Crowley, who risked life and limb alongside us. And Admiral Hiram Brown, who made numerous risky and career-threatening decisions . . . because he knew they were right.

As I've told you, I had no idea why I was back again. But now I'll tell you the truth: I had no idea why I was back again. However, in the aftermath of the past year, it's pretty obvious, right? There were things that needed to be done, rules that needed to be broken, and heads and minds that needed to be . . . adjusted. Was that my job? I don't know. But did that happen? Damn straight it did!

The nonsensical illogic of the human brain is . . . mind-numbing. (That might be stating a redundancy . . .) To have the intellectual capacity to make proper, sensible decisions, and waiving that capacity in favor of following the rantings of zealots, bullies, and, sometimes, psychopaths, is . . . stupefying. To toss intellectual advancement in the trash, in favor of "sameness" is . . . inexcusable. And in that, I think we made a difference.

In my reading over the past year, time and again I came across rationalizations for the concept (and practice) of 'mutual mass destruction'. I confess, I paid no attention to the issue in my first earthly go-round, as I was pleasantly occupied with resolving car title errors, and consoling people who lost their licenses because they were piss-poor drivers.

"Speaking of, Dad, are you still driving?" Andie gave him an elbow.

Michael didn't look at her. "Shut up. Concentrate."

The theory of building enough nuclear weapons to make your "enemy" think twice about nuking you because then you'll nuke him and destroy the planet, is insane. But it's consistent with human thought over the past several thousand years.

To knowingly destroy a planet by eliminating the tree growth that creates its oxygen is insane. And then to assure that destruction by poisoning the air . . . it's unfathomable. Humans are the only species on earth with the ability to consider the consequences of their actions and change those actions. But they say, "Aw, screw it."

However, we made some things better, didn't we? We convinced the religions of the world to stop killing each other based on the angry words of zealots. And we convinced them that relying on anecdotes and campfire stories instead of their intellects to guide their existence was stupid. People still believe in God, and they still go to church, but I think we highlighted the arrogance of deciding that God was an entity in human form, with the brain of a simpleton.

Granted, I was disappointed at getting shot, but it only hurt my pride.

We harnessed the free and constant power of the sun in a logical manner using one simple concept: "Git 'er done!" And now, hundreds of thousands of homes in the US have their own power supply up on their roof. And once the materials are paid for, it's free! Who woulda thunk it?

We convinced Hiram to repurpose a historical artifact—The USS Gerald R. Ford—into a rescue ship, and it's in service as I write this.

At great risk and effort, we found new homes for three scoundrel leaders, and there are tens of millions of people who appreciate . . . whoever made that happen. We simply took on the role of Allied movers or Three Men and a Truck.

And the greatest trick of all—nuclear fusion, in a year.

I admit, I'm disappointed that we couldn't get to speed-of-light space travel, or finding life (hopefully more intelligent than ours) "out there."

So, I guess I know why I was back again. I just truly don't know the how or the who. As Admiral Brown told me once, "That's beyond my pay grade."

I'd like to say, "See you all later," but, of course, I don't know that. What I do know is that I love you with all my heart, and I'm so happy that we were able to do all this together.

Much love,
Wendy/Mom

The fridge was humming, which helped fill the void in the room. All five of them sat still, not speaking, barely breathing, for four or five minutes. Finally, Michael broke the silence. "You guys hungry for some pizza?"

Andie looked up. "Meat lover's, stuffed crust?"

"Duh," Michael said, reaching for his phone.

Visit
WWW.JAMIESTOUDTBOOKS.COM
to be the first to know about upcoming releases.

Like the book? Please leave a review on
GOODREADS and **AMAZON**!

A review needs to be only a sentence or two long,
and it's a simple but powerful way to help an author.